THE SINGING SPY

Inspired by a true story of war, treachery, and one woman's selfless courage

FRANK MALLEY

FCM BOOKS

1st Edition

Copyright © 2025 Frank Malley

Frank Malley has asserted his rights under the Copyright, Designs and Patents Act 1988 to be identified as the author of this work.

This book is a work of fiction, and except in the case of historical fact, any resemblance to actual persons, living or dead, is purely coincidental.

This book is sold subject to condition that it shall not, by way of trade or otherwise, be lent, resold, hired out, or otherwise circulated without the publisher's prior consent in any form of binding or cover other than that in which it is published and without a similar condition, including this condition, being imposed on the subsequent purchaser.

ISBN: 9798264123580

For Carole and Michael

***

All royalties from The Singing Spy will be donated to Wigan and Leigh Hospice, who looked after my mum, Kathleen, with much dignity and compassion in her final days.

"In wartime, truth is so precious that she should always be attended by a bodyguard of lies"

WINSTON CHURCHILL

1

April 10th, 1941. Berlin.

THE pall of smoke refused to budge, clinging to the city as a frightened child holds tight to its mother.

Long faces, open-mouthed, lined the thoroughfare, transfixed by the devastation that British bombs had wrought. The raid had lasted no more than 15 minutes, around midnight, but under a full moon the bombers' aim and daring route had foxed the flak batteries. The incendiaries had found their targets and a beautiful, cultured city, blessed with fine art, historic landmarks and a haughty air of privilege, was burning.

Helena Schulz had eyes for one building only. The State Opera House on Unter den Linden boulevard, where the fumes hung like a shroud, the odd flame still licking through charred roof trusses, dancing in random defiance as firefighters trained their hoses. Alone, at the back of the crowd of observers, she spread a hand over her mouth but the pools of distress that filled her eyes could not be stemmed, every now and then a tear escaping, trickling down her cheeks, creating a salty residue on her lips.

Her mind wandered to the time, not long ago, when she first sang on that hallowed stage, her stomach tied in nervous knots, the spotlights blinding her to the dignitaries sat in the dress circle. Oh, what a night that was. *The happiest night of my life.* For a few moments she even sensed she could hear the applause once more and feel the systolic thump of her heart as the elation surged through her body. Never had she felt more joyous, or more German, than on that night. Or more certain of the extraordinary path her life had taken.

"Frau Schulz, excuse me."

A stranger, wearing a brown Macintosh, trilby hat and an expression of concern, jolted Helena from her reminisce. He offered a pristine white handkerchief, which she accepted, dabbing her cheeks, at the same time pondering the man's motive. Immediately, she disliked herself for suspecting such kindness, especially as he had warm eyes. His German precise.

"Forgive me for bothering you, Frau Schulz, but I recognised you. I saw you sing some months ago at the Opera House. A wonderful evening. I hate to see you so upset."

"You're very kind." Helena managed a weak smile. "It's a shock to see your place of work burn before your eyes, that's all. I'll be fine in a few minutes."

"This war has a lot to answer for."

Helena nodded.

The man continued. "I believe you're from England originally."

"Y-e-s."

"I read your biography in the opera programme." The man provided an explanation, having noted Helena's halting response.

"Of course."

"We're sworn enemies."

"I'm sorry."

"You're from Lancashire. I'm a Yorkshireman."

"Really?" Helena's eyes widened.

"Really."

The man offered his hand and they shook. He lowered his voice and spoke in English. "Jack Martin from Leeds." She recognised the flat tones, instantly transported to her homeland, although he quickly reverted to German. "Could we speak somewhere private?"

"Where did you have in mind?"

"A little bar I know."

"I'm married."

"Congratulations. I hope you're very happy."

"What I mean is, going to strange bars with strange men is not something I do."

"I get that, but, honestly, I'm not strange. Not when you get to know me. I'm not trying to be clever. You're a beautiful woman and have every right to be cautious."

She ignored the compliment. "Then say what you have to say."

His eyes flicked to the crowd. "Here's a little public for what I had in mind. But I think you might be interested. Don't worry, it's not far, and it's a café rather than a bar. I promise not to keep you long, or do anything strange."

Everything told Helena this was a bad idea. A stranger approaching her at a vulnerable moment. A man who had obviously researched her background, with uncertain motive, asking her to follow him to an undeclared destination. She should have run for the safety of home, but hearing a snatch of native English, from a northern enclave not dissimilar to her own, uttered by a handsome man with a mischievous smile and easy charm, had triggered her interest.

"Five minutes."

"That should do it. Follow me."

Jack led her away from Unter den Linden, dodging the throng, across the tramway, fortunately in the opposite direction from the densest smoke. A few minutes later they alighted on a basement café in a street untouched by the incendiary bombing the previous night. The café was warm and inviting, the smell of coffee enticing, although there were few customers. Most of the small individual booths, comprising leather bench seats that had seen better days, were empty. Jack chose one located towards the back of the building. As was his custom, he sat facing the entrance, Helena opposite. She noticed his dark eyebrows formed distinctive arches, slightly pointed, meeting in the middle as if supporting a heavy load, resembling the portal to a church. She liked that. He ordered coffees. And smiled. Jack smiled a lot. When the drinks arrived, black for Helena, white with a heaped spoonful of sugar for himself, Jack took a sip and said, "Frau Schulz. How long have you lived in Berlin?"

"No. You don't get to ask the questions. Not before I know who you are."

"Fair enough." Jack's intelligence reports had alerted him to expect a spirited woman with a sharp brain and a smart mouth. He realised the only way to gain her trust was to submit the truth, or at least a semblance of it.

"I like to think of myself as a representative, someone who can offer assistance to all the brave men from Blighty who, through no fault of their own, find themselves alone and helpless in enemy territory and need to get home. A sort of travel agent."

"Don't you mean a secret agent?"

He neither confirmed, nor denied, but she seemed unfazed by the possibility.

"Where's Lambert's Yard?" Helena snapped out the question, her jaw jutted, dark eyes dancing, daring Jack to answer.

"What does …?"

Helena interrupted. "Lambert's Yard. Where is it?"

"If you mean the oldest building in Leeds city centre, it's just off Lower Briggate. Can't say I've ever visited, but everyone in Leeds would know it." His eyebrows lifted and he fixed her with a steady stare, another wry smile on his lips, appreciating her quick-thinking. "Did I pass your test?"

Helena had sung in the Yorkshire city on several occasions, gathering snippets of history. Her shoulders relaxed. There was something intriguing, as well as engaging, about this stranger that aroused her curiosity.

"Almost eight years," she said.

"What do you mean?"

"That's how long I've lived in Berlin."

"Have you ever returned to England?"

"Not since the war began."

"That's understandable. Are you in contact with your family?"

Helena fidgeted with her spoon, stirring clouds in her coffee, for no reason, it seemed, other than to release tension. After a few moments, she shook her head, eyes downcast, the trauma of the previous night untangling truths that had tormented her greatly these past months. Her voice raised a notch in pitch, and she surprised herself, spewing out words that often swirled in the recesses of her mind but until now had remained unspoken. Words that she could only admit to a stranger.

"My father doesn't understand. He thinks because I've married a German and sung for the Führer, I'm a traitor. That somehow I've changed sides and don't love my own country. He's turned my mother and sisters against me. They no longer answer my letters. I feel as if they've disowned me."

"Have you changed sides?"

"No." A sudden fiery glint in Helena's eyes.

"Would you help your country if you could?"

"Of course. But I'm a singer. What could I do?"

He paused for a moment, as if in considered thought, although in reality he had choreographed this conversation over the past weeks, not knowing when or where it might take place but ensuring he was ready when it did.

"Through the opera, you meet and have access to high-ranking Nazi officers. Some say you are the Führer's favourite singer. Is this true?"

"I've heard that said, but the Opera House no longer exists. You saw the smoke and flames."

Two old men, one hobbling with the aid of a stick, the other hollow cheeked, sucking deep on a cigarette, the ash tip ready to fall, wandered in off the street. They shuffled into the nearby booth. Jack sipped coffee, computing whether the old men posed a threat. He watched the ash escape, depositing a powdery splatter on the stone floor, and quickly decided the men were harmless. He returned to his train of thought.

"I think you'll be performing again before you anticipate, Frau Schulz. Isn't the Opera House one of the nation's precious jewels, representing German talent and culture?"

Helena nodded. "Of course."

"The Führer won't allow a symbol of such magnitude to remain a charred ruin for long. Nothing screams defeat more than a burnt-out music palace. My bet is you'll be singing there once more within the year. In the meantime, the opera will find another venue, I'm sure."

"I hope you're right. Anyway, your five minutes were up ten minutes ago." Helena pushed away her empty coffee cup, clutched her handbag, and started to rise. Jack reached across the table, touching her forearm, a gesture for her to stay seated. His voice lowered to a whisper.

"All I'm asking is keep your eyes and ears open and report back anything, however insignificant or inconsequential it may seem. New factories, troop movements, where Nazi bigwigs are staying, snatched conversations on opera nights, that sort of thing."

"What about my husband?"

"You can't tell anyone, especially not your husband. He's German. A cog in the war machine. Once a Nazi, always a Nazi. I don't think he'd understand."

Helena glared, Jack's directness grating. "Siegfried's not a Nazi."

Jack shrugged. "He owns and runs munitions factories. Makes money from guns, bullets and bombs that kill British troops and airmen every day. I'm sure he treats you well and he might not have Nazi printed on his forehead, but I think it's obvious where his sympathies lie."

Helena's mind was racing, her instinct to defend her husband. By any romantic measure, their relationship was not passionate. They had met at an industrial rally at which Helena had sung, connecting over his appreciation of classical music. They talked for hours, dissecting the work of the great composers, agreeing to disagree on the merits of Beethoven's vast portfolio. Helena thought the composer's work overly complicated with unlikely harmonies and abrupt phrasing. Siegfried Schulz, like many Germans, considered it heroic. Yet a bond was formed, their polar opinions supplying energy and interest. Siegfried had supported her career ever since, opening doors when her Englishness had precluded her from typically Germanic roles. She owed him, and had grown to respect and cherish him for his devotion to her, but this was a chance to help her countrymen and women. An opportunity to exorcise the guilt, feel good again about her life of privilege and relative luxury. A chance to show her family where her true heart lay. She rose and made to leave. After a single stride, she turned. "I'll think about it."

Jack nodded. "I'll be in touch."

2

THE train journey home seemed to last forever, even though it was no more than 15 miles to the house Helena shared with Siegfried in Potsdam. Thankfully, the bombing raid had failed to damage the track, but explosions had weakened bridges and engineers were busy organising repairs. It meant the packed train was reduced to little more than idling speed.

The slow ride afforded Helena time to think. In normal circumstances, she wasn't overly reflective, but she was still immeasurably sad, the sight of the burning Opera House seared into her memory. When she closed her eyes, she could still hear the booming and persistent curtain calls on all those wonderful nights. Carmen, La Boheme, The Magic Flute. So many productions, so many triumphs. In front of the great and the mighty in German society. Generals, ministers, even the Führer himself on occasions.

Jack, however, had called it right. Around mid-afternoon, together with other members of the cast, Helena had met with management, who insisted temporary premises would be found and that the Führer, a frequent visitor to the state opera, had already issued a decree to restore the grand building to its former magnificence within the year.

That was a relief, but it wasn't the only reason her blood was pumping. She couldn't shake that Yorkshire accent out of her head. She had not stopped thinking about Jack Martin's proposition since she left the café. Revisiting his words. Weighing the risk and reward. Over and over. That surprised her. As a rule, she didn't procrastinate. She made quick, precise, decisions, the type her singing training demanded. There was no point sliding close to a note. In professional opera singing you either hit the sweet spot of the note first time, every time, or management would find someone who could. Cut and dried.

The smart move was to banish this stranger from her thoughts. She knew that. Don't jeopardise what you have. A wealthy, attentive husband. A career that could never have been dreamed of as a young girl amid the slag heaps of a Lancashire coal and mill town. Adoring fans. A country that had provided so much.

That's settled. She dug inside her handbag and found a small compact and a lipstick, proceeding to refresh her make-up as the train slid past the grey-green fields outside Potsdam. Mind made up. *A spy? How ridiculous.*

***

Helena was tall for a woman with long, honey-coloured hair cascading joyously onto her shoulders like waves crashing on a Cornwall beach. Not English-rose beautiful, but her face was attractive with a thin nose, big brown eyes, a full mouth and a pleasing symmetry, apart from a tiny mole on her left cheek that would have seemed a blemish on anyone else but somehow added to her allure. The sort of woman who turned heads when she entered a room, a wide smile radiating warmth and a sense of well-being even when she didn't feel like smiling.

She had become accustomed to swivelling heads and stares down the years, but had never taken them for granted. As the train chugged to a halt the passengers milled around the exits to disembark. A woman across the aisle dug her friend in the ribs, flicking her gaze towards Helena. Furtive whispers emanated from other passengers. Helena gathered the looks and sounds of recognition with an appreciative nod. There were times when the attention became wearing, but few would ever have known, other than Siegfried perhaps on the rare occasion of a sub-par performance. Helena was a prima donna on stage only.

Still, she was thankful to break free of the teeming throng and stride out for home, a large detached house on a gated plot of land no more than a five-minute walk from the station. It was a characterful house. Not too ostentatious. High ceilings, big windows, throwing light onto large portrait paintings of Siegfried's ancestors in the hall and up the stairway.

"I'm home, Siegfried." Her tone as cheery as she could muster. She kicked off her shoes on the black-and-white checked tiles in the hallway.

A man wearing a dark grey three-piece suit, waistcoat straining to contain an ample girth, emerged from the lounge.

"Hi, Darling. Sorry to hear about the Opera House. I hope you're not too upset." He kissed her tenderly on the cheek.

"It was dreadful, Siegfried. I watched it burn before my eyes. But at least it's going to be rebuilt and there's every hope of finding temporary accommodation within the month."

"The show must go on."

"Quite."

Another man, unknown to Helena, emerged from the lounge. Slim, close-cut black hair, he had the neck and muscular shoulders of a swimmer. He was also wearing a dark suit.

"I didn't realise we had company," said Helena.

"I'm sorry, I should have said. This is Thomas. Thomas Weber. He's one of the ministers responsible for ensuring the Luftwaffe have spare parts for their aeroplanes."

"Enchanted, Frau Schulz." The minister bowed, lifted Helena's outstretched hand to his lips and planted a kiss.

"Can I fix you a drink?" Helena was an attentive host.

"That would be most kind. A brandy, a little drop of water, would be fine."

"Siegfried?"

"Just a small one, we'll be in the lounge."

Helena fixed the drinks in the kitchen and carried them through on a tray, all the while detecting a sharp edge to the conversation. It seemed Weber was anxious to step up production at Siegfried's factory.

"Out of the question." Siegfried's tone animated. "We cannot double production overnight, let alone triple it. Impossible. We're working flat out as it is."

"I don't think …" Weber abandoned his response as Helena arrived with the brandy glasses. She laid them on a wooden coffee table and the minister presented a wide smile, although his eyes remained cold.

"You're most kind, Frau Schulz. Won't you join us?"

"I don't drink and it seems you have much to discuss. I'll leave you to your brandy. I have things to attend to."

"Such a pity." The response was glib, the sort of shallow remark that denotes wider insincerity. First impressions were important to Helena. Success or failure in her chosen profession rested almost always on a favourable audition. One chance. She prided herself on her ability to read people. The way Weber scrutinised the sway of her hips as she left the room, in full view of her husband, suggested that here was a man not to be trusted. A man who cared little for the feelings of others.

Maybe that's why, rather than proceeding to her study which doubled as a music room, she lingered in the hallway, bare feet silent on the marble floor. Normally, she had little interest in Siegfried's work. He never discussed it. Dry as the Sahara, he would say, always preferring to dissect Helena's latest production full of soaring arias and unmanageable egos. But visits from high-ranking ministers were rare.

The conversation resumed, Weber's tone increasingly steely.

"I think you misunderstood before, Herr Schulz. My visit here is not to make a polite request, although it is my intention to complete our business in a friendly manner." He raised his glass and took a deep slug of brandy. "I am here with the Führer's blessing. More than that, I'm here to state his express wishes. Do I make myself clear?"

Helena heard Siegfried clear his throat and inhale a deep breath. She sensed his caution as he pondered the minister's words. Siegfried was the sort of man who preferred negotiating a way around obstacles rather than facing them head on, but he was canny as a fox. Helena could tell he was wary of this visitor.

"Can I ask what you have in mind?"

Weber sniffed his brandy, his mouth pouting in contemplation.

"For many months our brave pilots have bombed London, and still the enemy's will has not broken, nor has the British war industry been decimated. We have lost hundreds of aircraft. The Führer wants to replace them with bigger planes and heavier weapons. He wants the Heinkel to carry bombs the size of a small bus. We will be stepping up production at our plant in Oranienburg. Thousands of aircraft. Your job is to keep those planes in the sky."

"I'll need more men."

"That's for you to decide. You're being paid handsomely. Do whatever it takes."

Helena heard footsteps approaching. She tiptoed across the hallway and as she disappeared inside her office she heard the lounge door shut. Sensitive details were about to be discussed.

It was then she decided. *Bombs the size of a small bus.* That's what she had heard. Bombs that would soon be falling on London and other British cities. Maybe even on her own Lancashire home town that was a hub for provisions required in the war effort. What if her family were struck? Pursuing her dreams had brought them nothing but pain. She couldn't bear to think of her parents going to their graves believing she was a Nazi. She didn't want to betray Siegfried, but she couldn't stand by and do nothing. She just couldn't.

She crossed to her writing desk and made a verbatim note of everything Weber had said.

3

AROUND a week later, Helena was staying over in Berlin as Siegfried was away on a business trip, touring his factories. The opera company had found new premises in which to rehearse and there was much to discuss late into the evening. She had joined members of the cast for a meal. Nothing fancy. Hot sausages and bread and butter, washed down with beer or weak tea. Helena opted for tea.

The air raid sirens had sounded earlier that evening, but proved to be a false alarm. For some reason the British bombers had deposited their cargo deep in the suburbs, possibly targeting ammunition depots.

Helena was walking back to her hotel when she heard her name. At first she wasn't sure. The wind was blustery, the sound indistinct. The hiss came again, this time louder, more urgent. She swivelled to her left and a man in a brown overcoat and hat, the tip of his cigarette glowing in the dark, stepped out of the shadows.

"Who's that?" A tremor in her voice.

"Come with me."

"Jack?"

"Do as I say."

The man disappeared into an alley off the main road. Helena's heart lurched, but not with fear as she might have expected. Instead, a sudden rush of excitement. She cast a glance up and down the road. A few soldiers at the crossroads up ahead, but no one close. She skipped into the cobbled street and followed Jack for about 30 yards, treading with care as the night was black. At the end of the alleyway he opened the passenger door of a battered old car.

"Get in and keep quiet." His tone urgent.

"That's a great chat-up line."

He ignored her sarcasm. She clambered into the vehicle. Jack rounded the car, flicked the butt of his cigarette into the night and slid into the driver's seat beside her.

He switched to English. "Sorry if it all seems a bit cloak and dagger, but the Gestapo have a tight hold on this city. They've spread fear in all quarters, pitched neighbour against neighbour. The next person you see could be the one to send you to the firing squad. It's difficult to know who to trust, so I don't trust anyone."

"That's exactly what a girl in a dark alley wants to hear."

Helena's night vision had kicked in and she could make out the silhouette of Jack's face. An attractive face, she remembered. Smooth features and a strong jawline.

"I'm a Yorkshireman. We might be stubborn and argumentative, but we're as honest as the day. Have you decided?"

"Straight to the point, I see. Is that a Yorkshire trait, too?" Helena was enjoying the interplay. With Siegfried, conversation was formal, conforming to convention. Kind and honourable, but essentially stiff and dull. With Jack Martin there was an edge. He could never be described as dull.

"Impatience is a product of the times, I'm afraid. Can't hang around waiting when bombs and bullets are flying. But before you give me your answer, let me say something." He paused as if memorising the contents of a prepared speech, before continuing, his flat vowels giving his message an appropriate earthiness. "Secret agents, or spies, or whatever you want to call them, are not interesting or glamorous. It's important you realise that. They are ordinary, fearful, mostly flawed individuals. They don't weigh up right and wrong. They do anything to get a result, sometimes dreadful things, not because they want to, but because they have to."

"I'm not spying on my husband."

"Pardon?"

There was a determined slant to Helena's tone. She'd wrestled with the conundrum since the visit of the minister. It had taken many hours, but finally she had come to a decision. "If I'm here because you want information on Siegfried's factories, then count me out. I don't get involved in his work. I owe everything to Siegfried. He made my dreams of becoming a professional singer come true. He's always been there for me. I won't betray him."

"I wouldn't ask you to."

There was another pause. They sat in the dark, the only sound Jack's fingers drumming lightly on the steering wheel.

"Oranienburg." Helena's voice was no more than a whisper.

"What about it?"

"All I know is there's a plan to step up production of planes for the Luftwaffe there, including one which can carry huge bombs. The source is high-ranking, reliable, and not my husband."

Jack whistled softly through his teeth. He knew the town of Oranienburg, around 20 miles north of Berlin, mainly because it was the site of one of the Nazis' earliest concentration camps.

"Does this mean you're in?"

She gasped, as if taking a leap into a dark and uncertain void. "I'm in."

"Great, fancy a drink?"

"What, now? I'm not sure a celebration is warranted."

"I'd prefer to call it relaxation. Better than going back to your hotel and worrying about what you've decided."

"I'm not worrying."

When she didn't protest, Jack turned the ignition and manoeuvred the car down the alleyway, masked headlights casting soft silhouettes on the brick walls either side.

Ten minutes later they pulled into a passageway leading to the back of a row of apartment buildings. Jack parked up and as Helena made to open her door, he gently grasped her arm.

"Some of the people you'll meet tonight work for me. They're on our side. Loyal and trustworthy. But let's keep our arrangement between us. No word to anyone. Safer that way for all concerned."

Helena nodded and Jack led her to the back entrance of a bar, steep steps winding to basement level. At the bottom of the steps, a sweet smell of stale beer mixed with a musty dampness and a murmur of conversation greeted them.

Jack pushed open a door, switching to German. "Welcome to Das Bar."

Around 30 people sat at tables, drinking beer, chatting, cigarette smoke fogging the air, the low ceiling damp with the breath and radiant heat of customers, an odd drop of condensation splattering on the stone floor.

"Jack, good to see you." The barman, beer-stained apron flapping around his rotund waist, waddled from behind the bar, extended an arm and shook Jack's hand vigorously. The barman's eyes immediately fixed on Helena, as if he didn't come across fragrant women of such obvious poise and beauty too often in Das Bar. "Well, well, who do we have here? You look familiar."

They shook hands and Helena noticed the top joint on one of the barman's little fingers was missing. She wondered what trauma had caused such an injury. Jack did the introductions. "This, Bo Schneider, is Frau Helena Schulz."

"Enchantée, Madame. Of course, I know now. I do apologise. From the opera. You're a singer. I've read the reviews."

"All good, I hope."

"Naturellement."

"You're French?" As well as the words, Helena detected sing-song vowels.

"Half French, half German."

"I'm half German, half English, at least by marriage."

"If only we could all live together in such harmony."

"Mine's a whisky, Bo." Jack interrupted the small talk.

"And, Frau Schulz, if you please?"

"A lemonade with angostura, if that's not too much trouble."

"My pleasure." Bo shuffled behind the bar while Jack and Helena found a small round table in a cramped alcove.

"He seems jolly. Nice to see a friendly face in this city for a change." Helena wriggled out of her overcoat, draping it over the back of her chair.

"Bo's a good man in a crisis. Can turn his talents to most things. Knows Berlin like the back of his hand. If you're ever in trouble, he's the man to visit."

"I'll bear that in mind, although I hope to stay out of trouble."

A barmaid with a pert figure and long golden tresses, who looked 15 but was probably in her twenties, arrived with the drinks.

Again, Jack introduced her. "This is Elke. Bo thinks he runs the place, but Elke is the boss around here. Isn't that right, Elke?"

She rolled her eyes and threw Jack an insolent look. Helena detected a gutsy character, a troubled undercurrent suggesting this was a woman who had endured much pain despite her tender years.

"Pleased to meet you, Elke." Helena gifted one of her warmest smiles. Elke managed a nod, which was better than her usual scowl.

When she had left, Jack said, "She likes you."

"What gives you that idea?"

"You've got a full glass and none of it is down your dress."

Helena, wearing a puzzled frown, enquired about Elke's story.

"Not sure. No family, I know that. Lives here above the shop which is lucky for Bo. He's always got someone on the premises. Elke's not the chattiest barmaid in Berlin, but she's done a few jobs for us and never let us down."

"What sort of jobs?"

Jack lowered his voice. "You'd be surprised at the number of British airmen holed up in this city after being shot down. Hiding in all sorts of squalid places. My job is to try to get the poor sods home."

"How?"

"Any way we can. Elke drives a truck as good as a man and, if necessary, shoots better than most. In your case, that won't be required. Your field of operation is somewhat more sophisticated."

"I sincerely hope so."

"What are you going to do until the opera resumes?"

"This and that. I'll keep myself busy. The commandant at one of the prisoner of war camps has asked me to sing there. That could be fun."

"Which camp?"

"A sub-camp in the south of the city. The commandant is Walter Reinhardt. Siegfried knows him."

"That's interesting. Let me know how you get on."

Helena sipped her drink, soaking in the ambience of a bar full of ordinary folk intent on friendly chatter, the sporadic laughter somehow at odds with the fact that bombs could drop at any moment. It wasn't her usual mode of relaxation. Normally, she would be driven straight home after an evening performance, where Siegfried would grill her on the dignitaries in the VIP box that evening. Somehow, such conversation now seemed shallow and frivolous.

"If you had your life to lead again, would you make the same choices?" Helena's question was spontaneous, as was Jack's reply.

"Are you talking about my job or your husband?"

"That's not fair."

"You asked the question."

"Both, I suppose."

Jack rummaged in his pocket, sliding a cigarette from its packet. His brow wrinkled in studied consideration as he lit it.

Savouring the nicotine buzz from his initial extended drag, he exhaled a plume of smoke along with his answer.

"I won't deny the job's a dirty, horrible, business much of the time. It's fraught with danger. Some weeks we lose more than we gain, but we give brave guys hope, a chance of getting home to their loved ones rather than rotting for years in a German prison. I like to think we make a permanent difference to their lives, and to the outcome of the war." He drained his whisky. "What about you?"

"No, I must get back. Early start tomorrow."

"I meant your husband. Would you make the same choice?"

She swung her coat off the back of her chair and grabbed her bag. "As I said, early start tomorrow. I'd better get back."

The streets were empty, Jack avoiding the main boulevards where soldiers were apt to man temporary roadblocks. He dropped Helena back at her hotel a little before 11pm. She went to retrieve her key from reception but was intercepted by the concierge, a tidy man with a spotless uniform and an earnest disposition.

"Frau Schulz, thank goodness you're back, could you follow me please?"

"What is it?" The concierge didn't answer, instead scuttling down the corridor, motioning for Helena to enter a small staff room. "What is it, you're worrying me?"

Two men stood to greet her, one was Thomas Weber, the minister she had met the week before, the other was a fellow director at her husband's company. Essentially, his business partner.

"Heinz, what are you doing here?"

The colour drained from her face as she recognised a dark cloud of concern distorting his features.

"What is it, Heinz, tell me?"

"Sit down, Helena." He attempted to usher her to a chair.

"Tell me, Heinz. Is it about Siegfried?"

"I'm sorry …I should have gone …" Heinz tried to explain, but the croak in his throat collapsed into a sob."

Weber stepped forward.

"Frau Schulz, I'm sorry to inform you that Siegfried was travelling on a train to Bremen this afternoon when it came under attack. He was on the way to visit one of his factories. The bomb missed the train, but a section of track was damaged and the train derailed."

"Is he alive? Please tell me he's alive." Helena gasped, an infusion of heat coursing through her veins. Her legs trembled. For a moment she thought she might succumb to the swirling foreboding in her brain. Instinct led her to catch the back of the chair to steady herself. She fought to concentrate, attempting to make sense of Weber's words. Hoping against hope they were untrue.

Weber shook his head, his icy economy and pragmatic detachment landing a sickening blow to Helena's stomach. "There were no survivors." For a minute or so he supplied sketchy details, informing that Siegfried's carriage careered down a steep embankment killing all 40 passengers and that the Luftwaffe would avenge their deaths in the fullness of time.

Helena heard nothing of his explanation, apart from her teeth chattering in shock. And, in the innermost recesses of her mind, a clang of regret.

4

January 21st, 1944. London.

GEORGE Bacon threw out the question as Sam Carter shuffled through the door of the MI9 base at the War Office on the corner of Horse Guards Avenue and Whitehall: "Where the dickens did you get to last night?"

"Had a quiet night in. Caught up on my beauty sleep." Carter's tone was teasing.

Bacon looked dubious. "First, one night's not nearly enough for that. Second, not even a deaf, dumb and blind man could have slept through last night's bombardment. Third, have you looked in a mirror this morning?"

"Why?"

"You're bleeding." Bacon shook his head, sighed, and pointed to Carter's face.

Carter caressed the bridge of his nose. "So I am. I wonder how that happened."

Carter had missed the scheduled meeting at the War Office the night before, mainly because he'd been caught above ground in an unexpected air raid and forced to shelter from flying debris, a fragment of which had found its target. He'd made his way to a nearby underground station, spending the night listening to anxious parents, wailing children, and an Irish woman strangling the life out of *Danny Boy* on a permanent loop while fiddling with her rosary beads.

It had left him a tad irritable, although his relationship with Bacon was tetchy at best. Bacon deemed Carter too cavalier, a liability, prepared to put the lives of agents in the field at risk. Carter, in turn, thought Bacon odd and stuffy, but conceded he was good at his job. He was a problem solver. Meticulous. Correct in dress and manner. You needed people like that in the military.

If war hadn't intervened, Bacon would have accrued pots of money furthering a career in his father's accountancy firm. Instead, he had become a civil servant in the War Office with a penchant for a train of lateral thought unusual in accountants. As such, he had come to the attention of the newly-formed secret agency, MI9.

Pretty soon, he had forsaken shuffling numbers and become one of the team tasked with dreaming up ingenious ways for soldiers to evade capture, or failing that to escape once they had been caught. His world consisted of odd but intriguing tasks, such as making compasses tiny enough to fit behind the top button of a uniform or hidden inside a fake boiled sweet. No longer did he work at the War Office, but at MI9's main headquarters in Beaconsfield, which was why Carter was surprised to see him in central London.

Carter pulled up a chair and sat at the polished oak table, big enough to hold a sizeable dinner party. He wiped his gashed nose with a handkerchief and couldn't resist a playful swipe at Bacon's former profession. "What's this all about, Mister Bean Counter?"

"I didn't come here to be insulted."

"Why, where do you normally go?"

"You're not funny, Carter."

"Lots of people would disagree."

"Well, I don't know any of them."

"That doesn't surprise me."

Before Bacon could continue the verbal spat, two uniformed men entered the room.

The first carried a briefcase, two pips on his shoulder insignia denoting the rank of lieutenant. The second man sported thick black glasses, a moustache and an air of authority. Everyone in the know respected Brigadier Harry Pritchard, mostly because he helped set up MI9, the organisation responsible for bringing home thousands of stranded airmen. Carter saluted and Bacon stood as he entered.

"Please, at ease. Everyone have a seat and let's get down to business." His cultured tones at once reassuring. Pritchard's presence confirmed the seriousness of this meeting.

Immediately, the Brigadier slid back his chair and extended an arm towards the lieutenant. "I think it best if I hand over to Lieutenant Harris. He's fully briefed on the sensitive nature of the mission we have in mind. It has code red clearance."

The lieutenant cleared his throat and rummaged in his briefcase. He flicked through a sheaf of papers, unfazed by the silence and expectant expressions. Finally, he alighted on the relevant paper. He fixed on Carter.

"Do you know Jack Martin?"

Carter nodded. "We trained together a few years back. Good man. From Yorkshire, I think, but I didn't hold that against him. He was good at his job and could hold his drink. No bottle of whisky was safe if Jack was around, but I never saw him drunk. Hollow legs Martin. Last time I heard he was heading out east."

Lieutenant Harris took a deep breath. "I'm afraid it's not good news about Colonel Martin. He went missing in action."

"Where?"

"Berlin."

"What the devil was he doing there?"

"Last we heard he was planning to lead Allied airmen to a safe place. They'd been hiding in a forest for weeks after being shot down. But he's not transmitted for more than a fortnight. That's not like Jack. He's always meticulous and punctual, our best asset in the area."

In Carter's peripheral vision, he saw the Brigadier studying him, weighing his reaction.

"Maybe he's lying low. Maybe he's injured somewhere and can't get to his radio. There are all sorts of reasons an agent in the field can go dark."

"That's true, Carter, and we've considered all of them, but we have to face the most likely possibility. The odds are he has been captured, or worse."

"What about the team he was working with?"

"Teamwork wasn't really Jack's style. We know he had locals helping him, but he never identified them. He planned the missions, recruited resistance fighters, liaised with MI9 when he needed money, but it was always the Jack Martin show."

Carter nodded, remembering his former colleague's unyielding trait. They'd spent a week together in a tiny cave on Dartmoor hiding from a make-believe enemy, honing survival skills. Sharing food, conversation and a makeshift hole-in-the-ground toilet. You get to know the real man at such times. Warts and all. Stubborn as Yorkshire stone. That was Jack Martin. But with a sense of humour that endeared him to everyone he knew.

"Poor Jack. I didn't know he was out there. Didn't know he still worked for us. Lost touch with him, to be honest. Must be hairy operating in Berlin right now. Not just the Germans trying to get you, you've got to dodge our bombs too."

"Precisely." The Brigadier thumped the table. "Jack's a brave lad. One of our top operatives, responsible for saving countless lives. Been running that patch for nigh on three years. We can't afford to lose men like him."

They sat in silence for a few seconds, as if in tribute to their missing comrade, before Lieutenant Harris returned the conversation to pragmatics.

"The thing is, Jack's one of the reasons our raids over Berlin have been so successful. He's been feeding us coded information, including precise coordinates, allowing our bombers to pinpoint weapons factories, engineering plants, all manner of key targets. As far as we know, the Germans had no idea what he was up to."

"Good for Jack." There was genuine respect in Carter's response.

"That's not the whole story." The lieutenant glanced at Brigadier Pritchard, whose eyebrows collided in concentration before an almost imperceptible nod supplied permission to continue.

"Jack was working with the resistance. We know that. He used them when necessary, especially a contact he only ever refers to as Le Droit."

"As in *the right*." Carter translated the French.

"Yes, we believe this individual was as close as Jack came to a right-hand man, hence the codename. We believe he facilitated many of Jack's operations with a detailed knowledge of the area and potential escape routes. Jack never revealed his true identity, probably to protect him. There are no photos, no detailed description. All we know is that he is around forty and the top joint of the little finger on his left hand is missing. A souvenir from a disagreement with the Gestapo."

"Another brave guy."

"That's right," said the lieutenant, "but Le Droit is an operative, a facilitator. We don't believe he's Jack's secret source, the someone closest to the action, privy to the most sensitive of useful information. The person who has been supplying pinpoint coordinates."

"Any ideas who that might be?"

"No. And since Jack went dark, no coded messages have been received."

"Do we think the source has been killed or captured?"

"Perhaps."

"But not definitely"

"No. The information Jack supplied was so precise. Everything points to a source that knows how we work. Where the war is poised. The importance of Berlin. It's almost as if a British officer has been directing clandestine operations."

That twitched Bacon's antennae. Thus far, he had listened with dutiful attention, but shown neither emotion, nor much interest in the fate of Jack Martin. Bacon's civilian world had little empathy with men of action, but the possibility of an informant using sophisticated methods of evasion was up his street.

"That's a good theory, but surely we'd know if it was a British officer in Berlin. Are we talking about a downed airman, someone who has evaded capture and taken it upon himself to spy for us? Without the proper gear, they're unlikely to have access to reliable information on a regular basis. And why wouldn't they reveal themselves?"

The Brigadier smiled. "Don't underestimate the resourcefulness of the British soldier, Bacon. Once a soldier, always a soldier. That goes for the battlefield, in the comfort of their own home, or in enemy territory. Wherever he or she is, it's their duty to fight with whatever means at their disposal."

"I didn't mean to …"

The Brigadier raised a hand, stemming Bacon's apology.

Lieutenant Harris again dug in his briefcase, emerging with a thick piece of paper which he unfolded several times and laid on the table to reveal a large map of Berlin, on which he had daubed several crosses in red ink.

He pointed with his pen to one of them. "This is the area we believe Jack operated from. We have an address that he supplied in code some time ago. There's no certainty he's still there, or if the property even exists considering the weight of bombing in recent months."

The pen swept to another location. "This is Grunewald Forest, a sprawling mass of trees and tangled vegetation close to the city centre, perfect for airmen to hide. The problem is the Gestapo and the SS know this and continually sweep the area. We believe Jack may have been operating in this area when he went missing."

The Brigadier strolled over to the window. It was festooned with sticky tape to prevent flying glass in the event of a blow-out. His eyes strained through the dust and grime, watching firemen and other services searching for survivors in a mound of rubble, all that remained of a collapsed building across the way. He gritted his teeth. When he turned to address the room, his voice contained gravity and passion.

"It's our duty to help anyone to evade capture. Not only because it's the right thing to do. How much does it cost to train a fighter pilot?"

Carter's brow furrowed. Bacon shrugged.

The Brigadier supplied the answer. "Fifteen thousand pounds. A bomber pilot around ten thousand. Every one we help get back home saves us time and money."

"Makes sense." Carter agreed.

"Jack Martin's main objective was the escape of stranded pilots. He had a small network of German resistance fighters helping him, men and women who oppose the Nazis. From his coded messages, we know they've been operating out of a bar in Berlin, running airmen out through Sweden to the north and some with forged travel warrants into occupied Netherlands. Results have been impressive. But Jack was the driving force. Without him, the network would dissolve or disband. What we do know is that his most valuable information came from his secret contact, who must have been, or still is, well-connected."

"Sounds like we need to identify this contact."

"Spot on. Except Jack only ever referred to the contact by codename."

"Which is?"

"The Wolf."

"What can I bring to the party from here?" Carter's question hung in the air for what seemed an age, so long that he wondered if his comment were too flippant, if it had angered the Brigadier. Finally, Pritchard laid his knuckles on the table and looked him in the eyes.

"We need to find out what happened to Jack Martin. We need to identify this contact, to carry on the good work. We need you to bring us the truth."

The word *Bring* rattled around in Carter's brain. It suggested a journey, the perilous purpose of the meeting finally registering.

"You mean go to Berlin."

Both Pritchard and Lieutenant Harris nodded.

A sudden infusion of emotion sent a shudder through Carter's body. He grabbed his knee under the table to stop his left leg shaking.

For a moment, he was back on the beach at Dunkirk, face buried in sand as the Luftwaffe strafed his column. He lost 15 men that day. Fifteen. In fewer than five seconds. That sort of loss stays with a man. Burns into an officer's psyche. *Could I have saved them? Could I have done anything different? Why did they die? Why did I survive?* He shivered at the memory. When his evacuation boat arrived, he had stood for six hours in shoulder-deep water, his bones stiff as iron, his will almost spent. But he was alive. He had been filled with regret and suffocating guilt ever since.

He wanted to tell the Brigadier he wasn't the man for the job. That he felt physically sick. These days he was a desk jockey. No longer could he cope with the terrors of working undercover. That the last thing he wanted on God's Earth right now was to go to Berlin. But he couldn't say it. He couldn't admit it. Not even to himself. So he fumbled those dark thoughts back into their box and he lied.

"Of course, Sir. Happy to help. I'll bring you the truth."

5

January 24th, 1944. Berlin.

EYES shut, Carter concentrated on the dull drone of the Dakota's engines. A tap on the shoulder and the American drawl of the jumpmaster yelling in his ear roused him. "Ten minutes to target."

Carter jabbed a thumb in the air, accompanied by a nauseous lurch in his stomach. It had always been like that, ever since his initial parachute course, jumping out of static hot air balloons. He'd never got used to it. Never would, despite having performed dozens of jumps.

As always, he'd packed his own parachute. The science of it appealed to him but there was also an art in smoothing the white nylon, folding the fabric with precision. He tugged on the aircraft's static line, hooked to the parachute's ripcord, to ensure no snags. One in 20 jumpers experienced packing problems. He was aware of the statistics, but wasn't carrying an extra safety chute. Too bulky.

"Two minutes." The jumpmaster held up two fingers, in case his holler went unheard.

Carter clambered out of his metal seat and edged towards the Dakota's rear door.

Lieutenant Harris's team had conceived the plan at MI9 HQ in Beaconsfield the day after they'd all met at the War Office. Carter had considered taking a train to Paris, travelling through occupied France and on to Berlin, but abandoned that idea after realising how long it would take and how often his false passport and papers would likely be scrutinised.

The Dakota was Bacon's idea. "The only way," he had asserted with a confident shrug. Easy for him to say, thought Carter. He wasn't the poor sap who had to drop into Berlin with several hundred tons of Allied bombs for company.

The strategy was to fly a few miles behind Allied bombers and bale out before German fighters intercepted.

"Okay, Sir." The jumpmaster released the door and beckoned Carter. Cold, wet air flooded in. Carter's teeth chattered as he braced himself against the wind pressure, managing to stay upright, despite the weight of his pack. The jumpmaster ticked through the safety precautions as if he'd done so a thousand times, which he had.

"Steady, Sir, steady. Wait for it."

Carter felt a strong hand on his shoulder. He could sense, rather than see, clouds scudding by and readied himself to jump. No need. The jumpmaster's shove verged on violent. "Go, go." Then he was falling, tumbling in the blackness, sucked into a vast hole. At least that's how it felt, gravity straining at his neck, tearing his shoulder muscles until it seemed his bones would surely crack. The uncontrolled spinning lasted seconds but felt like minutes before the static line yanked the ripcord, the jolt of the opening parachute triggering a manic chuckle of intense relief followed by a comforting stillness.

A shimmer to Carter's left confirmed RAF incendiary bombs were wreaking vengeance. He took no pleasure from the sight, even though two days before he had been on the receiving end of a similar pounding. Too busy searching for a suitable landing spot.

The Dakota pilot had done a professional job, avoiding the populated outskirts of Berlin, as well as the thick forest that scarred their route. No point evading most of the trouble, only to end up dangling, vulnerable and helpless, from the branches of a tall tree. A pathetic target for German patrols searching for stranded airmen the next morning.

Carter's night vision kicked in, helped by a half moon playing hide and seek with the light cloud base. Tugging hard on his straps, he slowed his descent, edging right on the light crosswind, another surge of relief as he realised he was heading for an open field.

Then he was down, left ankle twisting on impact, but the pain was fleeting. Flat on his face, the chute dragged him across wet grass towards a wall of mouldy hay bales. He stopped 20 yards short, a handy spot as the hay formed a natural barrier from anyone observing in the distant farm house.

He lay still for a few seconds, sucking in oxygen, before jettisoning his pack and hurrying to gather the billowing chute, hiding it among the hay.

Happy with his work, he sat with his back to the bales, glad of the wind break from the January chill. Taking stock. Reactivating his senses after the pitch and sway of the plane and the trauma of the drop. Listening to the crump of explosions, echoing and rolling like distant thunder.

There was no need for one of Bacon's compasses to point the way to Berlin. The RAF had done that already, but he took the compass from his pack anyway and checked his bearings with the light of a miniature torch. Fifteen miles at most, he reckoned. A few hours' walk under cover of darkness. He brushed down his flight uniform, debating whether to reverse it to transform it into a civilian suit. If he ran into a German patrol in flight uniform, he would be captured as a downed airman and imprisoned. If he was captured in a civilian suit he would be shot, almost certainly, as a spy.

But existing undercover was an integral part of his training. And even though the world of secret agents now set nerves twitching, it was who he was. Part of his instinct. He ripped off boots followed by his jacket and trousers, cursing as the chill bit into his flesh. Flipping the clothes around, he pulled on his civilian attire.

A sound jerked at his senses. He paused, still as a statue, a German accent knifing through the night air.

"Berlin's taking a pounding tonight." The gruff voice of an old man. Twenty yards away. Maybe more. Difficult to gauge amid the rumbles.

A young boy replied. "Is Papa safe, Grandpa?"

"Yes. Papa's safe, Helmut. He's nowhere near Berlin. He'll be home soon, don't worry."

Through a gap in the bales, Carter glimpsed the glow of a lantern and two shadowy figures, the younger one balanced on the middle stay of a wooden fence. Faces tilted to the night sky, observing distant flashes.

A low growl, almost within touching distance, sent a spasm of fear down Carter's spine. A black and white sheepdog, bared teeth gleaming in the moonlight. In normal circumstances, Carter had a way with dogs. His father kept spaniels and had taught him as a toddler. *Never show fear. Remember, boy, you're the leader of the pack. Stand tall, show them who's boss.* But these circumstances were far from normal.

He pulled a Webley .38 revolver from his pack. He didn't want to use it. If he did, whatever the outcome, his presence would be compromised. The dog crept closer, hackles raised, growl deepening. Protecting its territory. A snap of teeth confirmed its threat.

"What is it, Perle? What have you found?" The boy's high-pitched voice.

"It'll be a rat's nest. She loves chasing rats." The old man had farmed this plot for half a century. He'd seen most things. Foxes in the hen house. Bats in the cow shed. A couple of Czech airmen hiding in the barn a year or so back. They'd run off sharpish when he'd grabbed his pitchfork. He swung the lantern higher, sweeping light over the bales.

Carter heard the boy jump down from the fence and run towards the dog.

"Leave them alone, Perle."

Two options. Shoot the dog and run, although Carter's heavy pack rendered that option neither attractive, nor pragmatic. Shoot all three of them. Several of his special forces' colleagues would be comfortable with that scenario, but Carter wasn't one of them.

Another sound piqued his attention. The unmistakable click of a shotgun engaging, accompanied by a gruff cry.

"Let's see if I can bag a couple." The old man had sensed some sport to liven up the evening even more. He clambered over the fence.

The mission was in danger of ending before it had even started. Carter tightened his grip on the revolver, the swish of boots on grass and the swinging lantern heralding the old man's approach. A couple more seconds and he would round the hay bales. Carter extended an arm, pointing the gun at the growling dog, barely three feet away, his finger gently squeezing the trigger. It was the only way.

***

The explosion blew Carter off his feet. For many moments he had no idea what was happening as earth and mud rained down. His ears jangled. The smell of explosive stung his nostrils. Plumes of flame and smoke rose from the adjacent field, but the growls were gone and when his hearing returned the sound of distant barking and excited voices filled the air.

"Get in the shelter. Perle, you too, get in here." An old woman's voice emanating from outside the farm house.

Carter slumped against the hay, fingers combing mud from his hair, shaking grass and grogginess from his head.

He peered into the night sky. A faint drone. Returning aircraft. One of them must have jettisoned its bomb load, probably having taken fighter fire or flak before it could reach its target in Berlin. A common occurrence. Lightening the load was the first and obvious practicality for the pilot of a stricken plane, increasing the chances of the crew's survival if the aircraft had to ditch.

Thank God for friendly fire.
***

Carter pulled on leather gloves and trudged north for almost two hours, mostly across fields and along minor roads. Despite the weight of his backpack, his loping stride devoured the miles.

When he arrived at an intersection between several minor roads and the main highway, he paused to rest on a large rock. Traffic amounted to the odd car or truck, crawling along with masked headlights, the city no more than six miles away.

He could have continued on foot, but the chances of running into a German patrol searching for downed airmen would increase with each mile. Considering the pounding the city was taking, the mood of the hunters would be seriously bloody. Time for a lift.

Fishing a cigarette lighter from his pocket, he waved the flame above his head. The first two vehicles ignored him. The third, a truck, stopped. A middle-aged man with meaty forearms, a ruddy face and the suspicion of a lisp, wound down the driver's window. "What's the problem?"

"Broke down a few miles back. Any chance of a ride into the city?"

"Sure you want to go there, most of Berlin's on fire?"

"I've come from Leipzig. I'm on business."

"Must be important"

"It is. War stuff."

"Okay, jump in. I'm Gunther. But I'm not driving into the centre until we get the all-clear."

Carter threw his pack into the back of the cab and swung into the passenger seat.

"What happened?" The driver's tone contained a hint of suspicion.

"Pardon?"

"To your car."

"Not sure. Could be …." For an instant, Carter considered his own flustered response and thought it unpersuasive, before regaining his equilibrium. "I'm useless with anything mechanical. Engine spluttered, came to a stop. Wouldn't start."

"Sure it didn't run out of petrol, or oil. Not easy to come by these days."

"That could be it."

"Fuel's not what it used to be. More like weak piss these days. Wrecks the engine. Can't get the good stuff anymore."

Carter noticed Gunther relax, a satisfied smirk on his lips, proud of his diagnosis.

As the truck trundled on, they chatted about the state of the war and the daily poundings German cities were enduring. Carter sneaked a peek through the curtain at the back of the cab. The truck was carrying provisions. Canned food, bottled water, blankets.

Spotting his interest, Gunther jabbed a thumb behind him. "This load is on its way to a central warehouse before being distributed to air-raid shelters. Some people are so scared they're practically living underground these days. If this bombing continues, there'll be nothing left. Too many of our great cities have been reduced to dust and rubble." Gunther stuck to facts, careful not to criticise the ruling regime, although Carter formed the distinct impression he wasn't a big supporter of the Nazis. At one point, Gunther's curiosity turned to Carter's accent, intrigued by the harsh consonants.

"Don't take this the wrong way, my friend, and no offence intended, but you sound Swiss. I've never been a fan of Swiss-German. All the right words, well, most of them, but the accent's not always attractive to the German ear."

Pot and kettle came to Carter's mind, but he managed a diplomatic smile. "No offence taken. I can't help where I come from, but I live in Leipzig now. I'll try to speak better." Carter mimicked a posh German accent.

Gunther chuckled.

Carter relaxed, confident now that his German was good enough to convince a native speaker, especially as he hadn't spoken the language for several years.

Although detonations had receded, the sky's permanent glow and the cloying smell of smoke suggested fires were still raging.

Two miles out, the truck rounded a corner to find vehicles queuing at a roadblock manned by troops bearing rifles and machine guns. Confident the bombing had ceased for the night, their undimmed headlights blazed, torchlights dancing as they checked papers.

The taste of panic rose in Carter's throat. He swallowed hard, glancing behind to clock the masked headlights of a queue of cars. No escape. The truck hemmed in. He squirmed in his seat and contemplated lunging for cover amid the scrubby vegetation that lined the road, but realised that was a bad idea. Such a move would alert Gunther and almost certainly he would report him.

Nothing for it but to put his story to a sterner test.

The truck chugged towards the inspection point, the leading soldier's shoulder strap denoting the rank of captain.

Gunther's greeting was cheery. "Good evening."

"What's good about it? Didn't you hear the bombs and can't you see the fires up ahead?" The soldier's surly reply accompanied by a hand motion to present papers.

The captain flicked through Gunther's in disinterested fashion before returning them.

"Quick." The soldier jabbed a palm at Carter through the open window.

Cold sweat slithered down Carter's back. He prayed Bacon's handiwork in Beaconsfield was as proficient as he had boasted. This time the captain studied the papers closely, snorting twice, his upper lip curling with what Carter took to be disdain.

"Herr David Schmid. Swiss?" He spat out the nationality.

"Yes," replied Carter.

Switzerland, despite its Germanic connections, had stayed neutral in fighting terms for the duration of the war. Despite two thirds of its arms sales going to Germany during that time with the other third to Italy, not all Germans considered the Swiss as friends. Many could not understand why Germany had not invaded its pacifist neighbour, although the mountainous terrain was one obvious reason, while rumours circulated that perhaps it was a haven to hide Nazi gold.

The captain was of the persuasion that the Swiss should stand and fight alongside his comrades.

"These papers say you're a banker in Zurich. You're a long way from home. What's your business in Berlin?"

Instinct persuaded Carter a flimsy comment would not suffice. Instead, he recited a scenario concocted with Bacon back in Beaconsfield.

"I work for UBS, the Union Bank of Switzerland. I'm here to meet officials of Deutsche Bank."

"With bombs falling?"

"My visit is important."

"For what purpose?"

"That's confidential. I'm sure you understand. I don't think the Führer would want Germany's financial details divulged. All I can say is that it's material to the progress of the war and of special interest to Herr Himmler."

Carter detected the mention of the Führer and Himmler stab home. Nothing dramatic, a tiny twitch of an eye, a more significant tensing of the man's jaw.

Flicking again through the papers, the captain raised his eyes a couple of times as if weighing the veracity of Carter's story against the peril of incurring the wrath of powerful men such as Himmler, whose reputation as Reichsminister of the Interior and head of the Gestapo was fearsome. Still, he persevered.

"Why is a banker travelling in a truck?"

Carter motioned to Gunther. "My friend took pity on me. A few miles back, my car broke down. It's a horrible night to be stranded by the roadside."

"Water in the fuel pipe, I reckon." Gunther added his diagnosis, as if in corroboration.

With obvious reluctance, the captain returned the papers, jerking his thumb. "Move on."

Three miles down the way they stopped again. This time a squad of air-raid wardens, trained in fire-fighting, blocked the highway. Metal signs informed drivers the road was temporarily closed to allow fire engines and ambulances access to the carnage in the city. The wardens didn't carry guns but their grey paramilitary uniforms with black trims and red armbands, inset with a swastika, exuded a level of intimidation. One of the wardens had a whistle, a long stick and a short temper, a fraught combination as he directed proceedings from a strategically-placed wooden box in the middle of the road. Flourishing his stick, as a conductor might control violins, he took obvious delight in ordering vehicles into gaps in the makeshift lay-bys.

Gunther slotted the truck into a tight space, careful to avoid the deeper mud. "I'm not getting stuck here for a moment longer than necessary." He wound down the window, immediately gagging on the toxic smoke. Covering his face with a spare tee shirt, he took a deep breath and shouted to one of the civil defence league, although the gist escaped Carter amid the blustery breeze.

The man's reply was clear enough. "No one's moving before morning, unless you want to walk."

For a moment, Carter contemplated doing exactly that. But Gunther had parked on high ground and from their elevated position they could appraise the handiwork of the British and American bombers that night.

Tongues of flame, as far as the eye could see, licked high into the night sky, tracing the Allied aircrafts' route. On either side of the devastation, darkness denoted areas undefiled by high explosive. Three, in particular, flanking either side of the inner city, caught Carter's attention.

"Flak." Gunther's curt explanation.

"Pardon?"

"That's where Berlin's biggest flak towers are housed. If you were flying low in a slow bomber would you want to fly over the top of them into a cloud of jagged metal?" Gunther didn't wait for Carter's reply. "No, neither would I. That's why the only streets and buildings relatively undamaged in the city are in areas around the flak towers."

"Makes sense."

Gunther nodded towards the burning city. "By the look of that, so does camping here for the night."

"If you don't mind, I'll join you."

"Glad of the company."

Gunther pulled out a thin mattress from the body of the truck, and laid it in a gap behind the seats. Obviously not the first time he'd used the truck as a hotel.

"Sorry, I only have one. You'll have to sleep where you sit."

"No problem. Sleeping's my party trick."

Gunther threw Carter a blanket. "You'll need this. Fearful cold at night this time of year."

They settled down, the constant whistles and revving of vehicles eventually subsiding, replaced in Carter's mind by thoughts other than the mission ahead.

He drifted to childhood and happy holidays in sunny Devon where he loved crabbing with his big sister Susan. He thought of his parents. Julian, a Swiss national and a teacher at the local primary school, who taught him his native French and German as a child. And his mother, Angela, a stalwart of the Women's Institute. They had encouraged him to become a doctor because he was inquisitive, good at science and possessed a caring nature.

If they were disappointed when he decided to abandon his medical studies and stay in the Army after his national service, they never showed it.

They were proud to have a soldier and a proficient linguist in the family and although they were not aware of his secondment to the Special Forces Support Group a few years ago, and subsequently to MI9, they were pleased that no longer did he seem in daily danger.

He'd visited them at Christmas, dinner table chat turning to the hope that the Allies were at last showing signs of winning the war. His father had toasted fallen heroes with cheap sparkling wine and they had listened to King George's speech lauding the spirit of the people.

We know that much hard working and hard fighting – perhaps harder working and fighting than ever before – are necessary for victory. We shall not rest from our task until it is nobly ended.

Amid his gentle snoring, more fearful thoughts infiltrated. *Is my Swiss-German really good enough? Can I still deal with the pressures of life undercover? Am I up to this mission?*

6

THE smiles and sound of chatter surprised Carter.

He'd always thought of Germany in stereotypes. As a country devoid of laughter. A nation full of engineers, scientists and stern expressions, one in which obedience and organisation were cherished and humour frowned upon. Where light relief was confined to beer festivals or had been stolen from English traditions, such as men dressing up as Morris dancers. Yet, as the truck edged its way into the city centre next morning, negotiating rubble and smoking ruins, women were everywhere.

On one side, at least 50 formed a human chain, most dressed in brown overalls or dungarees, passing chunks of debris along the line before a supervisor at the end chucked them into a parked lorry. One sweet-looking girl caught Carter's eye. Rosebud lips, long brown hair, alabaster skin and the freshest of complexions. Fifteen at most. In another life, most likely she would have attended school this morning, studying without a care. On the other side of the road, a burnt-out tram leaned precariously, metal buckled and twisted. Another group of women edged around it, backs stiff, arms and legs straining, wheelbarrows laden with debris, depositing their loads in a growing mound off the roadway.

The only men were air-raid wardens, clawing through rubble. It was unlikely anyone was trapped. The shopping area was not residential, the raid the previous night was anticipated, most people would have been safely underground in shelters.

Carter hadn't expected the obvious camaraderie. It reminded him of London in the Blitz, without the Cockney curses. Some women even waved at the truck as they passed. Gunther seemed to sense Carter's surprise.

"That's what we call community spirit. Never underestimate German women. I learned that many years ago. They are strong-minded, lively, hard-working, harsh, gentle, arrogant, sincere, lazy and loving. Like women the world over, it's hard to generalise."

"You're not wrong there, Gunther, although I expect the same goes for men."

"Except, wars are waged by men, not women. Women are left to pick up the pieces." He nodded towards the chain gang swinging bricks and timber, the swaying rhythm oddly hypnotic.

Carter hadn't figured Gunther for a deep-thinker, but he had warmed to him these past few hours as they munched through the remnants of a packet of shortbread biscuits.

By the time they reached Gunther's destination, it was mid-morning.

At the far end of the street, Gunther spotted a space uncluttered by rubble near the Hotel Central. He pulled in.

"This is as far as I go. The underground warehouse is around the corner. It will take all day to unload. Good to spend some time with you, Herr Schmid. Take my details." He pressed a business card with numbers and address into Carter's hand. "If you ever need stuff to shift, Gunther Hagen's your man. Give me a call. I hope you have an agreeable meeting at Deutsche Bank. It's on Mauerstrasse, isn't it?"

Carter's antennae twitched. Gunther's tone was matter-of-fact, amiable even, but his question was unnecessary. Sounded like a trick, a test to gauge the veracity of his story. Germany, in common with France and Belgium, was teeming with spies, and no shortage of locals prepared to report them to the Gestapo.

Fortunately, MI9's research had been extensive, Carter memorising the geography as well as the specifics of his 'new' banking career. "That's right," he said. "On the corner with Franzosische Strasse. Thanks for the lift. Don't know what I'd have done without you."

As the truck door swung open, the smoky taste of Berlin hit the back of Carter's throat. An open-topped military vehicle turned the corner, heading in their direction, followed by five more, each carrying at least 30 men. They bore rifles, wore hard helmets, but many were dishevelled. Dirty faces, scruffy beards, solemn expressions and ragged uniforms.

"Back from the Balkans, looks like." Gunther surmised. "Hell on earth out there, by all accounts." The trucks trundled past. Carter jumped from the cab, dragged out his pack, and slammed the door. Gunther waved, a cheery farewell, prompting Carter to dismiss his suspicion. At first, the broken landscape was disorientating, the classical bay windows of the nearby hotel providing elegant normality from the front, until he realised one side was open to the elements as if sliced by a gigantic carving knife. Twisted staircases were festooned with trailing wires. Torn canvasses, broken chandeliers and a thick layer of plaster powder rendered the building's plush interior grey and ghostly.

It was a far cry from the city Carter had visited years before as a student. He'd done the usual tourist stuff. The Brandenburg Gate, the Reichstag, Berlin Cathedral. He remembered strolling along the famous boulevards, all the way from the Spree River to the Brandenburg Gate, He'd enjoyed a picnic with his girlfriend and they'd marvelled at the towering lime trees that lined the route.

This was so different. Another world. Back then, Berlin's palatial buildings and huge statues were a barometer of the wealth and engineering precision of Germany, each street oozing class and status. His visit had coincided with the week in September, 1930, when the Nazis were voted into parliament amid torchlight parades, rousing speeches and all-night parties. The posters and newspapers promised full employment, prosperity, a brighter future, and Germany's return to political power. Wherever you looked, there was a swastika. In his idealistic youth, the atmosphere was beguiling. Fresh, vibrant, and he fell for it. At least he did until he learned the swastika had been stolen from Asian culture, principally Indian religions, including Hinduism and Buddhism, where it represented divinity and spirituality.

Carter forced himself to concentrate on the present. He approached a young woman on the edge of a group of workers, taking a breather from shovelling debris. An unlit cigarette dangled from her lips.

"Excuse me Fraulein. Is the U-Bahn open?

She withdrew the cigarette, twirling it in her fingers. "Yes, why wouldn't it be?"

"I thought …" He motioned with a sweep of his hand to the devastation.

"Take more than a few bombs to shut the Underground. The tramway may need some repair, but the Underground's fine."

"Do you need a light?" Carter fumbled in his pocket, producing a lighter.

"Nein!" The force of the response, along with her obvious panic, caused Carter to jump.

"Can't you smell gas? A main's damaged. They're still trying to find the source of the leak. Didn't you see the sign?"

"Sorry, I didn't mean to … Thank you, Fraulein."

He hurried away in the direction of the U-Bahn, the encounter only serving to emphasise the perilous nature of his mission.

Half an hour later, he emerged from the underground station. Despite all the training, the action he'd encountered in France and Belgium, all the lessons in tradecraft as an undercover operative in enemy territory, there remained an icy sense of foreboding.

The weather didn't help. A chill wind blew a flurry of sleet into his face. He hunched shoulders, buttoning his jacket. He had checked his appearance on the train. Not bad, considering he'd landed in a field, yomped 10 miles and slept in a truck. Jacket and trousers rumpled in places, but the tie he'd fixed in place and the thick glasses he wore conformed to the stereotype of a Swiss banker.

He assumed a confident stride to fit the persona and the first significant landmark he noticed was the drab, dirty, concrete slab of the Flakturm II tower, scarring the skyline ahead of him. Gunther was right. Despite several derelict buildings and windows blown out in the streets around, the devastation was not as extensive in properties adjoining the flak tower.

There was even a semblance of normalcy. A bartender lobbed bottles into a skip, an old man with bandy legs towed items of luggage down the middle of the street, little puffs of breathy steam accompanying his effort. A row of women sat in an office, collars turned up, coats buttoned against the cold, noses glued to their desks.

Dolziger Strasse. Carter squinted to identify the street name. He trudged as far as number 96, a tall building, brickwork bearing scars from flying shrapnel but no obvious structural damage. By the numbers on the side of the entrance, it housed 10 apartments. He pushed at the big oak doorway, the opening creak setting nerves on edge.

From Lieutenant Harris's briefing he knew he was looking for number seven. The bare wooden stairs groaned as he climbed to the second floor, the only light emanating from a ragged hole in the roof several floors above where a tile was missing, the wind whining and sleet falling like fine mist through the aperture. At number seven, he knocked softly, waited, and then rapped a little harder. No answer. Pulling Bacon's modified version of a Swiss Army knife from his pocket, he fiddled a blade into the lock, and twisted. On the third twist the lock disengaged and Carter entered a drab room with crumbling plaster walls, threadbare linen curtains wafting in the breeze slicing through broken glass panes. A single bed snuggled against one wall, crumpled blankets and a head-shaped depression in the pillow suggesting it had been occupied recently. An easy chair, a small table and a sideboard formed the only furniture, the latter's drawers revealing a few woollen jumpers and several items of men's underwear.

Carter poked his head into a small kitchenette and spied a half-full bottle of Johnnie Walker Black Label whisky and two glass tumblers lurking in a corner of the worktop. A tiny bathroom completed the apartment, but there were no photos, no personal items, no indication as to who might live there. He edged to the window and parted the curtains a fraction, revealing a perfect view of the street below. Carter had already noted the metal fire stairs to the right of the doorway which provided a fast route to the rear of the property. In the world of the secret agent, this was a decent hideaway. A neighbourhood afforded significant protection by the flak tower, away from political buildings, with clear lines of sight.

The chilling click of a cocking gun hammer interrupted his musing.

7

HIS body tensed, a sudden bolt of adrenalin causing his heart to pound, his first thought for the whereabouts of his Webley revolver. At the bottom of his pack to elude any superficial search.

What an idiot. First rule of agent tradecraft: Don't enter strange premises without a weapon to hand and a means of escape. He couldn't remember the last time he'd needed that advice, but the gun trained on the back of his head served as a reminder that he had better sharpen up his act. If it was not already too late.

"Don't move." The language German, but the man's accent laden with softer overtones. "Turn around, slow and easy."

Carter toyed with replying, 'Make your mind up.' Instead, he parked the glib quip, and swivelled. The man in the doorway matched the gloom, his clothes dark, a belt and buckle hanging loosely from his overcoat, wide-brimmed hat too big so it cast a shadow across his fleshy features. But Carter caught the determined, dead stare, and the easy manner with which he handled the pistol. He'd seen that look before these past few years. This was a man accustomed to working in stressful times. A man almost certainly who had killed and would not hesitate to do so again.

"Who are you?"

"I'm a friend of Jack." Carter blurted out the information. It occurred to him to continue the pretence that he was David Schmid, the Swiss banker. That's what his spymasters would have advised, but his gut instinct kicked in. The man wore no uniform. He was obviously not a member of the SS, nor the Gestapo, as he spoke with a foreign accent, the sing-song type Carter had last heard in a Parisienne Tabac. While the man had demonstrated deftness and cunning to corner Carter, that did not mean he was necessarily an enemy. Playfully rocking the pistol's trigger, the man motioned for Carter to sit on the bed.

"Who's Jack?"

Carter snorted, attempting to convey a carefree air of derision. "Who's Jack? We both know Jack's the man who runs the show. I'm guessing you must be Le Droit."

Carter watched for recognition in the man's eyes, but detected none.

"One more time I will ask. Who are you? Be very careful how you answer." The man's right arm was fully extended, black gun barrel trained on Carter's head. All those lessons on how to negotiate stress and retain equilibrium in perilous positions raced through Carter's mind. In the office, on the range, they always seemed perfectly reasonable. Ingenious even. In reality, it was different. It came down to gut instinct and Carter's grumbling gut was telling him to stick to a semblance of the truth.

"I've told you, I'm Jack's friend." Somehow, his voice sounded calm. "Jack's a brave man. He's saved many lives. I'm here to help him continue his good work."

It was the calculated move of a master poker player, a confident, all-in play on an uncertain hand. Dangerous, potentially disastrous if wrong, but with rich reward if correct. For several seconds, the man held his pose as if ruminating, the silence chipping away at Carter's psyche. Slowly, the man's arm lowered and he eased the hammer on his gun.

Carter sucked in a lungful of relief as he noticed the tip of the man's left-hand little finger was missing. He grabbed the initiative. "Good to meet you, Le Droit. I've heard a lot about you."

"My name's Henry, but everyone calls me Bo. Only Jack called me Le Droit. It was his little joke."

"That sounds like Jack, always having fun. You said *was*."

"Pardon?"

"*Was* his little joke. Past tense."

Bo fixed him with a piercing stare, but Carter detected exhaustion and an aching sadness behind those dead eyes. The longer he stared the mistier they became. Four years of war had obviously exacted a psychological toll, but it was also the moment Carter concluded Jack Martin was not coming back. Stowing his gun inside his belt, Bo walked over to the window, parted the curtains and scrutinised the street. A tremor in his voice betrayed his emotion. "Forgive me for the welcome, but we're all a bit jumpy. We've been waiting for someone to take over. Without Jack, things have become a little disorganised."

"That's why I'm here. To find out about Jack. I have a transmitter. I can pass information to the right people in the right place at the right time. All safe and coded. Like Jack did. That's what I'm good at."

"What's your name?"

Carter pondered for a moment, before deciding there was no merit in lying. He fished his wallet containing forged papers from his inside pocket.

"Look." He handed the papers to Bo. "As far as the Nazis are concerned, I'm a Swiss banker. David Schmid. But my real name's Sam and I work for the same people as Jack."

Bo nodded and returned the papers. "You'll be staying here then." There was a lilt of encouragement in his tone.

"It's not the London Hilton, but it's well located and apparently as safe as anywhere in this ruined city. I guess I could stand it for a month or two."

Carter walked through to the kitchen and swiped the whisky bottle and tumblers off the worktop. He poured generous measures, handed one to Bo and motioned for him to sit on the easy chair. Carter perched on the edge of the bed and took a slurp of whisky, the fiery liquid immediately burning the back of his throat.

"Okay, Bo." An extra rasp in his voice. "Tell me exactly what happened to Jack."

For the best part of an hour, Bo related the circumstances surrounding Jack Martin's most recent mission. Members of the resistance had alerted him to a bunch of Allied airmen hiding out in a makeshift shelter in Grunewald Forest. Two Britons, two Americans, a Czech and a Polish pilot, the latter having spent almost six weeks dodging attempts to snare him. Two of the men were wounded, one suffering from a broken leg. The others refused to abandon him.

Jack had arranged for a truck to pick them up in the early hours under the chaotic cover of an air raid. The plan was to drive to Potsdam and lay low at a safe farm house for a few days to await the arrival of forged papers, train warrants, and civilian clothing. Dozens of airmen had escaped using a similar plan along the same well-tried route.

"So why didn't it work this time?" Carter knew Jack was meticulous in everything he did. Something catastrophic must have happened for his plan to fail.

"Jack ran out of luck. As simple as that."

"What do you mean?"

Bo licked his lips, his voice lowered and Carter leaned across the table to recharge his glass. They both took a slug.

"I should have been there. I know Berlin like the back of my hand, but I was taken sick that night. I could have got them out."

Carter looked puzzled. "Just tell me what happened, Bo."

"I only know what I was told by one of our group, the truck driver, who escaped. An American bomber came down on the road out of the forest. Burning fuel everywhere. It blocked their escape route. They had to abandon the truck. Jack helped carry the Czech guy with the broken leg, but it was hard work and the downed plane attracted half the German Army. An SS unit swarmed all over the forest. There was no way out."

"But Jack must have realised there was no point fighting. What happened?"

Bo didn't reply, his eyes fixed on the wooden floor. Carter had already calculated the likely scenario. Bombs falling on Berlin, soldiers and civilians dying by the minute. Humanitarian rules of engagement are not always observed in such circumstances. And this was a war in which German soldiers, particularly the SS, had forged a reputation for ruthlessness and brutality.

"The truck driver said it was quick." Bo's voice lowered to little more than a mumble. "He was about one hundred yards in front and saw it all from behind a tree at the top of a mound. There was nothing he could do, but hide. He saw Jack and the Czech caught in the soldiers' search beam. He thought he heard a warning, although he can't be sure. At first he was relieved. He thought they were being taken prisoner, but a burst of machine gun fire and it was all over. Like I said, Jack was unlucky. If that plane hadn't come down …"

Bo trailed off. They both slung back several more slugs of whisky, the mood melancholy, although Bo took the opportunity to explain he worked out of a basement bar not far from where they sat. At Carter's insistence, he supplied directions.

As Bo rose to leave, Carter threw out a thought he'd been trying, without success, to shoehorn into the conversation. "Does The Wolf mean anything to you?"

Bo chewed his lip for several seconds in contemplation, eventually shaking his head.

8

A FEW hours later, the light was fading. Carter had used the time since Bo left to pore over a map of Berlin.

Dolziger Strasse was east of central but well positioned to travel to any part of the city as long as the U-Bahn remained open. He committed the underground map and the streets around to memory. A straightforward task. If anyone asked, not that they ever would, he could also pinpoint the capital of every state of America on a map, as well as every football league ground in England. His training had schooled him well in the art of storing mental images.

Lying on the bed, he tightened the rough blanket around him to shield against the biting draught, and thought of Jack Martin. Ten years had passed since they shared a cave. He had seen him since, but not for several years. They had always enjoyed lively conversation, jokey banter, and could have been good friends, he reasoned, if war and geography had not prised them apart.

He fell asleep, the tension and discomfort of the night before having induced a seeping tiredness. A few hours later, he jolted awake in a state of confusion. For a moment, he struggled for his bearings, the bare plaster walls disorientating, head swimming, a heavy thump of boots resounding on the wooden staircase.

His training kicked in, first thought for the Webley revolver on the bedside table. He scooped it up and crossed the room.

Footsteps approached his door, accompanied by a light tapping and a scraping noise. Whoever it was paused for a moment. Carter strained to listen, but the footsteps receded and rhythmic thuds returned, this time ascending to the next floor.

Carter eased the door open, stepping into the passageway. The back of a big man in a long overcoat was disappearing around the curve of the bannister, white stick swinging side to side.

Good effort climbing all those steps. Carter watched in admiration before shuffling back inside.

"Who's there? Is that Jack?" The man spun around, calling down the stairs.

Carter made to shut the apartment door, but the man's demeanour was non-confrontational. He stepped back into the corridor.

"I'm a friend of Jack's. He's not around at the moment, but he's been kind enough to let me use his apartment for a while. An unwelcome visitor dropped by at my place."

The man chuckled. "A bomb, you mean?"

"That's right."

"I've not spoken to Jack for weeks. Used to enjoy our chats. Hope he's not got caught in an air raid." Carter detected genuine concern in the man's tone.

"I think he can take care of himself."

"Not if his name's on a bomb, or a bullet, he can't."

"I suppose you're right."

"If you see him, tell him I was asking about him. If you ever need anything I'm in number nine."

"I'll remember that. Nine. Thanks."

He ducked inside and shut the door. Carter had been in the building a few hours only and already two people had admitted to knowing and liking Jack. He found that surprising. After all, Jack Martin was an MI9 agent whose mission in life was not to be seen or heard.

Carter sat on the bed gathering his thoughts. The first requirement was to hide his spy radio transmitter. There was nowhere obvious, apart from under the floorboards, which was probably too obvious. but at least would require a comprehensive hunt rather than a routine glance.

After dragging the sideboard away from the wall, he set about prising out nails, taking care not to leave tell-tale splinters as he gently gouged the wood. It was a time-consuming task but an hour or so later he had loosened enough boards to slip the streamlined transmitter into its hidey-hole. Replacing the nails carefully, he returned the sideboard, content with his work.

He considered leaving the Webley revolver alongside the transmitter but decided against it. The gun was his one comfort. A friend in need. It might betray him to the Gestapo or SS if stopped and searched, but it could also save his life. He stuffed it into its slim-line holster inside his coat and set off to explore his surroundings.

The streets were dark, blackout blinds and curtains in place in anticipation of another raid. An electrical hum emanated from the direction of the flak tower, reminding him of bees hopping from plant to plant. Doubtless a generator supplying light and heat to the air raid shelter below the concrete tower as well as power to the anti-aircraft guns.

He arrowed his body into the wind, walking south for a couple of blocks towards the Spree River, before turning right. Too dark to see a street sign, although it was obvious the terraced properties at the end of the road were badly damaged, huge mounds of debris piled up against the jagged remains of the walls. His mental image of Berlin's map located the spot Bo had told him to meet.

A truck turned into the road, its masked headlights providing a shadowy glimpse of tall, imposing buildings, all with windows blown out. Most boarded, but some remained holes, dark and vacant like the empty eye sockets of the bomb victims that haunted Carter in his nightmares. At street level a row of shops, and several cafes, proved normal life had not been totally abandoned.

Carter spied a set of iron railings. Bo's directions were accurate. The railings protected a steep set of winding stone steps leading to the building's basement. An arrow painted into the wall at street level pointed downwards. A sign above it announced, Das Bar.

Grabbing a handrail, the sweet smell of stale hops sucked him through the entrance to the cellar. Two old men were sharing memories and sipping beer at the bar. Another group played cards, a bottle of obstwasser, a German fruit brandy, in the middle of their corner table. The night was young but the atmosphere was warm and friendly.

"My friend, you found us then." Bo emerged from a back room, the convenient timing convincing Carter he must have received an alert from a guard on the door. His ruddy face was wreathed in smiles, a grubby bartender's apron around his ample waist.

"Your directions were perfect. Nice place you have here." Carter's praise was genuine.

"We do our best, don't we Elke?" A coy smile lit up the sullen features of the girl behind the bar.

"We'll eat later, but first let us drink." Bo pointed to a bottle of schnapps and two glass tumblers. Elke delivered them to the table where Bo had led Carter. They sat with their backs to the wall, providing a clear sight of the entrance. Bo poured generous measures and while he threw his back, Carter took deliberate sips. The fog of sleep and whisky had not entirely cleared.

They spoke in generalities, their conversation light, focused on the history of the bar and how it served a double purpose in these troubled times, as an entertainment venue and safe haven, its basement location and thick walls protecting against anything other than a direct hit when the sirens blared.

After half an hour, Elke leaned over the bar. "I've set a table in the back if you fancy a bite to eat. Nothing fancy."

"Perfect. Let's eat, my friend." Bo led Carter down a short corridor, through to a room with a low ceiling. A soft lamp burned in a corner, illuminating a table laden with bread, cheese and a dish of roasted potatoes and sauerkraut. Rationing had begun to bite in Berlin. There were tales of people in the areas of greatest devastation, with no heat, water, or access to any amenities, eating rats trapped in the underground. Not Bo. Despite widespread shortages, he always managed to rustle up something acceptable.

They ate, Carter wolfing down the potatoes, realising his last meal had been the meagre remnants of Gunther's shortbread biscuits.

When they had finished, Bo lit a cigarette, offering one to Carter, who declined. Instead, he turned to business, asking about the resistance operation, eager to know how many people were involved and the lines of communication.

"You must remember, my friend, it was Jack's operation. For the last three years, he decided everything. Everyone reported to him, whether marking out coordinates for a factory manufacturing engine parts, or smuggling airmen out of Berlin. He always seemed to know what to do."

Carter was beginning to appreciate the talents of his former Yorkshire friend extended far beyond spying. He appeared to be a leader whose personality inspired those who chose to work alongside him, a man of verve and charisma. Maybe too charismatic. Such individuals possess a tendency to believe themselves indestructible. Perhaps Jack Martin lowered his guard at a crucial moment. After all, no one could do everything and be everywhere.

Bo saw the glint of doubt in Carter's eyes, sing-song vowels assuming a mocking tone. "I know what you're thinking. You think Jack must have become too cocky, made a mistake. You're wrong. He was too meticulous for that. He wasn't arrogant like most English people." Bo reached across the table and tapped Carter on the forearm. "No offence, my friend."

"None taken, Bo. But where did most of his information come from? I can understand troop and tank movements. They're easy to spot. But much of Jack's info was more nuanced, some of it relating to new projects that only Nazis in the know would be privy to."

Bo shrugged. "I'm a simple bartender. I have two little girls who are safe with their mother. I sent them away when bombs began falling on Berlin. I had to stay. I know Berlin. I hate the Nazis. I don't ask where information comes from or what Allied airmen are up to. All I do is make sure that both reach their desired destination."

Carter detected a hint of sourness in Bo's tone as if reacting to implied criticism. He decided to switch the conversation but before he could there was a knock on the door. A light rap, repeated several times as if the interruption was urgent.

Bo swung the door open and a wiry man wearing a beret entered. Tufts of grey hair stuck out at odd angles, giving him a feral look, while a gold fang protruded from the front row of his top teeth, but his German was fast and idiomatic. Carter had trouble understanding.

The man spoke for several minutes, Bo's face registering animation and concern in equal measure. Carter looked puzzled. "What is it?" Bo raised a hand to quell any questions before giving instructions.

"Hide them in the store room for now, Karl. Tonight, use the truck to take them to the usual place and await instructions."

Karl disappeared, Carter noting his sprightly gait was hampered by a significant limp on his right side.

"What was all that about?" Carter asked again.

"Two Americans, a pilot and a gunner. Came down in the air raid last night. The city's been crawling with police and soldiers searching for them all day. One of Karl's boys found them hiding in a coal shed. Apparently, the pilot's badly hurt."

"What are you going to do?"

"Hide them in the back for now. Wait for the early hours. Karl will take them in the truck to a cemetery on the outskirts. We have a bunker with shelter and running water. There's been a lot of activity in cemeteries in recent times for obvious reasons. No one will question the comings and goings. We'll try to get a doctor to take a look at them. But we could do with your help to get them out. They'll need clothes, papers, money, and lots of luck. That was always Jack's domain."

"That'll take weeks." Carter blurted out his considered opinion, wishing it hadn't sounded so feeble.

"It's either that or years in a camp at the pleasure of the Führer. Believe me, I know which I'd prefer."

"Okay. I'll get on the case tomorrow, but I'll need pictures and details."

"You'll have them."

They headed back through the corridor to the bar, the sound of laughter and conversation suggesting it had filled significantly.

As they trooped into the light, Bo stopped, rooted, Carter almost bumping into him. Across the bar, emerging through the entrance, were four men. Two carried machine guns, one brandished a Walther PP pistol.

The fourth wore a long black trench coat. His spectacles were round with metal rims, his hat wide-brimmed, his entire demeanour bearing the arrogance of a Gestapo officer.

9

BO raised his right arm in the customary Nazi salute. "Heil Hitler." He shuffled across the room, wiping hands on his apron, assuming the obsequious demeanour of a hospitable bartender.

"To what do we owe the pleasure of your company? Can I get you anything?"

The officer ignored him, his gaze sweeping the bar, piercing the smoky haze. Around 30 drinkers had gathered while Carter and Bo ate, including a table with five young German soldiers in uniform enjoying a few days' leave.

An old couple sat at another table, the man's face a web of spider veins, his eyes bearing the rheumy demeanour of someone whose only pleasure in life was drink, which almost certainly was the case. The woman's jaw jutted in defiance.

The Gestapo men's entrance acted like turning off a tap. Conversation ceased. Feet shuffled. Eyes fixed on the guns and the officer's cold stare.

After several seconds, he broke the silence.

"You could get me two enemy airmen. Last seen in this area. Would that be possible, do you think, Herr Schneider?"

For the briefest of moments, Bo stumbled, his mind seemingly numbed by the officer's use of his surname.

Then it dawned. In all likelihood, this wasn't a search for airmen. This was a hunt for resistance members, Jews, or political activists, anyone not committed to the Nazi cause as the hardships of a prolonged war began to bite. The stranded airmen were a convenient excuse to visit individuals on the

Gestapo's hit list. Or at least individuals likely to hear gossip and rumours, or gather information detrimental to the state. Such as bar staff and their customers. This Gestapo squad was probably trawling the area.

"I've not heard anything about enemy airmen in this area. Were they shot down last night? We closed early, as soon as the sirens sounded. I was in the flak tower all evening." Bo's tone was even, although his mind whirled. He knew Karl would have deposited the airmen in the store room, no more than 50 feet away, probably hiding underneath sacks and empty flour bags. Enough to evade a routine glance, but not a concerted search.

The officer strode across to the bar, trench coat flapping, nudging tables on either side.

He leaned on the counter, fixing Elke with a scowl designed to discomfort, beckoning her closer with a crooked finger. She obeyed.

"Fraulein, you're very young to be working in a bar such as this."

"I'm 22."

"As I said, so young, and so pretty."

Elke's eyes retaliated with a momentary glint of fire, an insolent pout telling the officer all he needed to know. This was what he was searching for this evening, a bar with staff unsympathetic to the Nazi regime, an ideal rendezvous for members of the resistance.

"Fraulein, you would tell me if you had seen American airmen?" An inflection in his tone warned of sinister intent.

Elke picked up on it. Even so, the warrior within her couldn't restrain a sneer as she nodded.

"I can't hear you Fraulein."

"Ya, heil Hitler." Elke's right arm extended, fast and stiff.

"That's better."

Bo, sensing the exchange heading for dangerous territory, edged to the bar. "We're still training her, but she shows lots of potential."

A flick of the officer's right hand dismissed Bo's entreaties, but he persisted. "She's a good …"

"Enough!" The officer's snarl was accompanied by a violent swing of his forearm, catching the bartender full in the face, sending him staggering, blood pumping from his nose. Bo fell to his knees, hands cupping his face, a red stream trickling through his fingers. A couple of his regulars half-stood, as if to assist him. Berliners had grown accustomed to Gestapo cruelty these past years. The state police force was renowned for its brutality, especially to political opponents, dissenters, the disabled, homosexuals, and Jews. Which is why Bo's regulars thought again, slumping back into their chairs, heads down, attempting to avoid direct eye contact with the gunmen.

The guards moved in, training their guns on the body of the bar, the man with the pistol holding the barrel against the head of the old woman, ratcheting up the fear.

Carter's hand inched towards his revolver, and then relaxed. His instincts yearned to reward the officer's violence with his own brand of brutality, but training kicked in. Play the long game. A Webley revolver was no match for two machine guns and a pistol, especially when they were loaded and cocked, and his firearm was nestled in its hidden holster.

The officer turned again to Elke. "Now, let me ask you another question, Fraulein, and be warned I will remember your answer. If my men were to search the building, would they find nothing?" His head tilted downwards, his eyes narrow and piggy, minimised by the thick lenses in his spectacles, while his eyebrows raised in quizzical fashion.

"Go ahead. Search. Take as long as you like. We've nothing to hide." Buoyed by the fearlessness of youth, Elke was convincing. Carter admired that, but his fingers again itched for his revolver.

"That's settled then. No one moves. We'll search the entire premises and if we find anything then I will hold you all responsible." A flourish of his right arm swept the room. "You will all come with us." The officer waved two of his men forward to search, the clatter of boots adding to the tension as he slid his pistol from its holster.

It would take no more than a minute or two for the guards to reach the store room. But as the officer trained his gun barrel on the throng, the front door swung open, a disconcerting creak echoing around the bare walls. Everyone turned. Standing on the stone steps was a tall woman wearing a long black coat with collar turned up over a black dress. A pearl necklace formed a dazzling smile upon her chest, while her red lips reminded Carter of the buds that bloomed each year in his mother's rose garden. Carter gauged late thirties, but age on such a woman was of little significance. She looked familiar, in the way of film stars such as Marlene Dietrich and Greta Garbo.

Radiant came to Carter's mind. "Wunderbar" was the word that emanated from the officer's mouth.

Immediately, he approached the woman. "Frau Schulz, what an honour to meet you. I have heard you sing many times. Here in Berlin at the State Opera and in Munich and Frankfurt also. The Führer speaks highly of you, but you know that."

"Thank you." Her face broke into the widest of smiles. It reminded Carter of the sun rising on a summer's morning.

"But what are you doing here?" The officer's demeanour suddenly agreeable.

"I come here now and then. Everyone looks after me. I can relax from the worries of these times with a quiet drink in warm and friendly surroundings. If the sirens sound, I don't have to run for cover. It's safe. Sometimes, I even sing here."

The officer bowed his head, swivelled and bellowed orders to his guards. They emerged from the back seconds later.

"Frau Schulz, I must take up no more of your time. I hope to hear you sing again soon. One of life's great treasures."

"You're too kind." She offered her hand and he took it, delighting too long in the soft touch of her fingers before letting go. He bowed his head again and motioned to his guards to leave, following them out of the door with a parting tip of his hat.

When they were gone, several drinkers rushed to Bo, fussing over him. Bo shoved them away to shuffle over to Helena. He held a beer towel to his shattered nose, drops of blood escaping, splattering on the stone floor, forming a haphazard trail. He blurted apologies.

"Don't, Bo." Helena's caring tone stemmed his contrition. "Don't ever apologise for them. They're nothing but thugs. Come on, let's get you cleaned up."

She slipped a hand into the crook of his arm and led him past Carter, to the back of the bar, down the corridor to the dining room.

Carter threw Elke a puzzled look, but all she did was shrug, diverting to attend to a group at the bar demanding beer, as if confrontations at gunpoint with the State Police were an everyday occurrence at Das Bar. Maybe they were. The Gestapo men had seemed sure of their purpose. Certain that this was a bar worthy of investigation.

After making sure the gunmen were truly departed, Carter made his way into the back. He eased open the dining room door to find Helena dabbing Bo's nose with a wet flannel, having urged him to rest his neck on the back of a chair to stem the bleeding. She caught sight of Carter's silhouette in the doorway.

"Who are you?" The protective sting in her voice surprised Carter. It was at odds with the fragrance of her smile and sweet scent of her perfume.

"I was going to say the same to you."

Bo intervened, his voice distorted by coagulating blood and swelling to his nose. "Don't worry, Helena. This is Sam, he's here to replace Jack."

"No one can replace Jack." The response fired back instantly, laced with obvious respect and seemingly deep affection, such that Carter instantly wondered about his colleague's relationship with this impressive woman. But he had so many questions.

How had this woman of rare poise and beauty been capable of diffusing a visit from armed members of the Gestapo, obviously on the prowl for dissidents and spies as well as downed airmen? What was she doing in Das Bar? What was she to Jack Martin? Who was Helena Schulz?

10

CARTER sat at the table and watched her tend to Bo as she applied a pressure pad to the bridge of his nose. Gently kneading the wound. The distraction gave Carter time to think.

From the Gestapo officer's conversation, Carter had gleaned Helena was a singer. Music wasn't his forte. He appreciated the classical composers, in his opinion best consumed with an accompanying tumbler of 12-year-old single malt. But the big band era of the time did nothing for him. His one concession to popular culture were the songs of Anne Shelton and Vera Lynn, especially *The White Cliffs of Dover*, mainly because of its uplifting effect on soldiers' morale.

Opera had rarely troubled his consciousness. Unbearably long. At times, incomprehensible. At others, downright boring. Those were his kneejerk thoughts on the musical genre, although his instant impression of the lady before him hovered between wary and much more favourable. There was something about the way she held herself, head high, exuding a serene confidence, fingers working with delicate dexterity. An intriguing woman. For several minutes he sat in near silence, the only sound the hum of animated muttering filtering from the bar as regulars discussed the Gestapo's visit.

When at last she spoke it was a husky phrase, delivered in French with a hiss into Bo's ear.

"You must take care my friend."

Bo nodded instinctively.

"Are you French?" Carter could restrain his curiosity no longer.

She glanced up and laughed. Friendly, bordering on flirtatious, he thought, even if he detected a hint of derision as her head tossed back, thick curls lapping against her collar. She replied in English.

"French? No, I'm not French, whatever gave you that idea?" Carter's brain struggled to determine the source of the flat vowels. Then, it dawned.

"You're from England. Somewhere north. Yorkshire? Same as Jack?"

She shook her head. "That's an insult where I come from. I'm a Lancashire lass and proud of it."

"What are you doing here in Berlin getting bombed by your own compatriots? Your German's perfect. No trace of an English accent."

"Thank you. I'll take that as a compliment."

"That's how it was intended."

Bo intervened, easing Helena's hand off the pressure pad, holding it himself. "German please. We don't know who's listening. A report of an English accent would have the Gestapo back here at the double, shooting and asking questions, probably in that order."

"Sorry, Bo." They apologised in unison.

Helena reached for a bag of dressings, cut some tape and fashioned a makeshift cover for Bo's wound. He resisted until she pushed him down and he thought better of it. "Just until it stops bleeding. You don't want it to become infected."

When she had completed the dressing, Helena grabbed her bag and fastened the belt on her coat. "I can't stay long, Bo. I only intended visiting for a few minutes."

"I'm glad you did."

"So am I," said Carter.

Their eyes met fleetingly and Carter thought he detected sadness amid her serenity. "Excuse me, I have somewhere I need to be." Helena strode into the Berlin night, leaving Carter with questions unanswered.

He would have interrogated Bo, but a few moments later there was a tap on the door and Karl's head appeared. Almost immediately, an air raid siren sounded.

"Bombs dropping in the west", said Karl, "now's as good a time as any."

11

THEY drove east into the suburbs, distant rumbles more persistent. A large vehicle overtook them, headlights masked, big wheels soaking the truck in muddy spray. There was nothing else on the road. Carter sat in the front with Karl, whose driving was jerky, perhaps on account of his dodgy leg, although it was more likely the truck had not been serviced for years. Mechanics, even retired ones, no longer fit for active military service, were key workers in the eyes of the German war machine. Civilian vehicles were left to fend for themselves.

Mud smears formed the shape of plump lips on the truck's windscreen and the engine groaned as Karl negotiated potholes and ran over jagged items of debris. The journey should have taken no more than 15 minutes on good roads, but such a thing was non-existent in Berlin these days. It meant they would be out in the open, vulnerable to German patrols for twice that time. A flimsy curtain sufficed as a barrier between the cab and the truck's interior and Carter drew it back an inch or so to check on the occupants.

He watched Elke train a torch beam on the dirty faces of two American airmen, half-buried under flour bags and potato sacks in case a patrol stopped the truck. In brown dungarees, scuffed leather gloves and a black beret encasing her golden locks, Elke looked the part. An intrepid resistance fighter.

"What's your name?" Her tone firm but caring as she quizzed the gunner.

"Everyone calls me Tex."

"From Texas?"

"Yeah, Austin."

"Okay, Tex, think of me as your Mama. Do everything I say." Elke spoke slowly and deliberately, in English, as one might talk to a child, wagging her finger for emphasis.

"Our Mama?" An incredulous tone interspersed Tex's southern drawl. "You're young enough to be my daughter."

"And wouldn't you listen to your daughter? Don't they say a father never wins an argument with his daughter?"

"I'm sure you're right. I'll let you know when I have one."

The pilot, one side of his head glistening and raw, blood oozing from a deep wound, moaned.

"He's in a bad way. He needs a doctor." Tex's concern was obvious.

"Be patient. First, you need to be safe."

Carter replaced the curtain. His first impression of Elke had been favourable. She had handled the altercation with the Gestapo officer with composure beyond her years. He had also observed the youthful fire in her eyes, suspecting a similar inferno burned in her belly. A firecracker waiting for the fuse to be lit.

They drove on, past ruined buildings silhouetted in fleeting shafts of moonlight, Karl jerking the truck around tight corners with an authority that suggested he had travelled this route on many occasions. Carter breathed deep to stem a wave of nausea. He could have remained at Das Bar, where Bo had stayed to tend his regulars and his damaged nose. That would have been the smart move considering he did not know the area and his mind was fuzzy from lack of sleep. But the trip presented an opportunity to work with Jack Martin's team. A fast track to understand the operation.

"You're a good driver, Karl. Do you always drive the trucks?" Karl threw a suspicious sideways glance, Carter's question touching a nerve.

"Not always. We have other drivers. Sometimes, Bo drives."

"Were you driving the night Jack died?"

Karl pursed his lips. He didn't answer for many seconds and when he did it was prefaced by a curt nod. "I wasn't supposed to, but Bo wasn't well."

"What was wrong with him?"

Karl shrugged. "Don't know. But I know the route as well as him, it made sense for me to drive."

"What happened?"

Karl related the events of the night in the forest. The bomber crashing. The fire stranding the truck, German troops on the hunt, and Jack Martin's decision to make a dash for it, carrying a wounded Czech airman. The whine of the engine meant Carter failed to catch every word, but the gist was roughly the same as the story Bo had related.

"How did you manage to escape, Karl?" The question hung in the air and Carter endeavoured to study Karl in his peripheral vision. It was no use. Even with the odd shaft of moonlight, the night was too dark to surrender detail. But when Karl spoke, Carter detected a catch in his throat.

"I didn't want to leave Jack, but he ordered me to climb the rise up ahead, to watch for Germans. He wanted me to warn him. Give him chance to hide the wounded airman. I didn't spot the soldiers until it was too late. They were already upon us. I had no time to signal."

"But you saw what happened?"

"There was fire and smoke. Torch beams playing tricks with my night vision."

"So you didn't see exactly what happened?"

Carter sensed Karl bristling. He could hear his breathing deepen.

"Look, Karl, I'm not trying to blame anyone. I simply want to find out exactly what happened to Jack. He was one of our best agents and also a good friend."

The truck swung around another bend, one of the wheels clipping a kerb, jolting Carter, the side of his skull smashing into the metal stay of the window frame. He rubbed his head.

"Steady on, Karl." A strident note in Carter's tone. "We want to get there in one piece."

"I heard the machine guns. Saw two of the airmen fall." Karl ignored Carter's anger. "Then the soldiers were all around. I couldn't do anything but press my body into the ground and hope they hadn't seen me."

"So you didn't see Jack shot."

"I don't know."

"What do you mean?"

"After around twenty seconds I heard two more shots. Not a machine gun this time. Sounded like a pistol. A Walther Seven, I think. I raised my head and an SS officer with a gun was standing over two of the men."

"Was one of them Jack?"

"I don't know, but one of them was definitely the wounded airman Jack had been carrying. I could see the splint that had patched up his leg. Another man was lying half underneath him. I couldn't make out who it was, but it must have been Jack. He had been carrying the Czech on his back."

"What did you do then?"

"I crawled slowly, inching my way behind a bush until I heard them leaving."

"So you never actually saw Jack shot?"

"No, but I heard the SS officer ordering his men to drag away the bodies."

"Thanks for that, Karl."

A few minutes later, Karl swung the truck off the main road, onto a narrow lane. They followed the contours of a wood on their right, fields on their left, away from any buildings. In front of the trees, Carter picked out a row of iron railings, black, shaped like spears. He wound down his window, the sting of the night at once battering his cheeks. Karl muttered something but Carter missed the gist as the truck's tyres crunched on the gravel.

"Where are we?

"A cemetery."

Carter's military training immediately warned against entering unknown areas without reconnaissance, especially with people he barely knew, no back-up at hand. Karl sensed his caution.

"Don't worry. It's a pauper's graveyard. Or at least it was until the big socialists became celebrities. You must have heard of the great funeral here for Wilhelm Liebknecht in nineteen hundred."

"No."

Carter couldn't see Karl's face, but the timbre of his voice radiated pride. "My father was there. He told me all about it. Half a million people. Honest, working class people lined the streets of Berlin to honour Liebknecht for what he did for them. He founded the Social Democratic Party, gave the ordinary man a voice. He was a great friend of Karl Marx, who my father named me after. My God, Germany has taken a nasty fascist turn since those days."

The truck pulled up by an overgrown path leading to a small iron gate that years ago must have served as a back entrance for pedestrians.

Karl pulled back the curtain. "Okay, Elke. Let's unload the valuables."

It took around 10 minutes to ease the injured pilot out of the truck. His condition had deteriorated, low moans and incoherent mutterings his only means of communication. Carter helped Karl lower him to the ground onto a hammock-type stretcher, before carrying him through the gate to what appeared a gardener's hut, overgrown vegetation and rhododendron bushes camouflaging it from general view. The perfect hiding place.

Inside, two soiled mattresses served as bedding, but there were plenty of blankets and a cupboard in one corner containing cereals, nuts, and all manner of basic provisions. A small stove provided heating while a rusty outside tap supplied cold running water. It was far from palatial, but as a survival lair Carter had seen and occupied worse.

"Okay, listen to Mama carefully." Elke addressed Tex. "You'll stay here for a few days, maybe a few weeks. It's safe. Do not leave the hut, except for water. I'll bring a doctor tomorrow to look at your friend. Do you understand?"

The gunner glanced at Carter. He had an ear for accents and had detected an odd twang in Carter's conversation with Karl. "You sound like a Tommy, or maybe an Aussie?"

Carter's stomach lurched, doubts once more infiltrating his nervous system. He ignored the question.

"We've got to get home, buddy." The gunner sounded desperate.

"Do exactly as she says. We're working on a plan to get you both out." Carter had no idea what that plan might be, but the tremor in the gunner's voice alerted him that he required succour. "Don't worry, we've helped dozens of airmen like you."

"Any chance of a cigarette?"

Carter reached inside his jacket, but before he could dig out the packet he kept for emergencies, Karl tossed Tex a half-full packet of his own.

"There are matches in the cupboard," said Elke.

The gunner grinned, nodding his thanks, the promise of impending nicotine calming his demeanour. Not for the first time, Carter pondered the power of cigarettes as a currency of trust.

On the return journey, Elke sat in the cab between Carter and Karl. The distant rumble of high explosives had ceased and they all knew instinctively this was a dangerous time on the streets of Berlin. Hunting time for squads of SS troops and Gestapo officers, preying on downed airmen and resistance fighters. Carter noticed Elke twiddling her thumbs. A release, he decided, for pent-up tension.

"What's your story, Elke? What made you decide to help us?" Carter broke the silence.

"You make it sound like a novel, as if I'm some sort of fictional character." Elke's response was sharp.

"I wasn't being flippant. It takes guts and passion to do what you're doing, and there must be a reason behind it."

"I hate the Nazis and everything they stand for. That good enough for you?"

"Fine by me." Carter was not unduly surprised by the vehemence of Elke's reply, not after clocking the bitter look she threw the Gestapo officer in the bar earlier that evening. The rage of idealism, he knew, was not uncommon in the young, but it was still rare to hear it expressed in such direct fashion.

Elke's chin hit her chest. Her bottom lip quivered. For a moment Carter thought she might cry, the sudden outpouring appearing to have released an inner sadness. He considered giving her a fatherly hug, but thought better of it. He didn't have Elke down as a hugger. For many seconds they sat in silence, the truck pitching their bodies against each other.

"They killed my brother, Konrad." The revelation stumbled from her lips, awkward, but devoid of emotion.

"Who did?" Carter's tone soft and caring.

"He was at university in Munich, studying chemistry. Nothing to do with politics. Minding his own business. He was eighteen, a lovely, caring young man who wanted to do medical research. He wanted to save people's lives."

"Who killed him, Elke?"

"The Gestapo."

"Why?"

"They said they found him distributing anti-Nazi leaflets and daubing graffiti, denouncing the persecution of the Jews. They said he was a member of the White Rose resistance group in Munich. But he wasn't. He was an ordinary student, a naïve young man in the wrong place at the wrong time."

"Did he stand trial?" Carter knew members of the non-violent White Rose group had faced show trials after being arrested for distributing leaflets. Three of the leaders, Hans Scholl, Sophie Scholl and Christoph Probst, had been executed by guillotine.

"What do you think? He was shot in the back down a dark alley in the middle of Munich after he tried to run away from Gestapo officers. They said he had red paint on his hands, proving he'd been scrawling graffiti, but never produced evidence. That's the only trial he got. Trial by bullet."

"I'm sorry." Carter muttered his condolence, but before Elke could react the road was filled with beams of light. Karl, dazzled, slammed on the brakes. Fifty yards ahead, Carter spied two soldiers in the middle of the road, standing by a jeep, headlights blazing. One of the soldiers trained a machine gun on the truck, the other raised a hand, signalling them to stop.

"Christ, you can't move in Berlin these days for muck and Nazis. Not that there's much difference." Karl spat his indignation, but eased the truck to the side of the road. "At least we've dropped off the airmen."

Carter slid his hand inside his jacket to caress the comforting contours of his revolver. He had an uneasy feeling about this encounter.

Karl wound down his window and the lead soldier shone a powerful torch into the cab. He trained the beam on each of them for several seconds. "Do you know why I've stopped you?" His tone officious.

"No," said Karl.

"Headlights not masked correctly. Too bright. You know that's an offence."

"I'm sorry, one of the masks must have slipped. I'll see to it straightaway. It won't happen again."

A ragged scar on the soldier's right cheek intrigued Carter. It was neither new, nor old, though the skin was raised and still livid. Probably a shrapnel wound from the early days on the Front. His right eye twitched. Carter wondered whether the two were connected.

The soldier trained the torch once again. It lingered on Elke for longer than the others, a satisfied smirk eventually crossing the soldier's features, although his eyes remained hard and cold.

"Papers." The demand was curt.

"We're on our way to Lichtenberg. It's only …"

"Papers, now!"

Karl rooted under the dashboard and handed over his details. The soldier paid scant regard, returning them after a few seconds. He wandered over to the other side of the truck.

"You two, out." He motioned to Carter and Elke.

"Why? We've done nothing wrong." Elke's pitch was defiant and Carter felt a spasm of apprehension. If the soldier searched him, he'd discover the Webley revolver. Squaring that with his assumed profession as a Swiss banker overseeing stuffy monetary policy could prove a stretch.

"Out!"

They clambered out of the cab.

The soldier fixed on Carter, fingertips beckoning for his papers. Carter fished them out of an inside pocket, calculating whether he could draw and fire his revolver before the soldier with the machine gun at the front of the truck cut him down. All his battlefield experience told him that was less than likely. He handed over his details, surprised and relieved when the soldier thrust them back into his hand with no apparent examination.

"Fraulein, show me what you're carrying in the back of the truck." There was a playful confidence in the soldier's demeanour, at odds with his dismissive attitude towards Carter and Karl.

"Empty flour bags and potato sacks, that's all. We've made our deliveries."

"Show me."

He stepped aside to allow Elke to walk around the back of the truck, before following close behind. By the light of the soldier's torch, she drew back the tarpaulin and released the catches on the tailgate.

"See, I told you there were only …"

A burning rush of fear mixed with rage scorched through her body as the soldier's torso pressed hard against her back. He dropped the torch on the flatbed, the weight of his body pinning her against the truck. His arms encircled her, hands pawing at her breasts, rubbing with clumsy intent. She could taste his foul breath, hot and wet, smell his rank sweat, hear his grunts, as he buried his head in the back of her neck. For several moments she couldn't move. Paralysed. She tried to scream but no sound came. Then the rage within Elke fought with the fear, and in that contest there could be only one victor.

As the soldier's searching hands dropped lower, so did Elke, wiry and writhing, feeling for the blade strapped to her calf. A flailing right hand strained for it. She brushed the handle but he yanked her upwards, albeit unaware of her purpose. She reached again with all her strength and this time her fingers curled around the hunting knife.

The soldier sniggered. It had been a long night amid an interminable stretch away from home in a miserable city that increasingly offered little comfort or pleasure. On a lonely road on the ruined outskirts of Berlin, he had determined to take some for himself. He had picked the wrong girl. As he lifted Elke once more, she used the momentum of his drive to thrust the blade upwards, into the soft, fleshy portion of his belly, twisting the knife back and forth, savouring the tearing sensation as it entered his intestines, ripping through his stomach.

He let out a short gasp, followed by a gurgling sound, before slumping to the ground, with a scrape of heavy boots that alerted his colleague with the machine gun. The soldier trained his sights on Carter, fear in his eyes, alarm in his shout. "Hans, Hans … is everything all right?"

They were the last words he spoke. Karl leaned out of the truck window and shot him dead.

12

CARTER showed his ticket to the railway guard and ascended the steep steps of the Pankow-Schönhausen station.

When he reached the top he swivelled sharply to ascertain whether anyone was following. A woman holding a young boy's hand trudged up the steps. She had weary eyes, the boy wailing and tugging at her coat. On the other side of the steps an old man clung to the iron hand rail, negotiating his climb in a painful sideways shuffle. They were the only other passengers alighting at the northern terminus of the U2 line.

Carter smiled at the thought that either of them could be Gestapo spies, but he accepted paranoia was a permanent friend of the secret agent. Never assume. Always check. Then check again. Trust no one. It was a simple protocol, not always guaranteed to ensure a good night's sleep, but it might keep an operative alive. The statistics were not in his favour. He knew that. Brigadier Pritchard had spelled them out back in the MI9 office in London. The life expectancy of a secret agent transmitting coded messages in enemy territory was currently six weeks. Not dissimilar from a pilot in Bomber Command.

A week had elapsed since the incident with the soldiers.

Elke had said nothing. Never referenced the fact that she'd gutted a human being as dispassionately as she might fillet a fish, while Karl had dispatched another without a second thought. Instead, Elke had jumped into the truck in matter-of-fact fashion, dead eyes, no mention of the assault, but a cheery "Let's get out of here." As if hailing a cab. Even in a city where

Nazi thugs dragged Berliners from their homes and summarily tortured, executed, or sent them to God knows where if suspected of harbouring Jews or not fully supporting the Führer, Elke's actions were troubling. Carter had tried once to enquire about her state of mind but received a glance of such disconcerting menace that he had gauged silence the best policy.

The next day Karl had revisited the graveyard complete with provisions and a doctor sympathetic to the resistance, who had patched up the pilot, but warned surgery in the clinical surroundings of a hospital was required. They all knew there was zero chance of that happening. Elke had returned to serving beer.

Carter used his time profitably. In the back room at Das Bar, over two nights, he had pumped Bo for information. Crucially, he learned Jack Martin's network included a Berlin doppelganger for George Bacon. The next evening when trade was slow, the bar almost deserted save for a small group of old-timers, Bo had introduced him. He went by the name of Felix. Looked like Bacon, thought like Bacon, and possessed many of the same pernickety characteristics. As with Bacon, nothing was outside Felix's orbit.

"Can you sort photographs and papers?" Carter had whispered in the back room, in hope rather than anticipation.

"No problem."

"What about train tickets?"

"No problem."

"Civilian clothes?"

"No problem."

"Is anything a problem?"

A shrug approaching indifference. Felix even shrugged like Bacon, although his features were lent a sinister slant by a glass eye on his right side.

Carter spent the next day compiling a list of requirements and formulating a plan. He quickly dismissed his first idea of encouraging the airmen to travel via train. The journey was too long, the pilot too weak. Besides that, the airmen spoke no German. A train guard or station inspector would rumble them at the first checkpoint and alert the authorities. The only way was by road to the Polish border, around 65 miles. A risky route for Karl to drive but no more than a couple of hours if German patrols could be avoided. Once there, they could link up with the Polish resistance, who could arrange an onward journey possibly to Sweden, which remained neutral but recently had accepted thousands of Jewish refugees.

The chances of the plan working were minimal. Carter knew that, but the alternative was a prisoner of war camp for the duration of the war, or worse. First, Carter needed to alert London that his operation was up and running.

The trip to Pankow was Bo's idea. In peace time, the area was a leafy suburb popular with intellectuals and celebrities, a district to hang out for a few hours with a cold beer, talking art and philosophy. War had extinguished that vibe, but swathes of the area had escaped the devastation of central Berlin.

Carter followed Bo's instructions, slinging his rucksack over his shoulder, pulling his collar around his neck to shield from a bitter wind, and heading north. He walked for 15 minutes up a gentle incline until he came across a small park. In carefree days, it would have been a haven for children, a green playground resounding with laughter, full of climbing frames and roundabouts, set around a duck pond guarded by iron railings. Inattention these past years had rendered it derelict and deserted.

He made his way to the only building, a pavilion-type structure once used to serve teas and snacks, eyes sweeping the area to make sure no one was around. A gentle tap on the back door. Nothing. He checked his watch and knocked again, this time harder. After half a minute, a bolt slid on the door and it creaked open. An old man's face appeared, full of craggy lines resembling dried-up river beds.

"What do you want?" The voice whining, like an old saw.

"Käsekuchen." Carter rattled off Bo's favourite cheesecake dessert. An appropriate password for the venue.

The old man stepped back, allowing Carter to pass.

"Go ahead." He directed Carter into a small room, probably a pantry cum kitchen, a window wearing the grime of many years, but still allowing a comprehensive view of the building's approach. The smell of damp and rat was unpleasant, but not overwhelming.

"Perfect." Carter wrestled the rucksack from his back, setting it down on a wooden worktop.

"Shut the door when you leave. Remember, no more than twenty minutes." The old man shuffled away, again muttering "No more, no more than twenty" as he departed.

Carter slipped a miniature suitcase-type container from his bag. Known as the Paraset, it was Bacon's favourite toy. The smallest and most powerful transmitter available to the secret agent. It weighed nine pounds, tiny compared to earlier models.

"Type three, mark two, brackets B two," Bacon had told Carter when he picked it up in Beaconsfield. "A range of more than five hundred miles, and you'll need every one of them and more."

Carter had yawned, for no other reason than to wind up Bacon, but while the model specifications were of little interest, he had memorised the salient characteristics and heeded Bacon's warnings. The transmitter's range could be increased by an elevated position, which is why he'd chosen the park in Pankow. Carter had no experience as a wireless operator in enemy territory, but he'd used transmitters before and was aware of the crucial details. Always transmit on a different day, at a different time, from a different place. Always remember to spell a chosen word incorrectly. Carter's chosen word was *when*, spelled *wen*. It was a simple but effective device. If a transmission contained the word spelled correctly, London would know Carter's mission had been compromised.

Most important, as the old man warned, was to keep any transmission shorter than 20 minutes, if possible half that time. The Germans had become adept at tracking transmissions. In urban environments they could pinpoint radio activity and be banging on, more likely knocking down, the operator's door within half an hour. Interrogation, torture and execution were certain to follow.

Carter fumbled inside his coat, tugging out what resembled a silk handkerchief. On it was written a series of single-use ciphers. MI9 held an identical key back in London. He started tapping in Morse Code's dots and dashes, substituting each letter of the alphabet with the content of the cipher. Using a one-off cipher was the operative's preferred method of communication. It meant the message was indecipherable without the key, which Carter intended to cut out and destroy after each transmission. The benefit of silk was that it reduced the chances of detection. It would not rustle if an agent was searched.

The taps echoed in the empty room, the sound of hail battering on a tin roof, each flurry fraying his nerves that little bit more. He breathed deep. No one's around, he told himself. No one can hear.

He kept the message short and simple.

Up and running. Two birds in bag. No word on The Wolf. Will advise as and wen.

Carter was not a professional wireless operator. He was far from an expert in Morse Code, but he was capable, routinely tapping and sending at around 20 words a minute. He glanced at his watch. The code key slowed matters down, but 10 minutes after knocking on the pavilion door he was slipping the transmitter back into its case and packing it into the rucksack. Next, he dug in a bag pocket, locating a box of matches and a pair of small embroidery scissors. He cut out the silk cipher, struck a match and set light to the material, dangling it above a sink until the flame lightly burned his fingers. The smoke smelled like charred meat as the silk shrivelled to a black powder residue. If the water had been connected, he would have swilled it away. There was no need. It no longer held any secrets.

For a few moments, he checked the window, his gaze sweeping a line of trees in the distance, searching for signs of movement. Content the exit was clear, he slipped out of the back door and headed for the U-Bahn. No sign of the old man. Within the hour Carter was back in his apartment.

13

THE air in Das Bar was thick, blue cigarette haze rising in the shadowy light cast by a single electric bulb.

Back against a wall, Carter balanced on the edge of a rickety wooden chair at a table for two, having sneaked behind the nearest tables to avoid interrupting the plaintive melody emanating from the far side of the room.

The bar was almost full, several groups of young German soldiers enjoying beers and Schnapps. No one spoke, everyone's attention captured by the singer and the song that had become so familiar.

A bar stool, perched on top of a wooden pallet, acted as a makeshift stage. Helena Schulz wore a black dress with lacy sleeves revealing slender arms. Her long legs were crossed and a gold crucifix dangled from a chain around her neck. She radiated poise and confidence, but as she sang *Lili Marlene* acapella it was the voice that delivered enchantment.

Carter observed a tear run down a woman's cheek. Hard men, some mouthing the words, sat entranced at the verses recalling a German soldier's love for his girlfriend. Some even joined in, melancholy humming providing a bass line that somehow made the song even more evocative. By the time Helena reached the final verse everyone hung on each sweet note. The soldiers stood and applauded, one of them whistled. A drumroll of approval sounded as others banged fists on table tops.

Helena accepted the applause graciously, bowing and nodding, before easing off the stool and disappearing into the back room.

The bar returned to its usual drone of conversation and Carter ordered a beer from a waitress he hadn't seen before. A fulsome lady, with broad hips and thick thighs, who regulars called Millie. Bo and Elke were tied up serving customers.

He had taken no more than a couple of sips as he mused on the message he'd transmitted that afternoon when he sensed a sweet scent battling the room's stale odour. A familiar scent. He looked up. Helena, glass of water in hand.

"Okay if I join you?" Her smile friendly.

"Sure." He pulled up the other chair and pointed to her glass. "Don't you fancy something stronger?"

"Don't drink. Not good for the vocal chords."

"The song was beautiful."

"Thank you. I wish I had a Reichsmark for every time I've been asked to sing that song. I'd be a millionaire."

"Bo tells me you're a singer at the Berlin Opera."

She nodded. "I was. Sadly, more bomb damage means it's no longer safe. I am, as they say, between performances."

"What sort of stuff did you sing?"

"Stuff?" Helena sneered, although Carter thought he detected a coquettish lowering of her eyes.

"Sorry, I'm a bit of a Philistine when it comes to music. I don't think I was ever taught to truly appreciate it."

"People shouldn't be taught to appreciate or respect music. They should be taught to love music."

"Who said that?"

"I did."

"Sure?"

"What are you suggesting?"

"It sounds like a quote from a book."

Helena studied Carter, a mixture of curiosity and suspicion in her gaze. He chewed his lip, worried that he had offended her. For a brief moment, the conversation risked ending in mutual distrust. A girlish chuckle and a whispered explanation cleared the air. "All right, it was Igor Stravinsky, but I don't think it's prudent to talk about Russian composers at this time, do you?"

"In my case, that would be a very short conversation."

Helena reached in her handbag for a packet of cigarettes. She offered Carter one, but he declined.

"Isn't smoking bad for the vocal chords?"

She ignored his rebuke. Taking a drag, she threw her head back, blew a plume of smoke and watched it jostle for position in the cloud that already existed.

Carter seized his opportunity, although mindful to keep his voice lowered. "Tell me, how well did you know Jack?"

"Not that well. He had many friends. I sang here occasionally to keep my voice warm and he loved his music." She emphasised the word *love* as if to score a point from their earlier conversation.

"Did you know his line of work?"

"What do you mean?"

"I think you know exactly what I mean."

Carter had been intrigued since hearing Helena assert, "No one could replace Jack," in Bo's back room. Was she referring to his role as a secret agent, running an active pocket of the resistance to rescue downed airmen? Or did she mean romantically? Helena stayed silent.

"I saw the look you gave the Gestapo officer the other night as he left. He could have been something nasty on the sole of your shoe. True, he'd broken Bo's nose, but he was so kind to you. So *appreciative* and *respectful* of your singing." Carter deliberately borrowed the words from Stravinsky.

A fire burned in Helena's eyes, but it was the only indication that Carter's words had struck home. She licked her lips and forced a sweet smile.

"Do you know what I think?" she said. "I think some men struggle with women who are successful. They don't know what to say. They stab at things in the dark, hoping to impress. And all they do is show how little they know."

"Did you love, Jack?"

"I love my husband."

"Oh, I'm sorry, I didn't …" Helena's instant response jolted Carter. He'd not expected that. He realised Schulz was not a traditional Lancashire surname, but the existence of a husband hadn't featured in his musings. He had broken the first rule of a secret agent. Never assume. Always deal in facts.

"Don't be sorry. My husband was an industrialist. A very successful one. He was the reason I emigrated to Germany, the reason I was given the opportunity to sing at the world's greatest opera house. I owe everything to Siegfried."

Worry lines appeared on Carter's face. He paused for several moments, struggling to compose the next sentence. In the end he blurted it out.

"You said, *was an industrialist*."

Her lips pursed. For a moment, her gaze wandered, mist in her eyes. Carter thought she was about to shed a tear, but she didn't.

"One of Germany's finest." There was pride in her voice, composure instantly restored.

"Is he here in Berlin?"

"Siegfried died three years ago. He was on a train to Bremen when the railway was bombed. The train derailed and his carriage plunged down a hillside. Many others died with him."

"I'm sorry."

"Thank you, but it wasn't your fault. You had nothing to do with it. There's nothing for you to be sorry about. It was this damned war and the evil men that started it that killed him." Her voice had lowered to a hiss, as if mindful of the soldiers in the bar and the fact her words alone were enough to have her shot. But Carter's probing had unleashed a rage inside her. Her jaw jutted and she continued. "I used to sing for the Führer. He came to see me at the State Opera on Unter den Linden boulevard with Joseph Goebbels. I also sang at his retreat in Switzerland. He sent me flowers. We spoke of Wagner, Beethoven and the joy of heroic music. I thought he was cultured. Oh, how young and naïve I must have been. If I'd known then that he was mad and evil, I would …" Her voice trailed off, as if the danger of the conversation at last had registered.

Carter indicated with a hand, as a conductor might lower the pitch of an orchestra. His peripheral vision had spotted one of the soldiers approaching. The young man was tall and blond, but his gait unsteady. Beer had taken effect.

"Excuse me, Frau Schulz." The soldier offered a slurred pardon.

"Can I help you?" Accustomed to people approaching her in bars and stores for autographs, Helena slipped into artist mode. She no longer sang at the famous opera house, but was still in demand at various Berlin social events, her picture appearing from time to time in local newspapers.

The soldier motioned to his friends, who laughed and leered. One raised his glass and beer swilled, splashing on the stone floor. "We'd really like you to sing again. Lili Marlene, please."

"I'm tired, I'm resting my voice and I don't do requests, especially when there's no music. I'm sure you understand."

"Just one, for the soldiers. For the nation's brave boys. We're back to the Front tomorrow."

"Sorry." She shook her head.

Clumsy in his movements, the soldier grabbed Helena's forearm, not roughly, but as she pulled away she disturbed her glass. It tumbled to the floor, smashing, spilling water over the soldier's boots.

Carter sprang to his feet, his chair screeching as it scraped the ground. The soldier immediately squared up to him, taller, broader, a sneer daring Carter to fight. An uneasy silence had replaced the agreeable hum of the bar. All eyes focused on Helena's table. Carter's mind whirled, the chance encounter threatening to jeopardise his entire mission. He considered drawing his gun, but realised he was hopelessly outnumbered. Neither was fighting an option. Grovelling and apologising went against everything Carter held true, but it was the only possibility that made sense. Do whatever it takes. He couldn't allow his true identity to be compromised.

He started to mouth an apology, but before it could spill from his lips, Helena intervened. "I'll sing." This time Helena grabbed the soldier's arm and gently squeezed, her tender touch instantly drawing the sting from the confrontation. "You're right, it's the least I can do for the brave boys of the Wehrmacht."

The soldier glared again at Carter, but bowed his thanks to Helena. "That would be most kind, Frau Schulz." He returned to his friends. Helena strolled to the bar stool and launched once more into the opening bars of Lili Marlene.

A multitude of thoughts collided in Carter's mind. It had been a close call. The soldier's entitled attitude had triggered a rush of heat through his veins of such burning intensity that it demanded release. His training should have allowed him to deal with it. To suck it up. To survive. To wait things out as once he had done in the chill waters of Dunkirk. But if Helena had not intervened, he knew he would have lashed out.

All he could do was deal with the shame of being unable to protect Helena and the knowledge that he probably owed his life to her timely intervention and the fact that the soldier was of lowly rank, an ordinary fighter and not an SS officer, or a member of the Gestapo. On a positive note, he knew more of Helena's history. Yet, despite his attempted interrogation, few more details about Helena's relationship with Jack Martin.

14

CARTER spent most of the next week sheltering from a cluster of bombing raids, planning the airmen's escape.

Much of his work involved liaising with Felix, the Bacon doppelganger, who proved to be more interesting than at first meeting.

He arrived in the back room at Das Bar one day with the civilian clothes he'd promised in a sturdy suitcase, all cut to size and customised for the job in hand. They contained silk maps of the northern districts of Germany and Poland with button studs containing miniature compasses. Shirts, ties, and two pairs of shoes completed the outfits. He seemed particularly pleased with the polished brogues as he lifted them from the case, presenting them to Carter as an actor might show off an Oscar.

"Excellent. You can see your face in them." Carter dispensed his praise.

"One moment." Felix raised a forefinger to signify there was more. He grabbed a shoe, stripped a lace, wrapped it around a raw potato he grabbed from a sack and pulled from either side. The potato sliced in half, two clean-cut pieces falling to the table.

"Made of steel. A handy garrotte, if such a weapon is needed." A trill in his voice suggested Felix was proud of his invention.

"Any chance I could get one of those?" Carter was impressed.

Felix dug in his suitcase and produced a spare pair, which Carter readily pocketed.

Another dip in the case saw Felix spreading identity papers on the table, inviting inspection. Carter scrutinised them in detail, comparing them with the ones Bacon had prepared for him. They were almost identical, good enough to fool anything other than the most concerted examination.

"Good work, Felix. You were right, it wasn't a problem."

Felix beamed, delighted to have his expertise appreciated.

"Tell me, Felix, how often did you work with Jack Martin?"

"Many times. Jack saved lives here. Kept soldiers from prisoner of war camps. He was a good man. He saved my life."

Intrigued, Carter fixed Felix with a steady gaze, although that was difficult. Felix's glass eye tugged at Carter's attention, making his own pupils dart from side to side.

"Tell me more, Felix. What happened?"

Felix filled the seat opposite Carter, who studied him as a professional gambler might weigh up his opponents. Where did Felix fit in? What did he know? Was he an anonymous fixer like Bacon, content to stay in the background, fiddling with his gadgets? Or was he central to Jack Martin's operation? Difficult to gauge. There was a disconnect between his laconic manner and his precision work that told Carter not to underestimate him.

"Not much to tell." Felix sat back, hands laid flat on the table. "Can't remember much about the incident. I was with Jack and a couple of others, pacing out coordinates for a factory making parts for tanks. It was three in the morning when a routine patrol spotted us. We ran for the trees. They started firing and that's the last I remember."

"How did you escape?"

"All I know is what Bo told me. A ricochet from a bullet struck me. I was out cold. Blood everywhere. They thought I was dead, but Jack refused to leave me there, He stayed, drawing the fire, covering the others while they carried me back to the truck. The surgeon who took the eye out told me a tree splinter did the damage."

"How did Jack escape?"

Felix smiled, as if savouring a warm memory.

"Jack was like a cat. Always landed on his feet. It wasn't luck. He planned every mission with meticulous precision. Studied distances, topography, timings, escape routes. Nothing caught him out."

"Until he got caught out." The response slipped from Carter's lips before he could bite it back. Even to him, it sounded crass and insensitive, but Felix registered no disapproval.

Carter fumbled in his jacket pocket for his cigarettes. He offered Felix one and he took it. Carter lit his own and slid the box of matches across to Felix, at speed and deliberately wide. He noticed two things. Felix was left handed. He also caught the pack with the casual aplomb of an accomplished slip fielder. Not a skill he would readily associate with a one-eyed gadget expert.

They sucked hard on their cigarettes, blowing clouds of smoke. Carter was warming to Felix. He offered some context to his questions, explaining what Lieutenant Harris had told him in Beaconsfield. That it had taken a long time to build up a network in Berlin capable of gathering and deploying high-grade intelligence. Too many of the early agents had blown their cover within days. One ignored the basic rule, transmitting from the same place on successive days, gauging his messages too short and too speedy to track. The knock on his door early next morning came from an SS unit equipped with machine guns and torture aids designed to deliver the relevant key codes. Another agent had arranged a meeting with an informant in an isolated spot in woods to the east of Berlin. He parked his car, left the door unlocked and wandered into the forest for an hour or more, expecting a coded message to be left. When he returned there was nothing in the designated hiding place behind the passenger windscreen visor. For 10 minutes, he searched the vehicle for another spot convenient to conceal a small document. Frustrated, he jumped in the driver's seat, turned the key, and the vehicle and the agent disintegrated, blown apart by a small pack of explosive rigged to the ignition.

Jack Martin was different. He was a natural, capable of integrating in an enemy environment without drawing attention. Reliable and intuitive. A man who engendered trust in those closest to him.

"Trust." Felix plucked the word from Carter's lips, at the same time stubbing out his cigarette in an ash tray. "That's true. And it has to work both ways. For Jack, everyone was prepared to go that little bit extra. Not only when rescuing airmen, but also sending information that would make a difference to the course of the war."

The doorknob turned, breaking the conversation. Elke appeared. "Okay if I put these in the cupboard? We're running out of space in the bar." She carried a box of wine glasses.

"Of course." Carter waved her in.

"I'm not interrupting anything, I hope."

"No. I'm trying to get to know Felix a bit better."

"Good luck with that." It was a strange response, Carter thought, until he remembered Felix reminded him of Bacon. The same social eccentricity. Probably didn't register too well in a young woman's orbit.

They gathered up the papers and while Elke deposited the glasses they limited their conversation to general chit-chat. When she had left, Carter shut the door and signalled for Felix to sit once more.

"I'm trying to learn more about the operation, Felix. Specifically, how Jack came about his most sensitive information."

"You mean, who was his mole?"

"That's a little blunt, but yes, I guess that's what I do mean. His information suggests he knew, or had the ear of someone high up. Someone with connections, privy to secrets."

Felix shrugged. "Everyone is high up to me."

Carter grinned. This Felix is a canny fox, he thought. What better way of deflecting the train of thought than with a dash of self-deprecating humour?

"Okay, let me put it this way. Do you know The Wolf?"

Felix paused. Carter studied him closely, but to no avail. The more he tried to focus his stare, the more his eyes darted back to that glass prosthesis. With its pale, colourless iris and fixed expression, added to its distracting nature, it had rendered Felix unreadable.

"As far as I know, Jack never spoke of any Wolf."

Again, Carter thought the response too considered. It was neither a denial, nor a direct evasion. There would be no reason for Jack Martin to speak of The Wolf. If Carter had understood correctly, the name was reserved exclusively for coded messages. Yet it defied belief that Bo and now Felix, two of the big-hitters in MI9's Berlin operation, for that is what Carter had determined, would have no knowledge of its greatest asset.

"Okay, Felix. Thanks for all this. Good job." He pointed to the suitcase. "We'll let you know when we're ready to go. The pilot needs a few more days to recover."

Felix departed. Carter pondered if he had said too much, wondering who he could trust. His right knee began to shake. He calmed it with a firm hand. There was no stopping the sudden, uncontrollable, shiver across his shoulders.

15

THE next evening Carter took a short stroll to Die Küche, a small café on the corner of Dolziger Strasse

A damp, misty day had surrendered its light mid-afternoon and an icy wind sliced down the street, howling and whistling through the crazy apertures of several ruined buildings. Carter hunched his shoulders and pulled his woollen scarf tight.

Bo had recommended the café. Many such establishments had closed down for all sorts of reasons. Some owners had fled the city. Others had found food difficult to source as rationing began to bite. Most had simply been bombed out of existence.

It wasn't food that attracted Carter to Die Küche. It was the fact that Bo had told him it would be full around six o'clock with Berliners looking for a simple meal. As well as rescuing Allied airmen and intelligence-gathering duties, part of Carter's brief was to inform London of morale on the ground. The RAF had been dropping anti-Nazi leaflets for months in a quest to win the hearts and minds of the ordinary people and undermine Germany's leaders. There are few better places to gauge the mood of a nation than among a group breaking bread together. At least that's what Carter believed.

At first glance, Die Küche looked anything but appealing. A mine bomb had blown out the big plate window. The café's owners had replaced it with wooden boards and scrawled the café's name in white paint. It did the job, but was far from a work of art.

Carter entered and immediately the enticing aroma of sizzling sausages and roasting potatoes wafted through from the kitchen. Most of the long tables were taken, customers shoehorned on bench seats, most with overcoats buttoned, some wearing woolly hats and gloves. Even with heat from the cooking, the dining room was cold as a grave. Carter perched on the end of one of the long tables, exchanging nods and smiles with two old women nearest to him.

"Good to be inside. There's a bite in that wind tonight," said one of the women before returning to chat with her friend. The men on the other side barely noticed Carter. One had a red scarf tied tight around his neck. The other wore a wild grey beard that probably hadn't been groomed for years. They were deep in conversation and Carter attuned to the pitch of their voices.

He heard the name Heinrich Wittgenstein and immediately realised the men were discussing Major Prince Heinrich von Sayn-Wittgenstein, a German fighter pilot of international fame, who was thought to have destroyed more than 80 Allied planes. Wittgenstein was well known to MI9, if only because of the workload he supplied. He had recently received the Oak Leaves to his Knight's Cross from the Führer, a commendation awarded only to those displaying the highest military valour and leadership.

"Heard on the radio. Killed in action. Must have been worn out, poor fellow. They reckon barely a night went by when he wasn't on duty, hunting bombers." The respect in the scarf man's voice was matched by sadness.

"Beginning of the end." The other man's tone was even more solemn.

"What do you mean?"

"The British and Americans are bombing Berlin night and day." He pointed to his meagre plate of roast potatoes and cabbage. "We're eating meals like this, every day, if we're lucky. The Russians have broken through to Leningrad. Mark my words, the Russians will not stop there. What more proof do we need that the tide has turned?"

A short man with a chef's apron tied around an ample waist approached Carter. "You want the same?" He signalled to the scraps on the empty plates of the two old men.

"Is there a choice?"
"Potatoes and cabbage."
"I can smell sausage."
"Only for regulars."
"How often do I have to come to be a regular?"
The chef shrugged. Carter couldn't be bothered arguing.
"Potatoes and cabbage it is then."
The chef returned to the kitchen and the bearded man turned to Carter.
"What do you think?"
"Of what?"
"Of the war. When will it end?"
"Who knows? All I know is that there used to be twenty or thirty bombers over Berlin in an air raid. Now there are hundreds. If it goes on like this there won't be anything left." It was an obvious observation that triggered a response Carter wasn't expecting.
"You're right. The water pipes are burst, streets flooded, with huge craters everywhere. Half the buildings are destroyed. The city smells permanently of gas. I never thought I'd say this, but I can't wait for defeat. The noose is tightening. Germany is collapsing around our ears and when the war ends the country will be carved up. Partition. Families separated. All those lives lost for nothing."
The woman to Carter's left piped up. "Klaus, don't talk that way. Stop complaining. What would our grandson say if he heard you talking like that? He's fighting at the Front, and you're surrendering in a potato kitchen. At least you have food to eat and somewhere to shelter from the bombs."
The chef arrived with Carter's plate and the old couples left, Klaus chuntering as his wife hooked the crook of his arm and dragged him through the door. It wasn't a scientific survey, but the word on the ground, in Dolziger Strasse at least, supported the view that the German leaders were out of step with the ordinary Berliner.

Carter made a mental note to include his thoughts in his next message. He ate his roasted potatoes and boiled cabbage, wondering how Heinrich Wittgenstein had met his end. Perhaps in an aerial dogfight with an admiring nod to his adversary, in the manner books portrayed the flying aces of the First World War. Carter knew war was not like that. There was no glamour in death, however or whenever it arrived.

He paid for his meal in ration coupons and set off for his apartment. The streets were familiar now and he felt more at ease, although always adhering to his tradecraft. Training at MI9 HQ had ingrained the skills of the secret operative. The ability to look and sound at home in an alien environment. Blend into the wallpaper, or in this case the dirt and rubble of daily life in a ruined city. He knew the precise times the armed sentries at one end of Dolziger Strasse changed guard. He had memorised the entrances and exits of the Flak Tower. He even knew the names of some of the stewards who herded people to the safest positions. Back in London, Bacon may have thought him cavalier, but Carter had always lived by an old adage, even if he could not remember who was responsible for it: *Knowledge itself is power.*

As he arrived at his apartment block, the moon sidestepped a cloud, casting enough light to see a big man with an uncertain gait, carrying a large bag, attempting to push open the door. Carter held back for several seconds before recognising the reason for the man's struggles. It was the blind man from number nine. Someone had placed a large bin on the doorstep that he was attempting to shift.

"Here, let me help." Carter tugged the bin away.

"You're Jack's friend. I recognise the voice."

"That's right."

"Has he turned up yet?"

"I'm afraid not."

"He had a visitor today, about an hour ago."

"Are you sure?"

"Yeah. Whoever it was didn't knock, but I was at the top of the stairs. I heard someone outside his door, listening."

"How do you know?" Carter realised blindness often raised awareness of other senses, such as hearing and smell, but how could it detect whether someone was listening?

"When someone is listening for a period of time and doesn't want people to know, they tend not to move their feet, which they know would make a noise. Instead, they often rock back and forth on the spot. That's what Jack's visitor was doing. Rocking. I could sense the neck muscles tightening and relaxing and hear the creak of a joint."

"For how long?"

"A minute or so, no more. I heard a scraping sound. Then the person moved away and took the stairs."

"Man or woman?"

"Couldn't tell. But if it was a woman, most likely I would have detected soap or perfume. The scent of a woman. There was no such sweet residue."

"Do you want a hand with the bag?" It was the least Carter could offer.

"No thanks."

"What's your name, by the way?"

"Max."

"Okay, Max, you can call me David." Carter gave his Swiss alias.

"Yeah, but what's your name?" Max stifled a chuckle.

Carter ignored the jibe, brushing through the door, bounding up the stairs, a rush of scenarios churning through his brain. Who was the visitor? Gestapo came to mind, although that seemed doubtful. Gestapo officers were more inclined to pick locks or blow doors off their hinges, rather than listen outside them. Maybe it was Bo. He was the only other person who had visited since Carter had arrived. But he had recommended the café and knew where Carter was. Whoever it was may have been looking for Jack. That was another possibility, albeit unlikely.

He checked the doorknob first, to determine whether the strand of cotton he'd tied loosely before leaving was still in place. A tried and trusted operative's trick. The cotton was undisturbed. His makeshift key turned in the lock and he edged the door open. It took several seconds for his night vision to determine that the apartment was as it was when he left. He turned on a lamp and a sealed white envelope on the wooden floor caught his eye. From where it lay, the visitor had obviously slid it underneath the door.

Carter ripped it open, and read a message, neatly written in capital letters in black ink.

HOTEL ADLON. LOBBY BAR. TOMORROW. 2PM. THE WOLF.

16

THE murk had lifted and icy grip relented. Compared to the day before, the weather felt almost spring-like as Carter made his way from the underground station, across the bridge over the Spree River, into the cultural heart of the city.

He had debated the wisdom of following the instructions on the message. Clandestine meetings in his world were usually facilitated in seedy cafes, or dark alleys, nearer to midnight than midday. Attending to covert business before the sun was over the yardarm was not general practice for a secret agent.

But the message was signed *The Wolf*. That went to the core of Carter's mission. To find Jack Martin's most valuable contact. No way that message could be ignored, although it was natural to speculate.

As far as he could remember he had spoken directly of The Wolf only to Bo and Felix, although he was uncertain whether Elke and Karl had been in the vicinity at the time. Bo and Felix had denied any knowledge, but Carter knew neither of them well enough to afford them total trust. For all he knew, any of the main players at Das Bar could have been in touch with The Wolf and revealed his whereabouts.

There was also the possibility that The Wolf could have been watching Jack Martin's apartment. He may have spoken to Max, the blind man. Hell, he may be Max. What better way to go under the radar than posing as a vulnerable person who poses no threat?

Carter swept the tangle of thoughts from his mind. It served no purpose and, anyway, the chances were he would know soon enough.

His first sighting of Hotel Adlon caught him unawares. The address, not far from the Brandenburg Gate, should have afforded a clue. But the formidable stone façade, with its big windows and ground floor arches, was a thing of beauty, especially set against the devastation he had witnessed on the way. By fortune, the building seemed virtually intact, apart from windows boarded, some arches bricked up, and shrapnel damage to two corners.

As he neared the arch at the front entrance, he noticed security guards checking papers, prompting a nervous tingle. But he was wearing a sober suit and tie, together with a pair of spectacles to conform with his assumed identity as a Swiss banker. He looked the part, he had decided. He was right. Boring. The guard took one look at his papers, and waved him through with a comforting greeting. "Have an enjoyable day, Herr Schmid."

The concierge in the lobby was dealing with a query from a group of uniformed German officers, trying to arrange a meeting for their party in one of the conference rooms. Carter busied himself, pretending to study the building's architecture as several more groups of SS officers strolled past. He breathed deep.

When the concierge became free, Carter affected an ingratiating nod. He'd seen bankers do that chasing a client's money. "I'm looking for the lobby bar."

"Of course, Der Herr. Follow me."

"Why so many soldiers?" Carter put the question neutrally, as if making conversation.

"Since the Kaiserhof Hotel was bombed, many SS members have moved in here. We also have a military hospital ward in one of the wings at the back of the hotel. Doing our bit for the Fatherland."

"Of course. That's commendable."

The concierge led Carter through swing doors into a bar area with leather armchairs, a floral carpet and a lingering residue of furniture polish. Oil paintings of past German generals hung from the walls. "Are you meeting anyone in particular?"

"An old business acquaintance."

"Have a nice afternoon."

"Thank you."

The concierge left and Carter found a small table in a corner alcove with clear sight of the swing doors. He picked up a newspaper on the way and ordered a beer. Pretending to study the news, his gaze swept the bar. It was a few minutes before 2pm. A bunch of businessmen occupied the opposite corner. Several SS officers lounged in armchairs, a bottle of brandy on the table in easy reach despite the early hour. Two women, not young, not old either, chatted in animated fashion, waiting for their lunch companions. The ambience was convivial. The room exuded privilege. A photograph hung on the wall over an inglenook fireplace, depicting the day Charlie Chaplin stayed at the hotel in 1931, promoting his film, City Lights. A youthful Marlene Dietrich sat in an armchair beside Chaplin, wearing a double breasted jacket, tie, and brimmed hat. It was easy to forget the carnage enveloping Europe. And yet there was no sign of The Wolf, nor anyone who might look like him. Unless he wore jackboots and a swastika on his arm.

That bothered Carter. Everything he had gleaned about Jack Martin's prized contact led him to believe he would be precise and punctual. Of course, he had no idea what The Wolf looked like. That bothered him too. Set him at a distinct disadvantage. But he knew one thing. If The Wolf was happy to meet him amid such splendour, in a venue rammed with SS officers, then the chances were he was German and of some local standing.

Carter's beer arrived. He took a sip, the cool amber fluid easing his dry throat, calming his nerves. He studied the newspaper. It was an old edition, full of depressing news for Berliners, heavy losses on the eastern front making headlines.

A middle-aged couple pushed open the swing door. The man could have been a banker, his partner a personal assistant. They sat on the next table and Carter's interest raised. He waited for a nod, a wink, a gesture of recognition. None materialised. Several more couples came and went. After half an hour, the bar had begun to empty, Carter had almost drained his drink, still there was no sign. A sense of frustration swept over him, combined with a modicum of relief that at least the message had not been a trap. He ordered another beer, deciding Berlin's transport was no longer reliable and perhaps Jack's contact had been delayed.

Forty minutes later, hope extinguished along with the day's fading light. Carter wondered if it was possible he had missed a nuance, some secret code, in the message. Unlikely. Coding was one of his natural talents. He swallowed the final dregs of beer, paid his bill, and headed for the swing doors. As he passed through the lobby, he saw three SS officers fawning over a woman with cascading fair hair. The soldiers had a car waiting and were trying to persuade the woman to join them. She threw her head back and laughed, explaining she had work to do, but even though she faced away from Carter, her husky tone was unmistakable. Helena Schulz.

He watched the SS men depart and then Helena turned and their eyes met.

"Oh, how lovely to see you." Helena's warm greeting seemed genuine and spontaneous.

"*Lili Marlene*. We meet again."

"Please, don't remind me. I feel like Lili is my big sister, forever telling me what to do."

"Thanks for the other night, by the way."

"Why?"

"Your encore. Not sure how that would have panned out if you hadn't sung Lili for the soldiers again."

"They were simply boys with sweethearts at home they might never see again. If the song makes them feel close to their loved ones for even a short while, then why wouldn't I sing for them?"

"What are you doing here?"

"I was going to ask you the same thing."

"I was meeting someone, but they haven't turned up. The rail line's probably down."

"Fancy a drink?"

Carter knew he should have declined. Already, he had stayed too long, his face and characteristics embedding in the minds of waiters, barmen, and soldiers. But Helena's eyes sparkled, her rosebud lips glistened invitingly, and the natural sway of her hips made him yearn for a love long gone.

"All right, just one."

She skipped past him, her fragrance swirling through the swing doors of the lobby bar. He followed a couple of paces behind.

"What will it be. A beer?"

"No, I'm swimming in beer. A whisky, please."

"A whisky for Der Herr and mine's the usual, Albert." A sing-song call to the portly waiter drying glasses behind the bar. He returned an affectionate smile.

They sat in the opposite corner from where Carter had spent most of the afternoon. An alcove to themselves, the businessmen the only others remaining. He repeated his question. "What are you doing here?"

"I live here."

"Really?"

"Not all the time, but the opera company provide a room for some of the key performers. The Opera House is around the corner and it cuts down on late-night travelling. Even though there are no shows at the moment, the room is paid for, so when I'm in this part of Berlin I sometimes stay here."

"Lucky you."

"Exactly."

The waiter brought their drinks, a Sicilian lemonade with ice, a slice of lemon and a dash of angostura bitters for Helena.

Carter sniffed his tumbler. The malty scent had an immediate warming effect. He swished the liquid around the glass.

"I was sorry to hear about your husband the other night. The last three years must have been hard." His concern was genuine.

"Others have had it harder, much harder. No one has escaped this hell." Her clipped tone signalled she did not want to take that subject further. "Tell me about you. Is there someone waiting for you when all this is over?"

He licked his lips, his mouth dry as a fleeting memory jemmied a route into his consciousness. Images of his wife, Mary, and his young daughter, flashed chaotically in his head. Only for an instant, until his training kicked in, drawing a mental shroud over a previous life. Never let the past complicate the present.

"There was someone, but, as you say, everyone has experienced a personal chunk of hell. Never mind that. How did you become a singer?"

Helena laughed. "Some people never know what they want to do in life. That's so sad. I was lucky. My mother told me I was singing in my cot. I don't think I ever stopped. I sang in school productions and one of my teachers arranged for special tuition. I won a scholarship to the Guildhall School of Music in London and it all snowballed from there. Next thing, I was singing at Glyndebourne and Covent Garden and then Berlin, where I met Siegfried. It's all a bit of a blur, to be honest. Not many lasses from the cotton mills and coalfields of Lancashire end up as a prima donna in Berlin."

"How did you meet Jack?"

The smile and the trill in her voice remained, but her eyes flashed a warning. "How about we drink up and go for a walk by the river? It's not too cold. That's if you're not still waiting for your friend."

"But it's almost dark."

"Precisely."

"Okay." Carter drained his whisky. He hadn't known Helena Schulz long, but already he had discovered she was sassy, with a sharp intellect, a penchant for languages, a beguiling voice, energy to burn, and a gift for making those in her company seem the most important people in the room. Not an easy woman to turn down.

They grabbed their coats and left, the concierge bowing in farewell as they passed.

With the day's brightness faded, the breeze had once more gained a cutting edge. They buttoned up and headed for the Spree. Carter sucked in cold air to shake off the effects of the alcohol. He realised they risked running into air raid wardens, incurring their wrath for being out after dark and away from a shelter, but he needed more information on Jack's operation.

"Tell me more about how you got to know Jack."

"He was an opera lover. He used to come to Das Bar to hear me sing. We got talking about England and music and his love for the Yorkshire Dales and mine for the Lake District. I suppose we enjoyed the comfort of shared knowledge and similar experiences. When bombs are dropping that takes on added significance."

"I can see that, but it must have been more than that. I don't believe you sing at Das Bar just to keep your voice warm." Carter's tone carried a hint of accusation, but Helena let it go, changing the thrust of the conversation.

"Do you remember I told you I sang for the Führer?"

"Yes."

"He instructed me to sing Wagner, his favourite composer. I found that difficult. Wagner doesn't contain easy melodies. The music is relentless in its seriousness. Out of context, without the operatic setting, it can be dry, its emotion difficult to convey. But I sang and he was appreciative."

"What did you want to sing?"

"In Germany these days you cannot sing or listen to what you want in public, only what you are allowed. Only what pleases Herr Goebbels. We have lost so many great talents. No longer can anyone perform the music of Alban Berg, Arnold

Schoenberg, Anton von Webern and Gunther Weill. There are many others, even Mendelssohn."

Carter had heard of Mendelssohn, but was not familiar with the other composers, although he realised the reason behind the banning of huge swathes of music. "Anything with a Jewish influence?"

Helena nodded. "But it goes deeper even than that. Anything anti-German or deemed to be degenerate, such as jazz. Anything, it seems, that stirs the soul. You must know Lale Andersen, the cabaret singer, was arrested last year for singing *Lili Marlene* and banned from public performances for months."

"But everyone loves that song."

"Apparently, it undermines morale. Too nostalgic." Helena mimicked the clipped tones of a Nazi bureaucrat. "Do you know what happened when she was allowed to perform again?"

"No."

"The audience sang *Lili Marlene* to her, because she couldn't sing it for them. That's where music is at in Germany right now."

"Is it not dangerous for you to sing that song at Das Bar?"

A smoky haze in her eyes smouldered defiance. "You saw, you heard the soldiers. They love it too. I'm not going to sing Wagner and listen to Bruckner for the rest of my life."

"What do you love to perform?"

"Something from The Magic Flute. Probably the Queen of the Night aria. That's my favourite. Light and frothy, easy to communicate."

"That's Mozart, isn't it?"

"Yes. Wolfgang Amadeus Mozart." She emphasised the first syllable of the first name. They stopped walking, a shaft of moonlight shimmered on the Spree, and Helena's deep and meaningful gaze fixed Carter. His jaw dropped, mouth wide. He stared back, realising, at last, that he had not been stood up at lunchtime.

17

AN excited trill in Carter's voice. "The Wolf. You're The Wolf? You sent the message?"

Helena said nothing, but her gaze never wavered. She sidled closer to Carter, so close that he could feel the heat of her body and the mist of her breath. Her lips brushed his collar as she whispered. "Yes. Karl delivered the message. I have information that needs to reach the right people. I need you to help it get there."

For a moment, Carter was bewildered. The pursuit of *The Wolf*, Jack's prime contact, was the purpose of his mission. He remembered Brigadier Pritchard in London stating Jack's most valuable information had come via his secret contact. That meant someone well connected, working alongside or having access to the high echelons of the Nazi regime.

Carter had imagined a driver, an orderly, perhaps a disaffected officer, someone alienated by the Nazis' repressive rule. There were many such characters, Pritchard had determined, although not enough with the courage and fortitude to match their beliefs.

Yet here was an English opera singer, accustomed to entertaining the Führer and his most powerful generals, living a life of privilege in a luxury hotel, claiming she was Jack Martin's informant. Carter needed more proof. He needed time to think.

Around 50 yards ahead, a stone shelter, facing the river, acted as a refuge in happier times for sightseers to picnic or shield from sun or rain as they viewed the river. The iron railings encircling it had long gone, doubtless transformed into ammunition. A rickety wooden picket fence stood in its place, but the shelter itself had escaped the bombs.

"Come on, let's get out of the wind." Carter took Helena's arm. The bombers' moon had transformed the Spree into a silver sliver. Shafts of light reflected off roofs, silhouetting buildings, illuminating what remained of Berlin. Good. It meant most people would be inside or underground, anticipating an air raid siren at any moment. As they approached the shelter, Carter counted 10 wooden benches, most in a state of disrepair. A couple looked sound. After checking the highway to determine no one was heading in their direction, he made for the one furthest from the road.

"Talk to me. What information?" An anxious catch in Carter's tone.

Helena fished inside her clutch bag. She held up a folded piece of paper between thumb and forefinger, as a priest might offer a communion host. Carter took it, studying it for several seconds. No words, only lines of numbers.

"Looks like code, or coordinates perhaps. Degrees, minutes, seconds."

"Exactly."

"What do they represent?"

"I'm not sure."

Carter wasn't expecting that. Everything about Helena had been precise. A woman in total control. Certain of her destination and how to get there.

"What do you mean?" Carter's response contained a jolt of frustration.

"All I know is the source they came from and that Jack said they had never let him down."

"Who are they?"

Helena sighed. For a moment, her eyes shut, lips tightening as if steeling herself to tell the full story.

"Okay. For the last few years I've sung on occasions at a prisoner of war camp."

"Where?"

"Here, in Berlin. To be precise, one of the smaller camps on the outskirts. It's not your normal camp."

"In what way?"

"It has fences and guards, like the rest, but in the main the guards don't carry guns and there are no watch towers or searchlights. The prisoners are all well fed. Some of the British officers are even given passes to shop in the town by themselves and trusted to return."

Carter looked puzzled. "Sounds like a holiday camp, not a prison."

"You're right, the men call it Butlin's. I sing for them in the dining hall. They've erected a stage and some prisoners even play instruments. A piano and double bass. It's not the Berlin Opera, but the prisoners seem to like it."

"So what's this?" He held up the piece of paper.

"After one of the shows, I was talking to one of the British soldiers who helps run the camp, Sergeant Ripley. He was very appreciative and told me hearing a girl with an English accent was boosting prisoners' morale. When there were no guards watching, he slipped me a piece of paper and asked me to pass it to someone who could get it back to England. The only English guy I knew here was Jack at Das Bar. I knew what Jack did and I told him about it. He warned me about the danger. He said I could be shot if the Germans found out. I didn't care. I no longer had Siegfried and I think I've been in Germany long enough to know who is on the right side in this damned war. I've been smuggling out messages ever since."

That rang true. Carter recalled his briefing with Lieutenant Harris. He had spoken of the information stream supplied in code by Martin, including coordinates for munitions factories. What was the phrase he'd used? *Almost as if a British officer has been directing clandestine operations.* Maybe the British officer in question was in this prison camp, using special privileges to gather information. After all, as Brigadier

Pritchard had reminded Carter, a soldier's duty was to fight in any way he could, even when captured.

Helena continued. "When I'm handed the mess …"

Carter slammed his palm hard across Helena's mouth and put a forefinger to his lips. Immediately, her body went rigid, eyes fearful. Engrossed in their conversation, the sound of boots heading towards them on the grassy bank of the river had gone undetected. Three soldiers. Carter picked out their silhouettes. Helena's voice must have carried on the water, alerting a patrol. They sat, still as statues, but the soldiers were closing. They could hear muttering, but couldn't make sense of it. A powerful torch beam swept the shelter. Carter had a split second to react. He removed his palm from across Helena's mouth and replaced it with his mouth, one arm hugging her in what appeared a passionate clinch, the other hand running down her thigh, tracing and tickling the seam of her sheer black stockings.

For a moment, the taste of her sweet lips and the velvet brush of her tongue were so deliciously sensual that he was distracted even from the perilous nature of their situation. If he had to die, then there were worse ways to go.

Carter sensed the torch rays fall upon them. His embrace, if anything, became more ardent.

One soldier laughed, another made a lascivious comment that Carter construed as encouragement. Without breaking the clinch, he flicked a thumb in the air, sparking even deeper guffaws. It could have gone either way. The soldiers could have investigated further, could have asked for papers and demanded explanations. Instead, they stood for several seconds, swapping lewd remarks like naughty schoolboys, before moving on.

When the sound of their boots faded, Carter slowly disentangled himself. Helena gasped before pursing her lips.

"My God, who taught you that trick?"

"In war, sometimes you have to make sacrifices for King and country. You do whatever it takes, agreeable or otherwise." Carter kept a poker face, his voice devoid of expression.

Helena's eyes narrowed. "Which one was that?"

"Let's just say …" The howl of an air raid siren interrupted the moment. "We'd better get off the streets and into a shelter."

"But you'll send the message?" An anxious tremor in Helena's tone.

"I'm doing nothing until you explain exactly how you met Jack Martin. I need to know how you worked together and what's going on in that prison camp. I need to know everything."

18

A MAP of Berlin, curling at the edges, stretched across the table top in the back room at Das Bar.

Bo smoothed it out and pointed to eight red crosses, dotted in haphazard fashion. The light was dim and Carter strained to see. He was still wrestling with the geography and infrastructure of Berlin. Felix had no such problem. He knew the city as well as anyone.

"These crosses denote the location of the P.O.W. camps in and around the city." Bo paused to allow them to assimilate the pattern before continuing. "They are split into sub-camps and the best guess is that in total they hold more than fifty-thousand prisoners, most of them heavily guarded."

"Which one does Helena sing at?" Carter was impatient.

Bo pointed to a town on the outskirts of the city. Stalag III was underlined in bold capitals. Additional squiggles within brackets denoted the sub-camp's individual code but the letters and numbers were indecipherable.

"This is a sub-camp, attached to the rest but separated from them," said Bo. "It's around fifteen miles from the centre of Berlin, surrounded by barbed wire, but there are no gun turrets. Guards carry holstered hand guns but they stroll around, mixing with the prisoners. No searchlights in sight. Our information is that the food is palatable, which can't be said for other camps, and there's plenty of it. They even organise sing-songs and entertainment evenings."

"That's exactly what Helena told me. The prisoners call it Butlin's."

Bo and Felix looked blank. "It's a holiday camp on the east coast of England, opened by a businessman named Billy Butlin a few years ago. It's all the rage."

He didn't mention the prison camp was also where Helena garnered her most significant information. He still hadn't fully worked out Helena's relationship with the characters at Das Bar. On the rare occasions he had observed them together, she seemed to treat Bo as if he were a benevolent uncle. She was cool and business-like with Karl and Felix and as for Elke, a tetchy mother-daughter relationship came to mind. The more Carter saw of them, the more it became obvious the only person Helena had trusted was Jack Martin. As far as the others were concerned, she was merely Jack's singer friend, albeit a successful and moderately famous one.

Carter, however, now knew Jack had approached Helena back in 1941, the morning after the night the Berlin State Opera was bombed. Following their café meeting, Helena had agreed to be Jack's *eyes and ears* amid the Berlin socialite circle, including the highest ranks of the Nazi Party. She had become a prime asset.

Carter did not relay that news to London, but he did transmit the contents of the coded message Helena had given him following their Hotel Adlon meeting, using the silk cipher. A few days later he received a coded reply.

Bravo The Wolf.

He took that to mean the information had proved to be precise. For all he knew those coordinates had been used to guide the recent bombs falling on key targets in Berlin. He hoped so. It would mean his mission was on the right track. The purpose of the Stalag III sub-camp, however, bothered him.

"What I don't get is why the Germans would differentiate between the treatment of prisoners. Surely the enemy is the enemy?" There was a crackle of uncertainty in Carter's delivery.

Bo fixed Carter with a knowing stare. "Why do you give a dog a treat?"

"To make it sit, beg, obey, that sort of thing. Do what you want it to do."

"Exactly."

"Sorry, I don't get it."

"The Nazis are a devious lot. As a rule, they don't do soft, but they've isolated this camp, probably hand-picking the prisoners. Maybe they have skills they need, scientists, engineers, although the Germans are pretty well-equipped in those departments. I don't know the reason, but they're going to a lot of trouble. Using a carrot rather than the stick they usually prefer. There's method in there somewhere."

"We need to find out what they're up to?"

Bo nodded.

Carter considered his next move for a few moments. "When's Helena here next?"

"Tonight, I think," said Bo.

"I'll speak to her."

"I won't be around. Karl and I are doing the run with the American airmen."

"Good luck. It's time they were on their way."

***

Karl handed Bo a cup of coffee from a thermos flask and said, "How much longer? They should be here by now."

Bo said nothing, staring through the truck's windscreen at the forest clearing ahead of them, black and blurry in the midnight rain.

"We can't wait forever." A plug of frustration in Karl's voice.

"It's not like they're catching a train. There are no timetables. These things take as long as they take. They could be held up for any number of reasons." Bo's explanation sounded reasonable, but there was a snap of concern in his reply.

It was almost two months since the airmen had taken refuge in the graveyard hut. They had intended leaving much sooner but the pilot's injuries required more convalescence. His head gash had healed nicely, but he needed to walk unaided and the wound to his right thigh had proved difficult to treat.

Bo had suggested Tex make the trip to the border to link up with the Polish resistance by himself. He was having none of it. "We never leave one of our own behind. We stay together, we leave together."

The graveyard had proved the perfect hiding place. The only time the airmen had been disturbed was when a drunk, searching for a sanctuary to lay his groggy head, stumbled upon the hut and tried to force the door open with a spade. Drawing his service pistol, the gunner came within a hair of squeezing the trigger when the drunk predictably collapsed against the door, unconscious. Tex dragged him out of the back gate, across the nearby field, depositing him by the road to Berlin, where doubtless the drunk would eventually hitch a ride, oblivious to how close he had come to oblivion.

As the driver, Karl had chosen this night for good reason. Heavy rain was forecast. The chance of running into a patrol or checkpoint was minimised, and the weather would provide cover for the Polish resistance at the border handover. No moonlight to betray their position.

The plan was simple. The truck would drive to the meeting point and wait for the resistance to announce themselves, whereupon the two airmen would clamber out of the truck in the civilian clothes Felix provided and make their way to the resistance's vehicle. After that, they were in the hands of the Poles, albeit relying on Felix's identity papers if and when they reached the ferry to Sweden.

Another half hour crawled by, Karl constantly glancing at his watch. With rain lashing harder than ever, a glimmer from the forest caught his eye, soft and diffused, like the glow of a cigarette tip. He nudged Bo. Three distinct flashes amid the trees 150 yards ahead of them. The designated signal.

Bo drew back the cab's curtain, his torch beam settling on the airmen's faces, wreathed in apprehension. "You're good to go. Quick as you like."

Tex rose from the mound of potato sacks to grab Bo's hand. He shook it with what Bo thought was desperate vigour. "Thank you, my friend."

"No problem."

The pilot did the same, after which the airmen clambered out of the back of the truck and headed for the trees. Karl reached to turn the truck's ignition, but Bo grabbed his forearm.

"Give them two minutes, make sure they get away, then we'll be off."

The airmen hurried across the clearing, the gunner acting as a crutch for the pilot who limped as fast as his wounded leg would allow. Half way to the trees, Tex heard a disturbing metallic click in the blackness. Searchlights from the left, brilliant white and sweeping, flooded the clearing. Clipped voices in the distance shouted orders.

Tex glanced back towards the truck, shock and terror distorting his features, before clasping the pilot's shoulders and struggling on towards the trees.

The shooting started. Sustained bursts of rifle fire thumping into the soft earth around the airmen until fleshy thuds signalled several rounds had found their target. The pilot staggered, then slumped to the ground.

Tex tried to drag him to his feet, but the dead weight was too much to bear and anyway he realised instinctively his friend was gone.

Sprinting on alone, for several seconds it seemed Tex might confound the natural law of probability and make it to the cover of the foliage, but hope is rarely a match for a speeding bullet, and he too was hit. He pitched forward, stumbling a few yards before sagging to his knees and collapsing face down in the mud.

Karl gunned the truck's engine and swung the vehicle around.

"Zu dumm zum Scheissen." He hurled his German vitriol at the Poles in the trees, certain there must have been a leak at their end. Poor organisation and loose talk had happened before. Bo shook his head and muttered something similar, but in English. "Too dumb to shit."

19

THE guard on the gate wore a cheery smile as he waved the car into the prison camp.

Helena Schulz waved back. The staff and guards had become accustomed to Helena's visits. At first she had to make her own way into the Berlin suburbs, an unpredictable journey with increasing air raids, fractured rail lines and damaged infrastructure. But after witnessing the positive effect on prisoner morale, the commandant supplied a car, complete with an armed guard. Everyone, including the guards, enjoyed Helena's presence.

One of the staff had picked her up outside Hotel Adlon. She attended to her make-up on the way, noticing the driver's sly glances in the rear-view mirror. She liked that. Keep them guessing. Keep them interested.

This time she viewed her visit through a different prism. Carter had relayed his discussion with Bo and Felix. No longer was she there merely to sing, put smiles on faces, help men cope with the boredom and desperation of captivity, at the same time receiving the odd coded message to hand to Jack Martin, the contents of which she never queried. Carter had decided the comforts of *Butlin's* demanded explanation. It was time to ask questions. But with questions came danger, which is why Carter had coached Helena in the rudiments of his tradecraft.

His advice was basic: Watch, listen, probe vulnerabilities and exploit trusted relationships. Helena only met two men for any length of time on her visits. Commandant Walter Reinhardt, and Sergeant Ripley.

As she passed through the gates, she forced herself to analyse the camp through different eyes. A five-a-side football match was underway in the exercise area, men standing side-by-side to form the touchlines of a rectangular pitch. A guard acted as referee, his whistles battling with whoops of encouragement.

The car swung past the accommodation huts. A group of prisoners wielded a variety of tools, one of them at the top of a ladder, hammer in hand, attending to a roof repair. Others sat at a table playing cards despite the chill. A few, at a more distant hut, stomped the mud, engaged in animated conversation, but in the main a busy ambience of normality pervaded. As usual, the car pulled up outside the block housing the commandant's office. The driver walked around the car and opened the door for Helena, who bowed, dispensing a warm smile in gratitude.

"Ah, Frau Schulz, you're back again." Reinhardt stood in the doorway, uniform pristine, chiselled features forming a benign grin as Helena climbed the steps to his office block.

She gave the customary Nazi salute. The commandant responded likewise.

"I don't seem to be able to stay away." Helena offered a hand and the commandant shook it gently before raising it to his lips.

"Anytime, Frau Schulz. You're always welcome. It's a delight to hear you sing. Gives the men something to look forward to. We have many different cultures here and music is a powerful tool to connect people, don't you think?"

"Yes, of course." It was not a sentiment Helena expected to hear from a high-ranking German officer, but there was something about Reinhardt she had taken to when they first met. He wasn't your typical arrogant officer, full of business-like detachment and snide remarks. He was engaging and sympathetic. A man, she had decided, more likely to act on his own intuition rather than by the Nazi textbook. It helped that he had known her late husband, Siegfried.

"Have you time for a drink, Frau Schulz?" Reinhardt guided her down the corridor towards his office. In her many visits to the camp, it was the first time she had received such an invitation.

"I should be preparing for …"

"Nonsense. You're not singing for the Führer today. The men can wait awhile, it will only sharpen their anticipation."

"If you say so."

"I do."

Reinhardt's office was as neat and tidy as his appearance. The obligatory Nazi flag dominated the wall behind his desk. Family pictures adorned another wall. Helena crossed the room to sneak a better look.

"Are these your children?" She pointed to a photograph of Reinhardt with a woman and two youngsters playing in the snow.

He smiled. "St Moritz, nineteen-thirty-seven. Astrid was eight and Wilhelm only five. Seems a lifetime ago."

"And this is your wife?" Helena pointed to the woman in the picture. Reinhardt nodded, although Helena detected a mistiness in his eyes. He covered up, searching his drinks cabinet, proceeding to pour a measure of cloudy liquid for Helena.

"How did you know?" Helena posed the question as she accepted the glass.

"What?"

"That I drink Sicilian lemonade with angostura."

"We're a resourceful and meticulous team here, Frau Schulz. Our camp is run by intelligence personnel. There are few things we don't know, even when people attempt to hide them from us, which is never a good idea." His smile was fixed and tone even, but she took his words as a warning. What she didn't know was whether this was a fishing expedition. Did he know she had been smuggling out items of coded information, or was he merely warning her about the perils of doing so? Or had Reinhardt detailed someone to follow and watch her? In the lobby bar at Hotel Adlon, perhaps when she met with Carter. For all she knew, Reinhardt could have a dossier on *Helena, The Wolf,* in his desk drawer, just feet away.

A cold, clammy, shiver crossed her shoulders. She sipped lemonade, glad of the acid bite as it stung the back of her dry throat. "Well, I shall take it as a compliment that you took the time and effort to find out what makes a lady tick. If only all men were so attentive."

He laughed. "It's good to enjoy some nuanced conversation, Frau Schulz."

For around 10 minutes they chatted about music, including the relative merits of Johann Sebastian Bach and Richard Strauss, until the commandant's orderly knocked on the door to announce the hall was set up and full with men waiting.

Reinhardt waved the orderly away, announcing he would accompany Helena to the hall. It was quite a trek involving crossing the main roadway between the huts and navigating a myriad of corridors away from the main accommodation.

It took them close to a block Helena had not passed before, built of brick in contrast to the wooden huts. The main door was reinforced with a metal gate, iron bars guarding the glass windows, its fortifications incongruous with the relaxed levels of security in the rest of the camp.

"What's that?" Helena asked out of genuine curiosity.

"Nothing, just a home for some of our most valuable inmates."

Helena thought *valuable* a strange adjective to use, but her mind was on her performance and she could hear the murmur of expectation emanating from the hall as they approached. The commandant's impromptu drinks session meant she had foregone her usual warm-up routine and, as always, she needed the bathroom before the performance began.

"I must visit the toilets." As she glanced to Reinhardt for permission, she swivelled, catching sight of the silhouette of a figure staring out of one of the barred windows. It was the merest glimpse, little more than a blurred reflection before the figure receded into the shadow of the room. But it was enough to send Helena's heart pounding.

***

It was not the Berlin Opera House. But the music-loving men of Stalag III had done their best to create an intimate atmosphere in the hall normally used as a canteen. The carpenters among them had built a small wooden stage, which gave everyone an unobstructed view of Helena. They had placed several large plants to soften the canteen's drab and dirty walls. An upright piano stood at the side of the stage, complete with stool, manned by a Czech soldier named Michal. He looked barely out of his teens, but had performed at several previous concerts, Helena remarking on the soul and dexterity with which he played.

The men stood and rousing applause greeted Helena as she entered. With nods and smiles, she acknowledged the prisoners, slipping off her coat to reveal a lacy patterned dress, the top of which showed her bra straps. A crucifix on a long gold chain dangled from her neck, nestling above a hint of cleavage. If Helena had learned anything in her foray into the world of opera, it was how to tantalise and tease her audience.

Crossing to Michal, she handed him several sheets of music and pointed out the set list.

"Happy with that?"

Michal nodded.

Helena skipped onto the stage, savouring the mood of the audience. The rays of a spotlight played on her hair, little gold slivers dancing as her locks cascaded onto her shoulders. She spied Sergeant Ripley in the front row, smiles of recognition passing between them, before, hands on hips, she announced herself in English, vowels flat and friendly.

"I'm Helena from Lancashire. Do you want me to sing?"

Hundreds of boots performed a makeshift drumroll on the wooden floor. Several prisoners stuck fingers in their mouths, shrill whistles piercing the air. The din lasted so long that guards around the hall's perimeter moved to the front, raising and lowering their hands to motion for silence. Eventually, the hall quietened and the sweetest sound replaced the cacophony.

The set list was an opera lover's delight. Mozart, Bellini, Bizet's Carmen, a snatch of Erbarme Dich, the beautiful aria from Bach's St Matthew's Passion.

Helena sailed through the songs effortlessly, as did Michal. When the last bar of the final number sounded, many of the men were open-mouthed, trapped in their own thoughts, lost in wherever the music had taken them. When they realised the concert was over, the foot-roll sounded once more, the whistles louder, more plentiful even than before, the audience baying for an encore.

The guards called for order.

Helena, quite instinctively, did something she'd never done before. Moved by the fervent response, she marched on the spot, knees billowing her dress, one arm raised as if holding a flag aloft.

"*Land of Hope and Glory.*" The first line of Elgar's song burst from her lips, and the men snatched at the challenge, belting out the patriotic lyrics, the hall resonating with British fervour. Michal, his piano redundant, looked nonplussed.

By the time the final *"Make thee mightier yet"* sounded, the guards had abandoned trying to quell the bedlam. Out of the corner of her eye Helena spotted the commandant watching, along with several of his officers. A strange shape played on Reinhardt's lips. She took it to be a smirk of admiration, but couldn't be sure.

When the men had dispersed, Sergeant Ripley approached Helena and as usual invited her to his quarters. As the camp's leading non-commissioned officer he was afforded privileges, including a room of his own. A brief chat with Helena following her concerts had become custom and practice.

"That was brave," he said as he closed the door behind them.

"A bit of fun, Sergeant, that's all. The men seemed to like it. I think the commandant …"

Ripley interrupted. "Don't underestimate Reinhardt. He comes across as reasonable and in the main he is, but he answers to powerful people. His decisions are not always his own. In the circumstances, it's probably best not to draw attention."

Helena understood. She lowered her voice to the merest whisper. "Anything for me?"

Ripley fiddled inside a sock. He emerged with a folded piece of paper, even tinier than the last one. Helena accepted it and without care for modesty hitched up her dress in full view of the sergeant, revealing black sheer stockings held in place by suspenders below a strip of smooth white skin. Easing back the elastic of her black knickers, she slipped the paper inside, immediately smoothing her dress.

Ripley's face betrayed no interest, although inside something stirred. They spoke for a couple of minutes about the songs Helena might sing at the next concert, until Helena deemed it an appropriate time to leave.

"Very well Sergeant. I'd better be going. My driver will be waiting."

He nodded, but moved towards Helena, his mouth close to her ear as he whispered. "Next time, we need to speak. I have something big, really big. Something Britain needs to know." There was a tremor in his voice.

As he opened the door he spotted a small man with a surly expression and a bald pate, resembling a Benedictine monk, bent over in the corridor beside two heavy boxes.

"Yes, Private Cohen?"

"On my way to the kitchen, Sir. New plates. Just taking a breather."

"Very well, Cohen. Carry on."

20

CARTER lay on the bed, propped on an elbow, fingers wrapped around the contours of a whisky tumbler. Thinking.

He'd drained one glass and craved another, but the fate of the two American airmen kept detonating in his head. They had been his responsibility, his first mission since landing in Berlin. And it had all gone so far south he didn't know where to start with his report. Karl had related the bare facts of the shooting in the forest clearing. There hadn't been much to tell. All over in several blurry seconds, after which survival became paramount. The obvious conclusion was that the mission had been compromised. But how and by whom?

Carter toyed again with inflicting more damage on the whisky bottle, probably would have done if a gentle tap on the door hadn't roused him from his musings. He discarded the tumbler, reached for his revolver, swung his legs off the bed and tiptoed across the room. It was gone midnight. No one knocked at this time. No one knocked at any time. Standing to one side of the door, he whispered. "Who is it?"

A husky voice replied, "It's me."

He edged the door ajar, pulled Helena in, and waited several seconds, listening, to make sure she hadn't been followed.

"What the hell are you doing here?" Whisky, mixed with guilt, fuelling Carter's fire.

"Are you always this charming? And do you ever clean this place?" Helena glanced around, nose wrinkling as she clocked a pile of discarded food wrappings and a thick film of white dust on most surfaces.

"Oh, no, the maid must have missed a bit. I'll have to have words with her. She's not up to the Adlon's standards." His demeanour sarcastic.

Helena rolled her eyes. Carter looked sheepish.

"Sorry. I don't mean to be a jerk. I was thinking about two airmen we lost. A bloody business. They didn't deserve what happened to them."

"No one deserves this war."

"You're right. I just feel responsible."

"Did you shoot their plane down?"

"No."

"Did you kill them?"

"Of course not."

"Did you offer them a chance of freedom, rather than rot in a P.O.W. camp?"

"Yes."

"I bet they grabbed that chance with both hands and I'm sure they'd do the same again."

"I still feel …"

"You can't go around carrying the burden of everyone's personal decisions, not if you want to stay sane."

Carter knew Helena was right. He didn't always appreciate her direct approach, but in the short time they'd known each other he'd come to admire her zeal in recognising and attacking a problem. He drew a deep breath.

"Let's start again, Helena. What can I do for you at this late hour?" His tone just the right side of mischievous.

Helena rustled in a pocket of her handbag and took out the folded paper Sergeant Ripley had given her.

"First, another message, coded like the rest. I trust you can send it ASAP."

Carter took the paper. "Of course, first thing in the morning."

"Second, you said you needed to know everything about that prison camp."

Carter beckoned Helena to sit on the lone chair. He perched on the side of the bed. She had his undivided attention and like a consummate stage performer, she determined to make the most of it. She described the car journey through the gates, the positive interaction between guards and prisoners, the football match and the seeming lack of depression or boredom. She remembered a pile of Red Cross parcels she'd encountered on her way to the toilet in the sick bay. The room contained a long bench down one side, cupboards and a washing sink. It had an examining couch and stools for patients while being treated. There was also an old microscope and a hand driven centrifuge. Carter was particularly interested in her chat with the commandant and probed her on every nuance. He wanted to know the items adorning his desk and the subjects in the photographs. He also encouraged her to remember the topography of the camp. The relative distance between accommodation huts, how many prisoners each contained and the geography of the kitchen and canteen. He took notes with a pad and pencil as she spoke.

When she described the concert, she surprised herself. She had sung for the Führer and his generals at the Berlin Opera House, performed for presidents and prime ministers, graced the stage at Covent Garden, won bouquets of applause for her command of emotion, yet never had she felt so alive or appreciated as in front of the prisoners at Stalag III.

She told Carter how the performance ended in a hubbub of singing, stomping and whistling while she marched on the spot and belted out *Land of Hope and Glory*. He guffawed so much it was all he could manage not to fall off the bed.

"I'm surprised they didn't slap you in handcuffs and find you a cell for the night. Is that everything?"

"No, there's more." She told him about her brief chat with Sergeant Ripley and his warning that he had *something really big* to divulge

"Tell me again his exact words." Carter prompted her to remember.

"*Something Britain needs to know*. That's what he said, and it was the way he said it. It was almost as if he couldn't believe what he had discovered."

Carter scribbled more notes until a thought struck. "How did you get here?" An air raid earlier had shut down the trains and trams.

"On my bike."

"Your bike?"

"Yes, why's that unusual? It's only a few miles over the Spree. Women can ride bikes, you know. I keep it at the Adlon, it has come in useful on several occasions."

"Is that everything?" Carter checked once more, aware that it was easy to miss the pernickety details once the big stuff was recorded.

"Not quite."

"Go on."

"Well, I'm not sure, but I think I saw something strange. Something impossible."

"What do you mean?"

"I was walking with the commandant to the concert hall and there was a brick building, away from the accommodation blocks, with bars on the windows and doors."

"That's not strange. It is a prison."

"Maybe, but something caught my attention. When I turned, I saw a person reflected in one of the windows, someone I swear I recognised."

"Who? Helena, who was it?"

A pained expression settled on her features, there was a catch in her throat and she paused for several seconds to compose herself. When the answer came it was no more than a whisper.

"Jack. I think it was Jack Martin"

21

IT wasn't unusual for Sergeant Ripley to receive a summons to the commandant's office. The Germans had appointed him leader of the prisoners in Stalag III, with freedom to arrange the camp as he saw fit, as long as his decisions met with official approval.

The fact that he spoke perfect German was one reason for his elevated status. His civilian job as a former accountant also helped when it came to organising and budgeting. But there was another reason that crossed his mind as he tapped on the commandant's door.

"Come in." There was a steely edge to the commandant's command.

Ripley entered and was surprised to find two of Reinhardt's right-hand officers also sitting at the commandant's desk, either side of him. They resembled the disciplinary panel Ripley had once been hauled in front of as an errant teenager. Aloof stares and cold demeanours.

"Yes, Commandant. What can I do for you?"

"I'll come straight to the point." He motioned to the other officers. "I have asked the lieutenants here to listen to what you have to say."

"About what?"

"There has been an accusation."

"What sort of accusation?" A bead of cold sweat ran down Ripley's back. Three senior officers were not here to waste time on stolen provisions, the allocation of bunks, or who was entitled to Red Cross parcels. He was certain of that. This was serious. His first thought was for the coded messages he had handed to Helena. Over the last couple of months Helena had smuggled out one each time she performed. Most contained coordinates of bombing targets, key factories, anti-aircraft batteries and barracks, verified by Ripley himself following his journeys outside the camp to source provisions. He received passes for such trips, signed personally by Reinhardt.

"Frau Schulz." Reinhardt's mention of Helena's surname convinced Ripley his messages had been rumbled. His heart pounded. He swallowed hard, somehow keeping control.

"What has this to do with Frau Schulz?"

The officers fixed him with piercing stares, watching for a false move, a nervous flicker of an eyebrow, an involuntary shrug, a tongue in the cheek, anything that might betray an untruth.

"You spent some time alone with Frau Schulz in your room following her last concert."

"What on earth are you suggesting?" Ripley's tone conveyed shock. Inside, he was quite proud of how affronted he sounded.

Reinhardt waved dismissively. "Nothing like that. Frau Schulz is a sought-after woman. I'm sure she can find a man who, first, isn't locked up, and, second, has a physique more like a mountain than a mole hill." The two lieutenants smirked. Ripley was not the most muscular of creatures. Years sitting at a desk in captivity had fashioned a hunched disposition. His face was gaunt, pale, and lightly freckled, lank hair had a ginger hue, his body devoid of athletic prowess.

Reinhardt continued. "I'm wondering what you had to talk about. You're not exactly like minds."

"You're wrong, Herr Commandant, if you don't mind me saying so. I have always loved the opera. Each time Frau Schulz sings for us, we discuss the composition of her next performance. For instance, in two weeks' time she will concentrate on Mozart, pieces from *The Magic Flute* and *The Marriage of Figaro*. Hopefully, the men will enjoy the humour."

Reinhardt held up his right hand to signal Ripley to stop talking.

"Back to the accusation. How long did you and Frau Schulz speak for?"

"Five minutes, no more. She didn't want to keep her driver waiting."

"Did anything pass between you?"

"Absolutely not."

"I have it on good authority that your meeting contained much furtive whispering. What does Mozart have to whisper about?"

Suddenly, it dawned. Private Cohen. The man in the corridor, ostensibly carrying boxes of plates to the kitchen. He must have had his ear to the door, attempting to eavesdrop their conversation. There were two ways of playing it from here. Shrug it off and stick to the music line. Or go on the offensive. By nature, Ripley was not an aggressive character, but something told him Reinhardt and the others still required convincing.

"If your *good authority* is that no-good Jew, Private Cohen, then let me tell you, he's always creeping around trying to make mischief. When things go missing, he's the first person the men think of. He's not to be trusted. A liar and a cheat. He'd sell his grandmother for a cup of rice. The most dislikeable man in the camp. And I know you know that. I take it as a personal slight that you would listen to, or believe, anything he had to say."

Ripley's pale face had turned a livid shade of purple, partly out of his genuine distaste for Cohen, mostly from the blood pumping through his stressed system. Reinhardt turned to each of his officers, whose faces remained impassive.

"In the normal sway of things I would tend to agree, Sergeant, but there are those who doubt your commitment to the cause."

"Such as?"

"We needn't name names, but I feel I need to remind you that the privileges you receive while organising the prisoners are in return for delivering men willing and able to aid our cause, even fight alongside us. It is the Führer's express wish."

"I am well aware of that, Herr Commandant, but I can't force men to change sides. Ideology must be nurtured. You have professionals to do that job. The men on the radio. Men steeped in psychology and propaganda. I've heard them, and seen them here."

Reinhardt stood and walked over to the window, hands clasped behind his back as he watched drizzle dampening the hut roofs in the distance. He said nothing for many seconds, the void of silence unsettling almost to the point of inducing panic, which was doubtless his intention.

Finally, he turned and spoke.

"You were chosen to come here, Sergeant, like many of the camp's individuals, to enjoy our food and relative comforts, unlike many of your countrymen elsewhere, because of your previous association with the British Union of Fascists. You knew Oswald Mosley, I believe."

"I was young. I met him once. I couldn't pretend to actually know him."

"Your membership of his organisation suggested you were sympathetic to our Führer's cause."

Ripley's eyebrows knitted. He was unsure where this conversation was going.

"But, Sergeant, the proof of the pudding is in the eating, I think that is one of your quaint English sayings, is it not?"

Ripley nodded.

"So far, only twenty-seven men from our camp have signed up to our new unit. Twenty-seven out of thousands. That hardly constitutes a pudding, Sergeant. We need more, and quickly, if our Führer is to get his special unit to help fight the Russians. Think of that, British troops joining us to fight the real enemy from Moscow. What a statement that would make to Mister Churchill. What a propaganda victory that would be for Herr Goebbels here in Berlin."

Ripley seized on Reinhardt's mention of Goebbels, as a drowning man grasps a lifebelt. Courtesy of several radios smuggled into the camp via Red Cross parcels, Ripley had listened to many of Goebbels speeches and knew the Nazi's Minister of Propaganda to be virulent in his discrimination against the Jews. Stories and rumours had reached the camp suggesting atrocities and incidents of systematic genocide were commonplace. His response carried bite.

"I'm sure Herr Goebbels is interested in the propaganda value of British fighters extolling the ideology of the Führer. And I'm sure more will follow. But Herr Goebbels hates the Jews. He wouldn't trust one of them, especially not someone like Private Cohen."

Reinhardt sat again, eyes narrowed. For many seconds he gazed at Ripley, appraising. Either side, the officers remained impassive.

Where did Ripley's real loyalties lie? What did he love and hate? Was he sincere in his declared intention to enlist British servicemen to fight alongside the Germans on the Eastern Front, or was it all a sham? Reinhardt had seen such men before. Men in turmoil. At odds with themselves. Convinced one moment they were doing the right thing, that betrayal was honourable, only to recant when the enormity of treachery dawned. Was Ripley such a man? Would he employ lies and deception like the soldier on the battlefield uses bayonets and bullets?

On balance, Reinhardt decided he would, but the mention of Goebbels and the Jew had clouded matters. And there was also the subject of Frau Schulz. If Reinhardt continued to interrogate or act against Ripley, then the obvious inference was that Frau Schulz was part of the deception. The same Frau Schulz who was the singing darling of so many prominent Nazis, including the Führer and Goebbels.

For a P.O.W. camp commandant, that was a mighty wall to scale, with a dizzying drop in prospect.

Was Reinhardt prepared to risk that fall on the flaky evidence of Private Cohen, a Jew disliked and distrusted by his own compatriots?

Reinhardt rose again. He crossed the room, picked up a brandy decanter, and poured large measures into two glasses.

"Let's drink, Sergeant, to those with the foresight to share our vision. I think Private Cohen might enjoy a change of scenery. I know just the place."

22

THE train to Potsdam was full of Berliners, heading out of the city at the weekend to escape the bombs and toxic smell of gas and putrefaction on the streets. Potsdam, due to its location, 15 miles from the centre of Berlin, had attracted its fair share of attention from British and American bombers, although many of its historical palaces and castles had survived unscathed and the picturesque lakes dotted around its open spaces still afforded the city fresh air as well as an ambience of calm, splendour even.

As always, Carter sat in the front carriage. The central coach of the train routinely lined up with the station concourse. It meant he would receive early warning if an inspection party of Gestapo or SS officers was in position to board.

There was another practical reason for taking the train. Most travellers carried large bags or suitcases, cramming the overhead luggage racks. Carter's rucksack was small in comparison. It would attract no attention when he alighted.

It was a stuffy journey. An elderly couple sat opposite, the man constantly fidgeting in the pockets of his overcoat as if he had lost something. His wife urged him to desist, but the more she remonstrated, the more he fidgeted. A woman next to Carter tutted her disapproval, but it made no difference.

Carter closed his eyes, shutting out the distractions, trying to construct the jigsaw Helena had brought him.

The first piece was Sergeant Ripley. The coded information he had supplied via Helena these past months had proved accurate, providing the Allied air forces with pin-point targets. Now he claimed he had *Something Britain needs to know*. Such a statement from a reliable source could not be disregarded. But who was Ripley? What was his background? If Carter was to put lives in danger on the say-so of a prisoner of war, he needed to know.

And what of Helena's dubious sighting of Jack Martin? Carter's instinct told him she must have been mistaken. A rainy day, a shadowy reflection. Her eyes may have deceived her. Or it could be a case of concentrated attention, one of the laws of suggestion that maintains if spontaneous attention is concentrated on a particular idea, it tends to become realised. Helena had been troubled greatly by Jack's loss. It wasn't much of a stretch to suggest her subconscious mind had dwelt on his fate while in the process of another mission. An unknowing fixation, a quick glance, a furtive sighting, the perfect ingredients to dupe the conscious mind. Yet something gnawed at Carter, something he couldn't put his finger on.

The train jolted as the brakes engaged, signalling Potsdam station was approaching. He swung his rucksack from the luggage rack, at the same time offering to hand down the suitcase to the woman in the neighbouring seat. She accepted eagerly. There were no welcoming parties. He mingled with the passengers as they disembarked, then headed for the tram stop on the opposite side of the station square.

He boarded a tram to Babelsberg, home of Germany's major film production studio and an area with an imposing palace and tree-lined park. Karl had suggested the location and Carter understood why. It was elevated from the ground around, comparatively isolated with no heavy stonework to deflect transmissions. Much of the studio area had been fenced off and boarded to protect the buildings. The site appeared deserted. Carter made his way to Gate 15 and rattled the padlock. It was unlocked, as Karl had promised, and he made his way inside the perimeter to a small block with a sign above the door, Studio 3.

Again, he required no key, pushing the door open to reveal a reception area. He set down the transmitter on a table, referred to the appropriate version on the silk code and commenced tapping. Sergeant Ripley's latest coded message was first to go, comprising another set of coordinates. Next, Carter filed an encrypted request for information on Ripley's status, stating that he was the British camp commander at Stalag III. Finally, Carter warned significant news out of the prison camp was imminent. He added an encrypted capital 'U' to his transmission to alert London an urgent answer was required.

Carter had taken around eight minutes to send his message. Swift enough to evade tracking by anyone listening in an urban environment. He realised the open spaces of Babelsberg made locating a transmission marginally quicker. It was the one downside. He packed his rucksack and retraced his steps.

When he reached Gate 15 he replaced the chain on the padlock and was about to wander back to the tram stop when he heard the high-powered rumble of a van negotiating a bend up ahead. It was speeding in his direction. Instinct kicked in. Instead of crossing the road in plain sight, he turned and dived inside a low thicket of gorse on scrubland in front of the studios, and lay still.

The black vehicle pulled up no more than 30 yards from him, tyres screeching, opposite Gate 15. Three men with guns clambered out. Another man followed, restraining a German Shepherd dog on a short lead, panting and pulling, as it yearned to go to work. Two of the gunmen threw open the studio gates and sprinted inside with the dog handler. The remaining man, machine gun at the ready, stood guard at the gates.

How the hell did they know? How did they get here so quickly? Surely no one could have tracked a transmission that took little longer than boiling an egg. Could they? Carter's mind was racing, his heart pounding, the instant surge of adrenalin ensuring he felt no pain from the thorns scratching his arms and legs. He considered drawing his revolver, but the guard at the gate was too far away and anything other than a single kill shot would almost certainly seal his fate.

He watched through a gap in the foliage, propped on his elbows. The guard wore no uniform. Possibly Gestapo. A member of a snatch squad. That was Carter's best guess. Five minutes later, the other gunmen reappeared, frustration in their tramping gaits. One of them lit a cigarette and their eyes scoured the landscape, searching for hiding places.

"He can't be far."

"Maybe jumped a tram back to the city."

The debate continued for a short while before the man dragging on the cigarette strolled towards the thicket, scanning a lake and a line of trees beyond. Carter held his breath, front teeth biting his lip as the tension approached unbearable. *Please God, don't let the dog off the leash.*

The squad's leader, for that is what Carter had decided, stopped no more than two yards from where he lay. Carter could smell the sweet aroma of strong tobacco and hear the sound of bristles being rubbed as the man contemplated his whereabouts. Then he was sure he saw the man point in his direction. For one chilling moment, he thought the boss had rumbled him.

"Those trees could be a good place to hide, don't you think? Let the dog have some fun over there."

The men tramped past his position and Carter listened to their mutterings recede before he dared steal a glance above the thicket. He watched the men and the dog disappear into the cover of the trees.

Carter grasped his opportunity, swinging his pack over his shoulder and scurrying to the transport hub where a tram was about to depart.

As his heart rate returned to normal on the way back to Berlin, he considered two possibilities. Either German tracking technology had progressed in a short time beyond anything thought possible. Or, more likely and more worrying, the state police had received a tip-off. Someone on the train perhaps? Maybe the woman he had helped with the case? The fidgeting old man? Anyone who, for some unfathomable reason, had formed a suspicion. Who knows?

It was the secret agent's random nightmare. Part of the reason Carter had grown to hate this undercover business. Yet his instinct remained sharp. Not for the first time, he gave thanks for the fundamentals of his tradecraft. Never assume. Avoid complacency. Expect the unexpected.

***

Lieutenant Harris was working late in his Beaconsfield office when his secretary, a petite young woman with a sweet round face, popped her head around the door.

"What is it, Mildred? I thought you'd gone home."

"Sorry to bother you, Lieutenant, but I thought you should see the latest wire from Berlin. It's arrived from Bletchley, decrypted and marked *Urgent*."

"Of course, Mildred."

He scanned the sheet of paper for several seconds.

"Could you get me Brigadier Pritchard on the telephone please?"

"He's at the War Office tonight, Sir. High-level meeting with General …"

"Now, Mildred, please. This time *Urgent* means urgent."

Two minutes later the Brigadier was patched through to Harris's office. "This had better be good, Lieutenant. You've dragged me away from a twenty-five-year-old bottle of Macallan."

"Are we on a secure line, Sir?"

"I'm at the War Office, Harris. If it's not secure here, then God help us."

Harris proceeded to read Carter's message.

Pritchard listened in silence until the mention of Sergeant Ripley, whereupon Harris detected the Brigadier's curiosity pique, a couple of murmurs urging him to continue reading. When he had finished, the line remained silent for several seconds.

"Sir, are you still there?"

"I'm thinking, Harris. Don't badger."

"Sorry, Sir."

Almost a minute later, Pritchard had made a decision.

"Carter's life's on the line here. His info has been flawless so far. He deserves as much assistance as we can give him. Find out about the current status of this Sergeant Ripley and report back. Within the hour, Lieutenant, is that clear?

"Yes, Sir."

The line went dead. Harris bellowed across the office. "Mildred."

***

Seven hours later a shrill and stubborn ringing awoke Brigadier Pritchard. At first he thought it was an air raid siren, the whisky fog of the night before lying heavy. He fumbled for the light switch on the bedside table, lurched out of bed and pulled on his dressing gown, his arthritic right hip complaining. The doorbell persisted.

"All right, all right. I'm coming." His barks echoed on the bare walls as he negotiated the stairs, rubbing the painful joint. He threw the door open, a draught of cold night air stinging his cheeks, helping to clear his head.

"Sorry to call at this time, Sir, but in the circumstances I thought it better you hear what I've discovered in person, rather than on the telephone. I know you wanted to ..."

"Come in, Harris. Come in, stop blethering."

The lieutenant had worked through the night since his earlier call with the Brigadier. He had enlisted Mildred's help. In turn, she had contacted several secretaries and administrators in the War Office, MI9, even the Red Cross, to locate the officers Harris needed to speak to.

Some were uncontactable, out of the country, others not answering their phones. But Harris persisted, despite realising Pritchard's one-hour deadline was impossible. From P.O.W. records, he established that Sergeant Ripley had been captured in 1941 in the aftermath of Dunkirk, and moved to various

P.O.W. camps, eventually ending up in Berlin. His regiment had been recorded as the parachute division of the Royal Engineers, although no details of his activity with the regiment, apart from his capture, appeared to exist after July 1940.

A documentary error was Mildred's explanation. But the date resonated with Harris, prompting him to place a telephone call in the early hours to a high-ranking officer of one of Britain's most secret organisations.

"That was ballsy, Harris. How did you get on?" The Brigadier's fog had lifted. He led Harris into the lounge, a room with a high ceiling and walls filled with paintings of British monarchs ranging from Queen Anne to George VI. Pritchard invited Harris to sit on a settee under Queen Victoria. The lieutenant had his undivided attention.

"Better than expected, Sir. Sergeant Ripley is indeed commander of a P.O.W. camp. He also happens to be an agent in the Special Operations Executive."

"Christ. Who would have thought? A bloody Baker Street Irregular. I thought they were all about destruction, blowing things up, creating carnage."

"You're right, Sir, sabotage is the SOE's primary aim, but so is espionage. It looks like Ripley has been used to infiltrate the P.O.W. system and smuggle out information. He joined SOE in the summer of 1940, the express aim of his mission to allow himself to be captured."

"That's a hell of a brief. You have to be brave, smart, and dare I say a little bit mad to accept that sort of mission."

"Quite, Sir, but I think it might explain where all Carter's information has been coming from. And probably Jack Martin's before him."

"You think Ripley is The Wolf?"

"Possibly, but not necessarily. Ripley is supplying coordinates, that seems certain, and maybe his privileges as camp commander allowed him space and time to pass on information. But that info has been so frequent, as well as accurate and spontaneous, that we can't rule out someone else is involved in smuggling it out."

"Who?"

"No idea, I'm afraid, but this isn't an ordinary prison camp, Sir. Not according to the SOE."

"What do you mean?"

"It would seem this sub-camp of just a few thousand men has been selected, along with several others in the area, for one purpose as far as we can see. To turn prisoners. To get them to broadcast propaganda for the Germans. Even to fight alongside the Nazis. The conditions are good and the rations plentiful."

"Surely no-one switches sides for a few decent meals." Pritchard's look was dismissive.

"The Germans aren't stupid. It has come to SOE's attention that a section of British prisoners transferred to this stalag, and other sub-camps in Berlin, were either former members of the British Union of Fascists or sympathetic to that cause."

"Followers of Oswald Mosley, you mean."

"That's correct. Even though Mosley's organisation was banned and he was jailed, you can't jail an ideology. The Germans think they're clever. It looks as if they're busy rounding up captured soldiers and airmen, trying to persuade them to fight, probably against the Russians. Even if only a few of our boys turned traitor, it would amount to a significant propaganda victory."

Pritchard sank back in his armchair, pulling his dressing gown tight around his shoulders.

"Good God, looks like Carter's landed in the middle of a right old shit-show. But we need to know what's going on. We need to identify these traitors. Let him know the score. We must be there for Carter."

"Of course, Sir."

23

THE car arrived at the Hotel Adlon's front entrance in the middle of the afternoon.

Helena was ready, skipping down the steps before the driver could disembark to open the back door. A striking long white dress embroidered with big red rosebuds emphasised her statuesque figure, aided and abetted by high heels that caused her to totter a fraction, while the cutaway top of her dress allowed a heart-shaped pendant to dangle against her skin. A jacket wrapped around her shoulders, but it was hardly required as the sun radiated welcome warmth.

Admiring glances from the driver and guard approved Helena's wardrobe choice.

Several weeks had slipped by since she had received an invitation to the prison camp. She wondered if that was due to the raucous finale on her last visit. Had the Germans interpreted her choice of Elgar as a step too far? Had the commandant deemed she was a bad influence, even to the point of inciting insurrection?

She had relayed those fears to Carter, but he had advised her to keep calm and sit tight. "Play the long game, Helena. The commandant has more to fear from his superiors." Carter had also informed her about Sergeant Ripley's true identity, having received a message from Lieutenant Harris appraising him of the British commander's covert status. It was only right to do so. After all, Carter surmised, Helena was taking an equal risk in smuggling out information. A greater one, perhaps, considering Ripley, as a P.O.W., was covered by the conventions of war, while Helena would be considered a spy and a traitor by the Germans, a crime punishable by firing squad. She also knew of the Germans' attempt to turn some prisoners.

When Helena reached the camp, a guard waved the car through the gate as usual, but instead of proceeding to the block containing the commandant's office, the driver dropped her off closer to the concert hall where Reinhardt's orderly was waiting.

"I'm sorry, Frau Schulz, Commandant Reinhardt sends his apologies. He's been called to Berlin with several officers and will not be able to see you today. He hopes you have an enjoyable concert." The orderly was a small man, wearing a uniform that appeared too big, giving the impression he had been swallowed by his own suit. His head bowed to one side as he spoke, in servile fashion, as if in thrall to Helena's fame, which was probably the case.

As they walked past the huts to the canteen, Helena seized the opportunity to check out the white brick building with the barred windows. She put the same question to the orderly that she had asked the commandant. "What's that building for?"

"Prisoners in solitary confinement, Frau Schulz."

"Why?"

"Lots of reasons. If camp rules have been broken. Prisoners who have tried to escape. Prisoners who might be useful in other ways."

"Such as?"

The orderly looked around as if making sure he was not being watched and couldn't be heard. "Sometimes, we have prisoners we may be able to swap for our own brave soldiers."

"Spies, you mean."

"Not always, but yes, sometimes secret operatives."

"It's all very exciting."

"Not if you're confined to the same four walls for months, sometimes years."

"No, quite."

The concert hall was already full when they arrived and again Michal sat at the piano.

The welcome was rapturous and Helena launched into the performance. "I'm Helena from Lancashire." She burst into songs from *The Magic Flute* and *The Marriage of Figaro,* this time skirting anything controversial, even when the men threw out requests.

"*Land of Hope and Glory*," shouted one prisoner near the end, but Helena dodged the request with a coy expression, a shake of the head and a jerk of the thumb in the direction of the guards lined up at the side of the floor.

"You'll get me locked up."

The men laughed and cheered.

When the concert was over, the orderly returned to accompany her back to the car, but Sergeant Ripley intercepted. "We need some time to plan the next concert. It won't take long."

The orderly seemed dubious. He didn't say the commandant had forbidden such a meeting, but there was a definite reluctance to agree. He was on the point of refusing when Helena intervened.

"Five minutes, that's all. Please."

The orderly's lips tightened, but one plaintive look from Helena and he relented.

"Very well, five minutes."

The moment Helena and Ripley disappeared into the sergeant's room, the camp's band piped up for practice in the concert hall, seemingly impromptu but in effect part of Ripley's plan.

"Don't talk. Listen." Ripley's command carried instant authority. "I have more coordinates but I also have a dossier I need you to get back to England. It's coded and full of names, dates and evidence. Can you do that?"

"What sort of evidence?"

"I said don't talk, but I suppose you have a right to know what you're carrying. Put it this way, these papers could send men with treacherous intent to the gallows."

"Men in this camp?"

Ripley nodded.

"How big is this dossier?"

"Too big for one run. Half today. The other half next time."

Ripley slid out the top drawer of his desk. He fumbled inside the aperture, feeling the underside of the desk top, carefully detaching several foolscap sheets of paper.

Helena immediately realised they were too big for her usual hiding place. She fumbled in her bag, taking out the sheet music used at the concert. After folding a couple of the papers, she slid them inside Mozart's *Queen of the Night* aria, hiding the others in similar fashion inside several more of the song sheets. She tucked the bundle under her arm.

"A singer and her music. What could be more natural?"

Ripley marvelled at her smiling face, vibrant and determined, yet seemingly carefree. He wondered if she realised the contents hidden in the music she now carried would constitute a swift and merciless death sentence if caught. Before him, he considered, stood the definition of bravery.

"That should do it. Remember, act normal."

"Sergeant, you forget, Acting is what I do for a living."

A sharp rap on the door, loud enough to penetrate the drum pounding in the concert hall, signalled the orderly's return.

"Until next time, Frau Schulz." Ripley bowed his appreciation.

Helena followed the orderly down the corridor, past the concert hall, towards the road where the car was waiting. Suddenly, she stopped, turning towards the orderly.

"Would it be possible to use the toilet before I leave? All that fluid I need to drink to soothe my voice."

"Of course."

"I know where it is. I've been before."

The orderly nodded, taking up position with his back to the toilet block."

Helena disappeared inside, but instead of taking a right turn, she veered left to where she had spied a back door on her previous visit. She prayed it was unlocked. It relented at the first turn of the handle. The brick building was no more than 50 yards away and fortunately down a grassy corridor formed by the backs of two storage huts, shielding her route from the main body of the camp. She slipped off her heels and ran, restricted a touch by her long dress, but thankful the band practice still enveloped the site in a blanket of noise.

When she reached the end of the storage huts, she glanced around the corner, recoiling immediately. A guard, bearing a rifle, the first such weapon she had seen inside the camp, stood on duty outside the front of the solitary block. Fortunately, he was the only one. She made for the rear. No door. Just one window, open a fixed inch for ventilation, behind bars, but far too high for Helena to see into the block. The smart move was to retrace her steps, but for once she forsook reason. The reflection in the window had unsettled her these past weeks. Haunted her dreams. She needed to know.

She scooped up a small pebble and threw. It struck one of the iron bars, but the drum's pounding beat masked the metallic clunk. She was about to toss another stone when a face appeared at the window. Her heart leaped, so hard and joyously that she felt the thump rattle against her ribcage, blood rushing in her ears. She wanted to scream, but knew she couldn't. Instead she mouthed his name. "Jack!" And then, "You're alive!"

His dark hair was shaved, his face bearded and gaunt, weeks of deprivation having stripped the life and humour that had so attracted her to him when they first met watching the Berlin Opera House smoulder on Unter den Linden. But his eyes were still calm and kind. Labrador eyes. Exuding loyalty and wisdom.

Yet strangely, no shock at seeing Helena. Later, when there was time for consideration, she was to ponder that fact on many occasions, never truly discovering an appropriate explanation, other than putting his preparedness down to covert training. Instead, he put a finger to his lips, warning her to remain silent, then raised a hand as if imploring her to wait. He disappeared, returning half a minute later with a scrap of paper. He folded it and dropped it through the ventilation gap, mouthing something. His obvious agitation suggested the words were important, but with Ripley's band pounding Helena struggled to decipher anything intelligible. *Trust* was the only word she could lip-read with any certainty. She snatched the paper, hitched up her dress and concealed the scrap along with Ripley's coordinates. When she glanced up to urge him to repeat his message, Jack was gone.

For several seconds Helena was consumed by the intensity of her chance meeting. Her shoulders shook, her mind churning with sentiments left unsaid and actions unrepaired. She had never been entirely certain of her feelings for Jack Martin, but the face at the window of the man she was sure must be dead had triggered a yearning so deep and powerful that truly she felt her heart might burst.

Forcing herself to quell her emotions, she hurried back to the toilet block, snapped on her heels and took several deep breaths. Having composed herself, she emerged to find the orderly in the exact same spot, still waiting, far too obsequious to investigate why she had taken so long.

24

WHEN Helena reached the Adlon the first thing she did was lose the rosebud dress and pull on a pair of dungarees and boots. She fixed a beret on her head and dragged her bicycle from the shed at the rear of the hotel.

The light was fading as she pedalled over a bridge spanning the Spree, although the clear sky promised a moonlit night. Realising the bombers could arrive at any time, she stomped on the pedals, passing a column of tanks trundling in the opposite direction.

By the time she reached Das Bar, it was almost dark. Her back was wet with sweat and her thigh muscles complained. She parked her bike by the railings, swung the drawstring bag off her shoulders, and ran down the steps.

The bar was empty, apart from two old men in a corner. Elke, golden tresses pulled back and tied in fancy bows with a black ribbon, was busy washing glasses behind the counter.

"Hi, Elke. You look nice tonight. Love what you've done with your hair. Have you seen Sam?"

Elke studied her for a few seconds. It was the first time she had seen Helena wearing anything other than a posh dress and an air of finery. The barmaid's usual pout slowly softened. She almost smiled. "You don't look so bad yourself, Frau Schulz." She jerked her thumb towards the back room.

Helena knocked and entered to find Carter deep in conversation with Bo and Felix, all three sat around the table studying a map.

Bo was first to rise, fussing around Helena, offering a drink.

"No thanks, Bo. I need to talk to Sam."

"Of course."

Carter detected urgency in Helena's voice. He asked the others to excuse them, and ushered Helena out of the door, noting Bo and Felix swapping suspicious glances.

"You scrub down well." Carter studied Helena's casual look, arriving at much the same conclusion as Elke.

"We need to talk." Helena lowered her voice as they passed the two old men.

"My place?"

Helena nodded.

Carter left first, leaving Helena to follow on her bike, reasoning it was safer not to be seen together. It was dark when Carter reached Dolziger Strasse. He waited by the front door for Helena to arrive, scanning the street as usual to ensure he hadn't been followed. He helped carry the bike up the steps into the lobby.

When they shut the apartment door, Helena rummaged in her bag, sliding out a bunch of papers. An agitation about her demeanour concerned Carter.

"Are you okay? You seem a bit ... unsettled."

"I couldn't wait. I had to see you. It's about the camp today."

Carter noticed her hand holding the papers was shaking. "Let me fix you a drink."

She nodded. "A tea, that's all. Nothing stronger."

"Okay."

Carter disappeared into the kitchenette. While he fixed two cups of tea Helena set her papers down in a tidy row on the table.

"You've been busy, I see," said Carter.

She handed him the first folded note. "That's another set of coded coordinates from Sergeant Ripley."

Carter put it to one side.

Helena picked up the foolscap sheets. "Ripley also gave me these. He says they contain evidence he's been compiling for some time. He needs to get the information back to England."

"It's a lot to transmit. Probably too much. Did he say what sort of evidence?"

"His exact words were the dossier *could send men of treacherous intent to the gallows.*"

Carter whistled through his teeth.

"That's only half of it. He says there's as much evidence again. Told me I could collect it next time."

"Are you comfortable with that, Helena? You don't have to. This is becoming seriously dangerous, and ..."

A massive explosion in the distance interrupted his thought. The building shook, windows rattled, tea spilled from the cups. A couple of seconds later, an air-raid siren howled. An anxious frown crumpled Helena's face.

"Bloody RAF. Can't they give us a minute's peace?" Carter attempted to make light of the bomb.

"Shouldn't we head for the flak tower?"

Carter shook his head. "I've been here long enough to realise we're pretty safe. The bombers dodge around the flak tower to avoid the anti-aircraft guns. Virtually every house in this street is still standing. A bit of superficial damage here and there, but nothing compared to some parts of the city."

Carter pointed to the remaining scrap of paper. "What's that?"

Helena cleared her throat. "That's also evidence."

"What?"

"Evidence that Jack Martin is still alive."

"Seriously?" An astonished tremor in Carter's voice.

Helena went on to relate how she had seen Jack for certain at the white brick building.

"Was he wounded? Had he been shot?"

"I don't think so. He looked hungry and dirty. He had a beard and his hair was shaved, but he was moving fine."

"Are you sure?"

"Of course, I'm sure. What do you take me for?"

Carter didn't answer, but rolled his eyes in apology and gently gestured for Helena to continue. She described how Jack had posted the scrap of paper through the ventilation gap. When she said he had mouthed a message, Carter pressed her to repeat the events in order to remember the content.

"Stop! I could think about it a million times but I can't remember, because I didn't hear in the first place. All I could make out was one word."

"What was that?

"*Trust*."

Carter picked up the scrap of paper. It contained a jumble of random capital letters.

WLMGGIFHGYLGIZRGLI

Carter realised it must be code. But without a key, there was no starting point to decipher.

He had a thought. "How long did it take Jack to produce the scrap of paper?"

"Seconds. Twenty-five. Thirty, maybe. No more. Why?"

"Because to code something that quickly, it would have to be second nature to him. A simple code, one that could be cracked without a key, but not instantly obvious to the casual observer. One he's used before hundreds of times."

"I'm a singer, not a code breaker."

Carter smiled. "I know. A very good singer."

More explosions in the distance. The building shook as if shivering in terror.

Carter walked over to the window, pulling back the blackout drape a fraction. Fires burned as far as the eye could see to the west. Fresh plumes of flame and smoke detonated in all directions, while powerful searchlights strafed the sky, hunting targets.

Helena squeezed next to him at the window, observing the pyrotechnics. He could smell her fragrance, sweet and fresh in contrast to the cordite and dust seeping through the cracks in the window frame. He could feel the heat of her body, still moist from the effort of her bike ride. The memory of her tongue brushing his when they kissed in the shelter by the Spree came to mind. He tried to banish such thoughts. He was Helena's handler, as Jack had been before him. In the covert world, liaisons with colleagues were not wise. Fraught with danger. Emotions clouded rational thought. Feelings compromised action. All secret operatives knew that. Yet, at that moment, with instant death and fiery destruction all around, when the next breath could be their last, he couldn't remember wanting a woman as much in his entire life.

She must have sensed his yearning, for she turned and lay her head against his chest. For many seconds they stood, holding each other, taking comfort, watching the conflagration, their passion heightened in the catch of the moment by the uncertainty of what horrors the night, or even the next few minutes, might bring.

"You can't go back to the hotel now. Stay here."

She turned her face to his, reached up and kissed him on the lips. Their tongues touched, bodies entwined, at first slowly and then with increasing ardour, the explosions outside a metaphoric soundtrack to the feelings colliding inside their minds. Carter slid the strap of Helena's dungarees from her shoulders, his hands brushed her breasts, traced the contoured curves of her body, and, sensing no resistance, he was about to manoeuvre her towards the bed when she gently but firmly pulled away from him.

"This isn't a good idea."

"Why not?"

"It just isn't. You know it's not. Things are complicated enough."

25

AT first light, Helena padded across the apartment and let herself out.

Carter heard her leave, but pretended to be in a deep sleep, not wanting to cause embarrassment by referencing the night before. He had insisted Helena take the bed. He was a gentleman, after all. He hunkered down on the floor, using a spare blanket for warmth and the cushion from the armchair as a pillow.

He didn't know whether to feel dejected or rejected, or both. Instead, when he heard the front door slam, he crawled out of his makeshift bed, made a cup of tea and checked out the landscape.

The bombing raid had been heavy, hundreds of aircraft, their droning engines implanted in his brain. It seemed that was the way the war was heading, Berlin burning every night.

He washed and dressed, following the daily routine that had become his professional crutch these past months. Often a suit, or at least a jacket, and always a shirt and tie. His papers identified him as a Swiss banker. He had to look the part, play the part, feel the part, even when he was not on duty. Rather like actors often stay in character to feel and live the role they are playing. A secret operative was not dissimilar from an actor. That's how Carter viewed it. A type of deception. The difference with actors was once the curtain fell they could return to their loved ones and the emotions and banal protections of their everyday existences. Carter had no such luxuries. He had to stay in character. The thick, black-framed spectacles, helped. Without them, he was Sam Carter, the laid-back, charismatic, Middle-Englander, who no one really knew, but whose company everyone enjoyed. Once he donned the glasses he became the quiet, somewhat nervy, risk-averse, banker, with a head full of figures. A man everyone was happy to avoid. Living the lie kept him alive.

But it was tough to live the lie with Helena. His protection had slipped. The yearnings from the night before already swamped his thoughts, clouding his decision-making. How much more complex might it have been if Helena's timely jolt of reason hadn't saved him? If they had succumbed to their passions, he was certain his mission would have been compromised. As it was, Helena had secured more crucial coordinates, as well as vital evidence of potential British treachery.

What of Jack Martin? The thought of his one-time friend returned Carter to stone-cold reality. He sat at the table, gazing at the scrap of paper and the message Jack had written.

Why was he alive? That was the first and biggest question. Karl had been sure Jack was carrying the Czech soldier when the German patrol intercepted them. Shots were heard. Two dead men lay in a heap. Karl's evidence was compelling, even though he couldn't categorically confirm having seen Jack shot.

In Carter's opinion, there was only one reason Jack was alive, and the commandant's orderly had already confirmed as much to Helena. Secret operatives were sometimes held in the brick building, he had said, to be swapped for agents of their own. Officially, the authorities on both sides would always deny it, but there was little doubt it happened.

A tap on the door interrupted Carter's musing. He glanced at his watch. Seven o'clock. Too early. Nothing of benefit in his experience happened at this hour.

He reached for his revolver and crossed to the door. "Who is it?"

"Max, from upstairs."

He slid the revolver inside the back of his trousers and swung the door open.

"Sorry to bother you ... David ... Jack's friend ... or whoever you are. Just checking you and your lady were okay after last night. Thought the house was coming down, it was shaking so much."

Carter surprised himself. He was actually happy to see Max. A familiar face, a friendly one at that. "Step in for a second. And she's not my lady. Just sheltering from the raid, that's all."

"None of my business. I enjoyed the jasmine and vanilla fragrance though. Expensive taste for someone who rides a bike."

Max may have been blind, but he missed nothing. If Carter hadn't already checked out Max and discovered he was who he purported to be, he would have been worried.

"Never judge a book by its cover, Max."

"In my case, that isn't very likely, is it?" Max chuckled.

"Sorry, Max, I didn't mean ..."

"No problem, don't apologise."

"What are you up to today?"

The question took Carter by surprise. Not because he thought Max was prying. Quite the reverse. In a world in which each new day brought another wave of atrocities, it was a long time since he had been asked something quite as normal and mundane. What was he up to today?

"Well, actually, Max, I have a little conundrum at work that I'm wrestling with. Have you ever had one of those days when, however hard you try to solve something, you can't seem to come up with the answer."

Max thought for a moment. "I used to struggle finding my way around if I went for a long walk. That was a problem"

"How did you solve that?"

"A few years ago, one of my friends made a model of the area around here for me. I still have it in my apartment. I learned it by touch and by heart, like the alphabet. All the roads, the parks and the buildings. Both the route out and the route back. The route back was most important because although the roads and buildings were the same, it felt very different."

"What a great idea."

"Yes, and now the RAF have blown it to pieces." Max guffawed. "You can't win."

Carter laughed along, admiring the positive, light-hearted manner in which Max dealt with his disability.

"I must be going, glad we're all still here," said Max.

Carter opened the door and watched Max waddle down the stairs, presumably heading for his morning walk.

For the next hour, Carter stared out of the window, sipping tea, watching smoke residue from hundreds of fires the night before, pale and grey, track across the city. He kept one eye on Jack's message, praying intuition and training would intervene to provide the key to the code.

Carter put himself in Jack's position. No physical key. No time to plan a sophisticated code. Time only for a rushed sequence intended to deceive Nazi scrutiny at first glance. His instinct told him the jumble of letters must almost certainly constitute a substitution code, a simple technique replacing one letter of the alphabet with another. With patience, such codes were not difficult to decipher, especially if they contained repeated patterns. He sat up, a sudden infusion of excitement as he realised he did have a key. Or at least part of one.

Trust. That was the one word Helena was sure Jack had mouthed. Five letters, beginning and ending with the same letter 'T'. Carter scanned the message even more closely.

          WLMGGIFHGYLGIZRGLI

There were only two occasions where the same letter, 'G' was repeated exactly five letters later. If *Trust* was correct then logic decreed 'G' in the sequence would represent the letter 'T'.

It was a start, but even so, the letters were 13 places removed in the alphabet. That was too wide, Carter decided, for a precise and workable substitution code.

He scribbled and mused for many more minutes, at times sensing the solution as intangible as the drifting smoke discolouring the blue sky. At others, it seemed the solution was about to tumble. When it did, it came in a euphoric rush, in no small part courtesy of Max, and the description of his walk. The return journey, Max had said, appeared different, but was equally important to memorise on his physical model as the way out.

What if Jack's message was coded in the same manner?

What if 'G', the seventh letter from the beginning of the alphabet, corresponded instead to the seventh letter from the end of the alphabet, 'T'? The simplicity appealed to Carter and he rushed to apply the same logic to all the letters in the sequence.

It took him no more than 10 minutes to complete the task, writing the corresponding letters in a neat row on his pad. When he had finished, four words leaped out at him. He stared at them, at first disbelieving.

Then a shiver of anger and apprehension snaked across his shoulders. And a cold bead of sweat ran down his back.

26

July 20th, 1944. Berlin.

WHEN Carter arrived at Das Bar, Elke was leaning on the counter, customers huddled around her, listening to a wireless broadcast.

It was approaching 6.25pm.

Carter skipped down the steps. "What's going on?"

Elke's jaw set firm as she waved a hand to signal silence. The radio crackled and Carter joined the scrum. The announcer's voice was grave.

"Today an attempt was made on the Führer's life with explosives. The Führer himself suffered no injuries beyond light burns and bruises. He resumed his work immediately."

There were no further details. The broadcast cut to music, the huddle broke up, and Carter motioned Elke to the quiet side of the bar.

"Pity they didn't get him. He's got nine lives and then some." Elke sneered.

Carter grabbed her forearm to focus attention. "Don't let anyone hear you talking like that, Elke. You don't know who's listening. There'll be hell to pay after this. The Gestapo and the SS will be everywhere, hunting down resistance suspects in every city, including Berlin. Especially Berlin. Where are Bo and Karl, and Felix?"

"Out." Elke whispered. "Moving an airman to a safe location, I think."

"Will they be back tonight?"

"Don't know. It'll be late if they are?"

"I'll hang around. Any chance of some hot potatoes?"

"I'll have a look, give me half an hour."

"Great, I'll be in the back."

Carter used the time to familiarise himself with the map of Berlin. He needed new locations to transmit from. Following advice from Karl, he was growing adept at sourcing likely spots that did not require risky train journeys to such as Potsdam. About an hour later the savoury aroma of roasted potatoes and onions wafted in a few seconds before Elke, carrying a dinner plate. Carter was effusive in his gratitude and Elke unusually sat across the table as he ate.

"Do you want to know the latest?" Her tone teasing.

"Of course."

"Apparently, he's going to address the nation at midnight."

"The Führer?"

She nodded. "Lucky bastard. Some customers have heard reports that one of his officers planted a bomb in a briefcase. Killed a couple of his aides, but he got away with a pair of tattered trousers and a perforated eardrum. Some say there's a coup under way right now to overthrow him, using parts of the Army. Let's hope so." Elke rubbed her palms and radiated a wide grin of pure glee. Carter had never seen her so animated.

He chewed his food, considering the consequences, before offering his opinion.

"I shouldn't count your chickens, Elke. A coup either works immediately, or not at all. If the Führer is alive and well, it's unlikely to be successful. If it's not, then I meant what I said. The Gestapo and SS will be everywhere, poking noses and guns into bars like this, dragging anyone they suspect of having sympathies to the torture chambers, or firing squads."

"In that case, I'd better have bullets waiting for them." Glee had dissipated, replaced by vehemence. Elke's tone worried Carter. In his experience, hate stirred passion, but also blinded reason. She slid her chair back and headed into the bar.

The rest of the evening passed without incident, although rumours that high-ranking officers were among the conspirators and tanks from the Wermacht were on the streets continued to circulate.

Elke threw out the bar's lingering customers at 11.30pm, proceeding to wipe down tables and wash glasses.

It was well gone midnight when Bo and Karl returned from their mission, the tread of heavy boots in the corridor alerting Carter. The back room door swung open, Karl's eyebrows immediately knitting at the sight of Carter sitting at the table in the shadows, a lone candle bathing the room in flickering light. Bo followed Karl in.

"What are you doing here at this late hour?" Bo's question was friendly enough, although he also seemed puzzled at Carter's presence.

"Heard the news and wondered how it might affect us." Carter's voice was measured.

"There's something going on out there," said Bo. "Tanks, lots of them from Krampnitz, trundling around. Rumour is there's a coup to overthrow the Nazis, but the assassination attempt failed, so I can't see that happening. The Führer's already been on the wireless. Chances are the SS and Gestapo are rounding up the conspirators right now."

"Exactly what I was thinking."

Karl dumped equipment in a cupboard. Bo swiped a half-bottle of whisky and three glasses from the worktop and sat at the table opposite Carter. Karl sat beside Bo, who poured generous measures and slid one across the top.

Carter ignored it. Bo knocked his drink back in one noisy slurp, immediately pouring another. "Thirsty work tonight."

"I can imagine," said Carter.

Karl polished off his measure, immediately presenting his glass for a refill. Carter remained impassive, this time Bo becoming aware of an atmosphere.

"Is there a problem? Is something wrong?" Bo's sing-song accent made his query sound like a lyric.

"I think there might be."

"What do you mean?"

"History will record the last few hours as a night of treachery in so many ways." Carter fixed eyes on Karl. "Tell me, Karl. What happened the night Jack died?"

"We've been through all this. What are you dragging it up for again?"

Carter took a deep breath. "You said you heard shots. Single shots. You were very precise. A Walther Seven, if I remember correctly."

"That's right. I'm sure it was."

"But you didn't see anyone actually shoot Jack."

"No."

"That's funny, because the first time I met Bo he told me the truck driver saw everything, watched a German patrol kill Jack in a burst of machine gun fire."

"That's not true." A glint of fear in Karl's eyes. He didn't like the direction of this questioning.

"You were the truck driver that night, weren't you Karl?"

"Yes, but only because Bo dropped out at the last minute."

"Bo wasn't well, was he?"

"No."

Karl looked at Bo. "Tell him, Bo."

Bo shrugged, uncertain of Carter's intention. Karl slid back his chair as if intending to leave.

Carter reached below the table top and slowly drew his Webley revolver. He pointed the gun at Karl. "Probably best if you sit back down, Karl. I have something I want to show you both." Karl sat.

Carter rummaged in his pocket, pulled out a scrap of paper and tossed it onto the table. He slid the candle a little nearer to cast more light.

"What's that? Looks like a jumble of letters."

"A jumble of letters written by Jack Martin yesterday, to be precise."

"But, how? And why?"

"It's a code, Karl. Meaningless until deciphered."

"And then?"

"It turns into this."

He threw down another piece of paper, this time in his own handwriting, containing four words.

DON'T TRUST BO – TRAITOR

27

BO squirmed in obvious discomfort. The scar on the bridge of his nose turned a livid shade of purple. Beads of sweat formed on his bald pate and a squeak of fear sounded in his throat.

"You've got it all wrong."

Carter trained the revolver on the space between Bo's eyes. "I don't think so."

"You were sick on the night Jack was captured. That was convenient."

"I was ill, on my mother's life."

"You were there the day Tex and the pilot were shot with every opportunity to signal the Germans."

"Karl was there, too. I'm not a traitor."

"Sorry, Bo. I don't believe you."

Carter stood, outstretched his right arm, finger curling around the revolver's trigger. "Give me one good reason why I shouldn't shoot you here and now, or so help me God, I will." Karl slid his chair away from the table, out of the firing line.

The direct nature of Carter's ultimatum took Bo by surprise. His shoulders shook. His eyes darted fearfully around the room. Carter's finger tightened the trigger.

"No, no, don't shoot." Bo raised his arms in a vain bid to protect himself, sending one of the whisky tots tumbling. The glass smashed on the stone floor, the sound of breaking glass shattering Bo's resolve. A sob spluttered from his lips. He covered his face with his hands and for several seconds he was unable to speak. When he did so, he resorted to gabbling truth in a desperate attempt to save his life.

"They said they'd kill my girls. They're only five and six. They found the place I'd sent them with my wife in Switzerland. Told me what they'd do to them. All of them. I couldn't let that happen."

"Who are *they*?"

"The Gestapo. An evil bastard called Neumann. He was the guy who gave me this." He pointed to the scar on his nose.

"The officer in the bar?"

Bo nodded. "For appearances. So no one would suspect me. He enjoys hurting people."

Carter's stomach lurched. "Does he know about Karl, or Felix, or Elke?"

"No. I would never do anything to harm them."

"What about me?"

"No. On my life, no."

"But you sold out Jack Martin."

"I had no choice. They didn't know any details, but they knew something was going on. The others had jobs here. Jack didn't, yet he was always here. They'd been watching the bar and that must have been suspicious. Neumann wasn't interested in small fry. He demanded a big player. Someone he could trade."

Carter shook his head. "But you were friends. Jack trusted you."

A whimper struggled from Bo's lips, genuine guilt and shame escaping.

"What would you have done?" Bo's watery eyes fixed Carter.

Carter had already asked himself that exact question. What would he have done, in another life? His mind filled with images of his wife Mary and his three-year-old daughter Patricia, playing in the park on a Sunday morning under a warm sun, the smell of new-mown grass in their nostrils, feeding ducks on the pond, the promise of ice cream cones before lunch. What would he give for just one more morning like that? Anything. At least, that's what his heart told him, the yearning so real and painful that he felt his chest might burst. His head realised life was not so straightforward. His idyllic family had been torn from him in the most traumatic fashion, but just because they did not receive justice did not mean he could mete out retribution of his own. Bo was protecting his family. Carter understood that. Part of him admired Bo's devotion. Truly, he did. But he also knew that whatever Bo said, now or in the future, could never be trusted. He would say or do anything, betray his best friend as readily as his worst enemy, to save his wife and daughters.

Jack Martin must have had his suspicions about Bo, reasoned Carter. What would Jack do now?

"I can help you." Bo's voice was pleading. "They trust me. Neumann trusts me. He values my intelligence. You hear all sorts in a place like Das Bar."

"How often do they check in with you?"

"It depends. Once a month as a rule. I could feed them false information."

Carter paused in contemplation. For an instant, Bo sensed a corridor of opportunity. Carter closed it down, a pragmatic edge to his tone. "Too late for that. They'd smell a rat straightaway. We'd all find ourselves in front of a firing squad."

"But with what's happened tonight, the Gestapo will have their hands full. They'll be busy hunting down the conspirators. They won't be interested in me, not until all this has blown over."

Carter again took time to consider Bo's argument, quickly concluding that while the bartender had almost certainly divulged only a fraction of Das Bar's secrets he knew too much about the structure of the resistance movement. Too much about their secret routes, safe houses, communication codes, and hiding places. There was only one possible outcome, as unsavoury as that was to Carter.

He raised the gun.

"No, please no. My girls." Bo's whimper had turned to a desperate wail.

Carter closed his eyes, breathed deep, curled his finger once more around the trigger of his revolver, and steeled himself for the inevitable.

The shot in the confines of the low-ceilinged room stung Carter's ears. He saw the hole appear in Bo's forehead and parts of the bartender's brain explode through the back of his skull, splattering against the back wall. He watched Bo rock sideways in his chair before his body slumped with a heavy, fleshy thud onto the stone floor. Yet, for several moments, Carter did not understand.

Not until he turned to see Elke standing behind him, a pistol smoking in her hand, eyes hard and cold as a tomb.

"That's for Konrad." She spat out the name of her brother, killed by the Gestapo while studying at university in Munich. Dropping the gun on the table, she wandered casually back to the bar to wash more glasses.

28

CARTER did nothing for a week, apart from smoke cigarettes and drink whisky in Dolziger Strasse.

On the night Bo was shot, the night of the attempted coup, he had arranged for Karl to dispose of the body in the cemetery where they had hidden the airmen. There were heaps of open graves waiting for occupants, it was an easy task to dig one a little deeper to accommodate an extra tenant.

A fleeting pang of concern for Bo's daughters crossed Carter's mind, but this was a dirty war, full of innocent victims. Too many to expend emotional effort on those one had never known.

He met Max on the stairs on a few occasions and they discussed the details broadcasted of the plot to assassinate the Führer. The plotters had been part of the resistance, consisting mainly of Wermacht officers.

The leader of the conspiracy turned out to be General Claus von Stauffenberg, who had personally placed the briefcase containing the bomb at a military conference. By chance, the briefcase had been moved behind an oak table leg by Colonel Heinz Brandt, inadvertently saving Hitler's life. Brandt and two others, including a stenographer, were killed outright in the blast and while an attempted coup to take control of the Nazi Party was launched it fizzled out in chaos and confusion once news of the Führer's survival became general knowledge.

Carter and Max had drunk in the wireless reports. They had watched and heard the Panzer tanks of the Wermacht swamp

Berlin. They had dared to believe this might be the beginning of the end, but it soon became obvious there was no concerted coordination, or determination, in the attempted coup.

Within hours, the tanks were trundling out of the city as the Gestapo and SS predictably moved in, arresting and summarily executing hundreds of suspected conspirators.

Stauffenberg, who had lost an eye, his right hand and two fingers on his left hand in previous war wounds, had flown to Berlin, believing his plot had succeeded, but it was soon announced that he and a handful of high-ranking officers had been executed.

"The blind leading the blind. Idiots, the lot of them." Max was not shy in expressing his opinion of the plotters' plan, especially after sampling several tumblers of Carter's whisky. "Couldn't organise a Kindergarten party."

"A shame though. With the Führer gone, this godforsaken war would surely be over." Carter tried to reason with Max.

"Not a chance. The plotters would have tried to negotiate a new Germany after taking charge. The Allies would have nothing to do with that. Do you think Mister Churchill is going to leave men in charge who have presided over some of the worst atrocities in history? Hitler or no Hitler, it doesn't matter. Surrender is what the Allies are after, nothing less."

They decided to leave war talk to one side and concentrate on the malt. That was something they could both agree on.

Early next morning, Carter ventured outside, a walk required to clear his head. The guard no longer stood on Dolziger Strasse. That was the first thing he noticed. The second was a newspaper seller setting up a stand at a junction.

Carter loved newspapers. He didn't read books, neither fiction, nor non-fiction. His mind would wander. He couldn't remember characters and their place in the plot. It was all to do with concentration, his obsession with the world around him usurping any requirement for imagination. With newspapers, he read slowly, drinking in every fact and detail. So meticulous was his absorption that he could often recite every story on a broadsheet page almost verbatim. He watched the old man unfold a trestle table and arrange towers of newspapers, neat and uniform. The seller sat on a box, lit a pipe and blew smoke rings, blue and shimmering in the still air, waiting for customers. There was no good news for any Germans who supported the war. Carter could tell them that. Wireless broadcasts had already confirmed Allied troops had liberated Bayeux, Cherbourg and Caen in northern France. Paris was within their grasp. There was gathering momentum to the Allied charge to Berlin, each day bringing another relentless air raid, another arc in Dante's nine concentric circles of torment.

Trudging on towards the Spree, he considered making a detour and dropping in on Das Bar, but it was too soon. He had left Karl and Felix in charge, and warned them to look after Elke. Killing a man in cold blood was not something most people could shrug on and off like wearing or jettisoning an overcoat. It left scar tissue that numbs the mind. Elke may have avenged her brother in some small way, but Carter was certain her action in shooting Bo would have consequences. He had asked himself many times whether he would have pulled the trigger if Elke had not beaten him to it. Yes, or no? He didn't have the answer, and probably never would. What he did know was that Elke had solved a problem for him. He also expected the Gestapo to arrive at Das Bar's door, sooner rather than later, demanding to know what had become of Bo. In the circumstances, it was not a natural, or safe, venue for a Swiss banker.

Forty minutes later, almost without thinking, he found himself outside Hotel Adlon. He hadn't seen Helena for more than a week, since she had tiptoed out of his apartment the morning after the night that never happened.

He climbed the steps, heading to reception, the opulent surroundings of the hotel lobby in sharp contrast to the smoking ruins outside. The elderly man on the desk was bent over what appeared to be a large diary, writing in studied fashion. For a minute or so, he didn't acknowledge Carter's presence.

"Frau Schulz's room, please." A hint of irritation in Carter's voice.

The receptionist glanced up without lifting his head, eyes peering over round, rimless glasses, perched half-way down his nose. His manner aloof.

"And you are?"

"I'm an associate, a colleague, David Schmid."

"Frau Schulz isn't here."

"Are you sure?"

"She left earlier this morning."

Carter looked at his watch. 7.45am.

"Where did she go?"

"I cannot divulge that information. Do you have papers?"

Carter fished in his jacket pocket and produced his identity papers. The receptionist stood tall, slid his glasses up his nose, and perused the papers, studying the small print, his demeanour gradually becoming more servile.

"Union Bank of Switzerland. Are you here on business, Herr Schmid?"

Carter, who had donned his suit, tie, and black-framed glasses as usual back in Dolziger Strasse, explained he was in talks with Deutsche Bank to supply cash for munitions to aid the war effort.

"How does that involve Frau Schulz?"

Carter bristled, digging his nails deep into his palms. He yearned to bark that it was none of the receptionist's damned business. The man was a simple desk assistant. How dare he pry into a guest's personal affairs and demand identity papers as if he were a member of the state police? Instead, he bit his lip, cleared his throat, and assumed a coy expression. "We have a love for music and the opera. I'm sure you understand."

The receptionist handed back the papers, and scribbled in the diary. He looked Carter up and down for several seconds, as if assessing the details of his story.

"Frau Schulz left around six-thirty in a car with three soldiers."

Carter's heart thumped. "Where was she going at that time?"

The receptionist shrugged. "We don't ask such questions, especially as the soldiers were accompanied by an officer of the Gestapo.

29

THE walls were bare plaster, freckled with spots of mould and other, more sinister, blemishes. The room smelled of dust and damp.

A single bed was pushed up against one of the walls. A pail with an oval lid of stained wood perched in a corner. On another wall a small desk, on which sat a sheaf of writing paper and a pencil. No windows. A single light bulb burned in the middle of the ceiling.

Helena sat on a stiff wooden chair at the desk, her shoulders shivering in the cold atmosphere, trying to work out what was happening.

Shortly after awakening that morning, a telephone call from a member of staff at the Adlon had summoned her to reception. She had thrown on a skirt and top, slipped into a flat pair of shoes, wrapped a cardigan around her shoulders, and headed downstairs.

A portly man, devoid of charm or answers to her questions, apart from confirming he was from the state police, had demanded she accompany him. The three soldiers carried rifles and formed a guard as they marched her to their waiting car.

They had proceeded through the city centre to a group of grey buildings on Prinz-Albrecht Strasse. Helena recognised the properties, as would every Berlin resident, as housing the main office of the SS Reich Security and the headquarters of the Gestapo. She asked more questions, this time her voice betraying a tremor of fear. The man remained silent and impassive, gripping her arm tightly when she alighted from the car, leading her down several long, dimly-lit corridors to the room. The door had clanked shut behind him, followed by the turn of a key.

Three hours passed. Still no explanation, although she could hear distant shouting and what appeared to be screams. Shrill, but faint, as if emanating from a cellar.

Helena's sense of foreboding was approaching panic level when she first became aware of his presence. The smell of cigarette smoke alerted her, drifting through the gaps in the door frame. She padded over and listened to the sucking sound of his lips and the soft whoosh as he exhaled.

"Who's there?" She could bear the tension no longer.

The key turned, the door creaked open, and a tall man wearing glasses filled the doorway. He looked familiar. The angular frame, slight tilt of the head. She was sure she had seen him before, but her scrambled mind couldn't pinpoint the exact location.

"Frau Schulz, you don't remember me?" The voice gave it away. A soft tone with a sinister edge. This was Neumann, the man who had shaken her hand in Das Bar, the same night he had broken Bo's nose.

"I remember. The bar. You've seen me sing."

"Yes, Frau Schulz, on several occasions."

"I don't understand. Why am I here?"

"I work for the Sicherheitsdienst."

Helena looked blank. Neumann supplied more details.

"Put simply, the intelligence agency of the SS and the Nazi Party. I also have a role with the State Police."

Helena felt her heart race. The thought of any of those organisations would strike fear into the ordinary German citizen.

"I have questions for you and how you answer them will determine what happens next. Please, take a seat. I'm afraid the décor here is not quite what you are accustomed to at the Hotel Adlon."

He motioned for her to sit on the bed and took up position on the wooden chair, straddling the seat with his arms resting on the back. A smile played on his lips.

"I heard you sing in Frankfurt. The Magic Flute. A wonderful performance. Mozart has always been my favourite. I know he's not everyone's cup of tea in Germany. He was a Freemason, of course, but he wrote his first composition at just four years of age. Quite extraordinary. I think his work exhibits an interesting sense of humour, don't you think?"

"Yes, his works sparkle with clarity and soaring melodies. I love singing them."

"That's obvious to anybody who has heard you perform, Frau Schulz."

"Thank you, but I'm sure I'm not here to talk about Mozart."

"You're here to speak about all sorts of things. Let's start by talking about Das Bar."

"What about it? I sing there occasionally."

"Is that all?"

"Yes." Helena's tone was confident.

"So, you know Henry Schneider?"

"You mean Bo. Of course. He runs the place."

"Any ideas where we might find him?"

"Das Bar?" A puzzled frown set on Helena's features. It was some time since she'd seen Bo, but, as she'd not visited the bar recently and not spoken to Carter, she'd not heard of anything untoward happening to him. Neumann continued his interrogation. His voice measured, although Helena formed the distinct impression he was skirting around more significant issues. He asked about the bar regulars, enquired how Helena had met Bo, probed Bo's relationship with Elke. It was becoming obvious that he was working up to something sinister, although there was no mention of the resistance.

Half an hour went by. He dug in his top pocket, withdrawing a packet of cigarettes. He offered Helena one, but she refused. He made great moment of lighting his own cigarette, inhaling a deep drag and blowing out a plume of smoke, which rose, swirling in a haze around the light bulb. Looking around the room at nothing in particular, he picked at a tooth for a moment.

And then he fixed her with an icy stare and barked out a name. "Jack Martin."

He was searching for a reaction. A twitch of an eyebrow. A glance of recognition. Anything to connect her with the secret agent in solitary confinement.

"Pardon?" Helena's reaction was instant, her look of confusion dredged from the endless acting classes she had attended on her rise to the top opera houses. Those classes had been bolstered by Jack's own tuition in the art of deception once she had agreed to join the resistance.

There are only three things you must do if you find yourself under interrogation, Jack used to say. They are easy to remember and you can do them in any order. *Deny. Deny. Deny.*

That mantra ran through Helena's mind, calming her nerves, offering her something tangible on which to focus.

"Jack Martin worked with Henry Schneider at Das Bar. We know that. It's inconceivable you would not have come across him." Neumann pressed her.

Again, Helena perfected an expression of puzzlement. "First, I did not attend Das Bar with any degree of frequency. Second, I was there to sing the odd song, not to forge relationships with men. To my knowledge, I have not met this Jack Martin."

"You are English, Frau Schulz, isn't that correct?"

Beware the sudden switch in subject matter. A classic ploy, designed to unsettle. Another lesson learned from Jack.

"That's no secret. Anyone reading a programme at one of my performances would know that. I grew up in England. I sang at Covent Garden. But I made my home in Germany with my German husband." Helena did not need to act to speak with passion about the route her life had taken.

"And your family still lives in Lancashire. Twenty-one, Clayton Street, I believe?" For the first time there was a hint of threat in Neumann's tone. The address detail unnerved Helena.

Most of her friends would have no idea where her parents lived. The fact that an officer of one of the most feared security organisations in Nazi Germany knew the number of their house brought a plug of bile to her throat.

She swallowed her apprehension. "I've not seen any family for years. We don't talk. They don't answer my letters. They aren't exactly ecstatic that I'm living in Berlin, supporting the Nazi cause. My mother won't have my name mentioned and my father disowned me the day war began. I'm dead to them."

Helena surprised herself. Again, she didn't require acting skills. This time the words spewed from a place deep inside her psyche, the sadness that accompanied them almost overwhelming. A tear welled, glistening, until she blinked, when it rolled down her cheek.

"Frau Schulz, I didn't mean to upset you. Here." Neumann plucked a pristine white handkerchief from his jacket and handed it to her.

This was exactly what Jack's tradecraft tuition had warned against. A veiled threat involving loved ones, followed by an act of kindness. Neumann's methods were so transparent. Helena knew what was happening, but still she could feel her nerves fraying.

"I think that will do for today." Neumann sprang from the chair, swinging it around so it faced the desk.

"Can I go now?"

Neumann sniggered. "Frau Schulz, we're only getting to know each other. I think we need more time to talk." He pointed at the paper and pencil on the desktop. "If you think of anything I should know about Das Bar or Jack Martin, perhaps you would be so kind to write it down."

"I told you, I don't …"

He held up a hand to interrupt her. "Do not fear the judgement of others, Frau Schulz."

"What?"

"Take the advice of Mozart."

"I don't understand."

"Be silent if you choose, but when it is necessary, speak – and speak in such a way that people will remember it. Good advice from the great man, I'd say."

He backed out of the door and Helena heard the metallic scrape of the key in the lock. The light extinguished, leaving her in total, unyielding, blackness.

***

She lay on the bed, a rough blanket wrapped tight around her, for what seemed like ages. Every two hours, perhaps more, the light came on, dazzling, a physical jolt. After five minutes it went off again, returning her to a black world inhabited by her darkest fears.

Time slipped by. She had no idea whether it was day or night, or how long she had been lying there. Hunger pangs griped in her stomach. She had eaten nothing since the evening before the soldiers had come, but the thirst was worse. Her mouth dry and scratchy, all sorts of fearful scenarios revolving in her head, none of them with good outcomes. Neumann clearly knew about the resistance operation at Das Bar. How much was unclear. She was certain that knowledge would not have derived from Jack Martin. Unless. How does someone, even when trained in the ways of deflecting interrogation, cope when subjected to relentless psychological intimidation and physical pain? The thought swirled. Each individual must have their breaking point. She wondered about her own.

And then the screaming started. At first, whimpers, as a dog when separated from its master, followed by howls of agony on a scale she thought unimaginable. The sounds emanated from the cellars below, rising like the damp and mould in the walls, until she could almost smell the suffering. The basement, she decided, must house a multitude of dungeons.

Of course. That's it. The reason behind the screams was all over the wireless broadcasts. Following the attempt on the Führer's life, thousands of suspected plotters and resistance sympathisers had been arrested by the Gestapo and the SS.

Ordinary Germans had been encouraged to betray their next-door neighbours about any anti-Nazi activity, even if they had only the faintest of suspicion.

Rumours circulated that the purge had already seen scores executed and hundreds, maybe thousands, tortured. The fortunate ones died before they could be hoisted on butchers' hooks and slowly strangulated with piano wire, while they writhed and twisted in agony. It was said the killings were filmed and sent to Hitler's HQ where the Führer could gloat at exacting his revenge. As the plotter-in-chief, General von Stauffenberg, had flown directly to Berlin following the assassination attempt, it was likely the city's residents had suffered more than most.

Helena pulled the blanket over her head, stuck fingers in her ears, desperate to block the wails and thoughts of torture. The more she tried, the more they infiltrated her mind. She imagined beatings, suffocation with plastic bags, cigarette burns, industrial pliers ripping out nails and teeth, as well as electric wires wrapped around a person's most intimate parts. Jack had warned her of the Nazi security forces' deployment of such methods, not to shock or frighten, but to prepare her for the brutality utilised in the pursuit of information. In the world of the most sadistic Nazis, sometimes it seemed it was in the guise of fun. Now she was in the waiting room, for that is what it felt like. She shivered at the thought, her resolve wavering. As she yearned for unconsciousness, she employed one of Jack's distraction techniques, imagining herself back on stage at the Opera House, running through her most memorable performance.

At last, sleep came.

30

THE night of my life. May 6th, 1936.

Shouts of Wunderbar! Applause rolling like volleys of artillery fire around the Opera House. So many curtain calls I thought the night might never end. I didn't want it to. I could feel it in the hearts of everyone present. After years of training, I had at last arrived, accepted, adored even, as a prima donna in my adopted land. Everything I had ever wanted.

I had been nervous, especially when I caught a glimpse of him in my sideways vision, illuminated by a stray beam of light as I reached the outer edge of my vocal range.

It was always the most dangerous moment of the performance. If my voice faltered, it would be here, buffeted by the swell of emotion.

I'd sung Wagner before. At London's Covent Garden as a water-nymph. I found that role testing, requiring seduction and complex melody. But this was tougher, the first time as Brunnhilde, the leading lady and heroine of The Ring, at the Berlin State Opera, the world's original opera house with its sumptuous gold trims and Baroque architecture. With his eyes upon me.

At one point I saw him nod. A smirk, rather than a smile, played on his lips. I remember his angular features were set hard, eyes cold as iron, slicked black hair and severe moustache emphasising the pastiness of his complexion. He was difficult to read, but I recognised the nod as appreciation. At least, I hoped that was the case.

A few minutes after the final curtain call, I still felt drunk with elation when I pushed open the door to my dressing room.

I gasped. A blanket of red petals adorned the dressing table, long stems wrapped in a voluminous white sheet bearing a black swastika against a red background. The scent of roses, two hundred at least, filled the air. No gift card. My first guess was for dear old Siegfried. On second thoughts, no. Siegfried was generous and supportive, but a husband not given to ostentatious shows of affection. Behind me, I heard the gruff tones of a man clearing his throat. I spun around.

"Heil, mein Führer!" My reaction was instinctive, body tensing, right arm raising, hand straightening in the customary salute I'd been taught by Siegfried, as I addressed the man whose face I knew so well from newspapers and magazines, but whom I had never met. My skin prickled with anticipation, hairs standing to attention as if on a parade ground. I could hear a rumble of feet in the corridor, suggesting the man commanded a sizeable entourage.

He waved a hand, dismissing my formality.

"Frau Schulz, I have heard you sing many times, but never as haunting as this night. Please accept my gift." He nodded towards the roses.

"Thank you," I said. "They're beautiful."

He leaned towards me, in the manner of a benevolent uncle. "You soften the edges of Wagner."

"I've heard he's your favourite composer."

He nodded. "I was twelve years old the first time I heard Wagner. I've been addicted ever since."

He half-turned as if to leave, before pausing, as if a thought had struck. Finally, he spoke.

"When you listen to Wagner, or Beethoven, your heart swells with heroic German spirit, don't you think?"

I didn't know what to say, so opted for the truth. "It's a little serious for my taste." *Immediately, I wanted to bite back my response. Too naïve. Too honest. Too English. He smiled at my discomfort.*

"Perhaps that's because you're not German."

"Maybe."

"You're from a small mill town in the north-west of England, I believe, although I congratulate you. Your German is excellent."

"Thank you. I've lived here some years now. My husband is …"

"I know who Herr Schulz is."

"Oh."

"Do you feel safe in Germany?"

"Yes." *I felt fine frown lines form on my forehead. I was puzzled. I couldn't imagine where this conversation was heading.*

"I would like you to sing for me at my retreat. Would that be possible?"

My cheeks burned, so flushed I raised a hand to mask the glow, but my reply was instant. "Of course, I'd be honoured."

"My office will be in touch."

He clicked his heels, swivelled, and disappeared down the corridor, his entourage squirming against the wall to allow him passage.

I shut the door and stood with my back to it for many moments. I picked up one of the red rose stems, sniffed the petals, the scent fresh and sweet. Never had I felt so elated.

31

HE watched from a vantage point giving him a wide-angled view of the street. There were plenty of places to hide. A mine bomb had drifted beneath a tattered parachute the night before and taken out a couple of houses across the way from Das Bar.

A burst water main spilled its contents in a muddy stream down the gutter, although a bulldozer had scooped and shovelled debris into several big mounds along the pavement. Carter hid behind one of the makeshift hills, leaning against a felled roof joist that pointed to the sky at an awkward angle. The streets were relatively quiet, many residents too afraid to venture out, knowing Gestapo patrols roamed the city.

After around half an hour, Carter deemed it safe. He strode across the street and disappeared down the steps leading to the front entrance.

There were a few regulars toying with glasses. Elke was behind the bar, looking bored. She perked up when she spotted him.

"Hi, not seen you for ages." Her welcome warm, without the angst he had become accustomed to.

"There's a good reason for that." He was alluding to the shooting of Bo, but Elke was oblivious to the connection. "Are Karl and Felix around?"

"In the back. You're lucky to catch them. They're usually gone by this time."

Carter found them packing up, Karl stuffing provisions into a big hold-all.

"Good to see you, my friend." Karl gave Carter a bear hug which he wasn't expecting. "I wondered whether we would see you again after what happened."

"Did everything go okay? Taking care of the item." Carter lowered his voice, preferring to use innuendo.

Karl was more direct. "If you mean, burying the treacherous bastard, then yes, everything went to plan."

"What about the airman?"

"Shipped him out to Potsdam. He'll be safe there for a while, until we can find a route. No point trying at the moment, Nazi patrols all over the place."

"Have they been here?"

"Twice. Looking for Bo."

"What did you tell them?"

"Nothing. I wasn't here, but Elke fired them off with her personal brand of charm. She has quite a mouth on her. I'm surprised we get any customers."

Carter smiled. He told Karl about Helena's disappearance from Hotel Adlon with an armed guard and a Gestapo officer.

"Any ideas where they might have taken her?"

Karl grimaced and sucked in air. "I'm not going to lie. It doesn't sound good. Chances are she's been taken to Prinz-Albrecht. Many walk in there, not many walk out."

"Any chance you could ask around?"

"I'll try, but everyone's scared. Mere mention of the Gestapo is likely to get you arrested."

"Thanks Karl."

They shook hands, Karl heaved the hold-all onto his shoulders, and they bade farewell. Felix made to leave also, but as he brushed past, Carter grabbed his forearm. "Felix, could you do something for me?"

"What?" Felix looked suspicious.

Carter rummaged in his rucksack and pulled out an opera programme. He flicked through the pages until he came to a head and shoulders picture of Helena, with a small biography underneath, including details such as date and place of birth, as well as positions held in opera companies.

"Would it be possible to make new identity papers, using this picture, with the name Mary Schmid and these details?" He passed Felix a scrap of paper containing a Swiss address, a new date of birth and family details.

"Everything's possible, but Frau Schulz is well known. Someone could still recognise her."

"I'll take my chances with that, Felix. How long?"

"A few days, no more. It's not difficult."

"Good. When it's done, leave it with Elke." Carter knew the whereabouts of Felix and Karl were difficult to predict. By contrast, Elke worked and lived at Das Bar.

Carter offered Felix his hand. They shook.

Before he left, Carter took Elke aside and briefed her on his plan.

32

HELENA heard the switch click and dazzling light filled the room for what seemed like the hundredth time. It was accompanied by a metallic scrape and a rush of air as the door swung open.

She had no idea how long she had been confined to the room, or how many people had died in the building that night. A young boy's plaintive cries haunted her dreams, but she didn't know if the voice was just that. A dream. Mixed with the other dreams of singing at the Opera House. She hoped beyond hope that it was. She gauged it must be morning, but the bright light was disorientating and the man standing over her little more than a blur.

As her eyes adjusted, he came into focus. He wasn't wearing a uniform. Simple brown overalls matched his plain appearance, but he carried a bottle of water and a bread roll. He offered her the water and she clawed at the top, twisting it off, glugging the liquid almost in one gulp. The water gushed down, cold and refreshing, swirling away some of the horror of the night before.

He offered her the bread.

"I'm not hungry."

"You must eat." His voice high-pitched, squeaky even, but with a modicum of compassion that eluded Neumann.

Helena didn't think she would ever eat again. Her stomach growled, but she couldn't face food. The screams too close, the memory leaving a nauseous residue. She waved away the bread.

"Very well, I'll leave it here in case you change your mind."

The man stepped back and Helena was aware of a taller man, and the smell of smoke. Neumann.

"Ah, Frau Schulz. I trust you had a good night's sleep. Not too noisy, I hope." A smugness about his demeanour warned Helena to be wary.

Neumann had an odd face, she thought. Chiselled cheek bones, a thin nose, and rimless spectacles that made piggy eyes look even smaller. There was a dull pallor to his skin, as if the colour had left it long ago. Perhaps down to years spent in basement dungeons. If the separate characteristics were unimpressive, the whole somehow fitted together to form an unusual, yet formidable façade. She wondered whether he was married. If he had children. If he did normal things like reading bedtime stories, walking the dog, washing dishes. She decided not. Here was a hard man, she concluded. A loveless man with merciless intent, accustomed to giving orders and being obeyed.

He motioned for her to sit up. She swung her legs off the bed and ran fingers through her tangled hair. It felt like straw. As before, he sat on the wooden chair.

"Frau Schulz, I believe you sing at the stalag, entertaining the prisoners."

"Sometimes, yes. I was invited by Commandant Reinhardt. He thought it would be good for the prisoners. Give them something to look forward to. Help with morale."

"I'm sure it does. There's nothing like music to rouse the spirits. Boredom breeds disaffection, and disaffected prisoners are difficult to manage. Your performances will have been most beneficial. The commandant must be grateful. I hear the men call you The Angel of Berlin."

"I'm no angel."

"Oh come, Frau Schulz, you're too modest."

Helena's mind was racing. Neumann, she was certain, did not start any conversation without knowing the direction of travel. The mention of her singing at the stalag could mean only one thing. He knew, or at least suspected, she was involved in smuggling out information. She breathed deep, trying to control a rising sense of panic. Jack Martin had warned her of the consequences if she was discovered. A firing squad awaited, and before then hours of psychological torture and physical suffering in an attempt to exhort information. The screams of the night before invaded her thoughts. She blocked them out.

"I was happy to help once a fortnight. I'm not performing at the Opera House at the moment. It makes sense to keep my voice in good order."

Neumann clicked his fingers and the door swung open. Two men, neither in uniform, carried in an A-board, placing it in the middle of the room, directed towards Helena. A detailed map of Berlin was pinned to the board with red blobs highlighting specific locations.

One of the men handed Neumann a thin stick around two feet long. He pointed to a grey shaded area to the south of the map.

"Do you know what this is, Frau Schulz?"

"No."

"Really, no idea?"

"No."

"This is the stalag at which you have been singing once a fortnight."

He pointed again, this time to the red blobs. With a twirl of the stick he emphasised the circle the blobs formed around the stalag, at slightly different distances but forming a distinct pattern, rather as the planets orbit the sun.

"Any ideas?"

She shook her head, as if puzzled, which she was. Genuinely, she had no idea where this conversation was heading.

"Very well. Let me help you out a little more." He pointed the stick at the outermost blob. "This is, or was, a munitions factory." He flicked the stick around the blobs.

"Here, a steel producing plant. This one, a factory assembling tank parts. This one, the main plant producing engines for the Messerschmitt Bf 109, the most advanced fighter aircraft in the world. I could go on, Frau Schulz, but I'm sure you can see where all this is leading."

Helena's eyes were wide. "No, I haven't a clue."

Neumann's lips formed a tight, thin line. His patience was fraying, but he maintained his even temper. He signalled to one of the assistants, who promptly produced a foolscap piece of paper from a bag and pinned it to the map on the A-board.

"Take a close look at the dates written here." The stick pointed to the paper. There was a row of dates forming a column on the left hand-side and a corresponding row on the right.

Neumann pointed to the left row. "These are the last ten occasions on which you performed at the stalag." His stick flicked to the right-hand side. "These represent the dates on which the locations in red, including the munitions factory, the engines plant, and all the rest serving our war endeavours, were bombed and destroyed by the RAF. On each occasion there are no more than a few days between you singing and the bombing. I'm a pragmatic man, Frau Schulz. I don't believe in coincidence. Apparently, you sing and bombs fall."

Helena shrugged, triggering a reaction she feared, but still was not expecting.

Neumann rose from his seat, kicking away the chair violently. It scraped along the floor and smashed into the plaster wall. He strode over to Helena, bent forward, and for the first time since they'd met raised his voice. He yelled in her ear, so close that she felt his spittle warm and wet. "Don't take me for a fool. Tell me the truth. You've been supplying the British with coordinates. Information that has come from within the stalag."

Helena's body shook with the shock of Neumann's reaction, but in her head she recited Jack Martin's mantra. *Deny. Deny. Deny.*

"No. Never. I wouldn't do that. Germany has given me my career. I love this country." Tears ran down her cheeks,

"But you hate the Nazis. Admit it." His voice seethed with anger, a film of foam spilling from his lips. Sobs racked

Helena's chest, but she sucked in oxygen, desperately striving to stay calm.

For the next hour, Neumann repeated his questions, demanding answers, at times in a reasoned, dignified manner, at others with the feral and sinister shrieks of a man on the edge of his sanity. After her initial emotional response, Helena quickly became inured to his rants. It was all designed, as Jack had described, to destabilise her thought processes, to induce fear, to encourage her to grasp at any tiny reveal to make the interrogation end.

She gauged her repeated denials were beginning to frustrate Neumann. His pale cheeks had taken on a purple hue. He seemed to bite his thin lips continually and his breathing was laboured. But he never laid a hand on her. Nor did he order the men who stood by to indulge in physical violence. She found that surprising. After a night listening to the torture seeping through the walls, she had steeled herself to resist the brutal methods used by the Nazi regime. She deemed it inevitable. Maybe it would still come.

The interrogation ended as starkly as it had begun, Neumann signalling his men to leave the room. He picked up the shattered chair and carefully leaned it against the wall at a forlorn angle, as if massaging his frustration. He walked towards the door before turning sharply, stroking his chin in a gesture of contemplation.

"You may think you're clever, Frau Schulz. That you can fob me off with your denials. Many have tried to do the same within these four walls. It's only natural. But there are ways to make everyone tell the truth. We'll see what tomorrow brings. You can tell the truth and walk from here, still The Angel of Berlin, free to sing your sweet songs to an appreciative audience, or you can continue with your lies and …"

He never finished the sentence. Instead, the door clanged shut, the light extinguished, and in the darkness Helena was left once more to wrestle her doubts and fears. The more she assessed her predicament, the more she concluded there was no acceptable exit. If she admitted she had smuggled information out of the stalag, she would be shot as a spy. Of that she was certain. The information had led to the loss of many German lives and significant destruction of munitions and essential hardware. In Nazi Germany, that could not be allowed to go unpunished.

Yet, if she continued with her denials, she knew her own screams would surely echo in the chamber of horrors she now inhabited. In the luxury of the Adlon, in the anonymity of Das Bar, even on that fateful day she met Jack Martin three years ago on Unter den Linden, she had been confident her inner strength could resist all attempts at exhorting information. But that was before she heard the whimpers and howls of anguish. That chilling soundtrack had burrowed so deep into her psyche that all certainty was gone. She laid her head on the bed, hopelessness overwhelming her. She thought of her mother, her sisters, sunny days on the beach as a youngster when life was safe and uncomplicated, and peace was taken for granted. She thought of her father who had encouraged her to sing as a child, forever organising musical evenings around the family piano, but who now disowned her. He would never know the sacrifice she had made for the beloved country of her birth. A tear ran down her cheek, swiftly followed by another. Soon, her blanket was soaked in a swollen stream of emotion and regret.

33

CARTER automatically reached for his revolver. He was aware of footsteps descending the stairs, but it was a scraping sound that had jolted him awake.

The first full rays of a splendid dawn were breaking over Dolziger Strasse, its watery light slowly diluting the darkness. He glanced at his watch. Twenty past six. He swung out of bed to investigate and discovered a note slid underneath the door.

He perused it for several seconds. It simply read *Prinz-Albrecht*. A tick had been scrawled by the side of it.

Karl's instinct had proved correct. It was probably him on the stairs. Helena was a prisoner in the Gestapo fortress, no more than a couple of miles from where Carter stood.

He fixed himself a cup of tea and watched the sun rise over the neighbouring rooftops, his mind sifting every option. There weren't any. He couldn't think of a single way of helping Helena.

He knew she was strong, feisty and resilient. She would not betray any secrets. At least, he hoped not. But this was the Gestapo, whose officers were a law unto themselves, licensed for cruelty. Men, stronger and better trained than Helena, had broken, their will shattered after only a short time in Gestapo captivity.

He sipped tea and watched a woman cross the street and enter a public telephone booth, an unusual sight at such an early hour. It had impressed Carter how many of the red-and-white kiosks, dotted around the city like miniature havens, had survived the recent bombing onslaught in working order, some even with glass intact. He surmised the reason lay in the underground cables used by the German postal service's urban network.

The woman lifted the receiver and for five minutes or more her arms flailed, signifying an animated conversation. She reminded Carter of Elke, feisty and opinionated. When the woman left, her jaw jutted and her stride was confident, as if the call had been informative.

Again, Carter played back all his conversations with Helena, searching for something useful. Nothing extraordinary came to mind, apart from the revelation that the biggest fans of her singing included the Führer and top Nazi ministers. She had performed for them on numerous occasions. Carter couldn't imagine Hitler being pleased that right now the woman he had gifted red roses was being tortured by the Gestapo, doubtless screaming for her life in an underground dungeon.

He abandoned the dregs of his tea. His mind was whirring. He had an idea.

Two hours later when the working day was under way, he wandered down to the street and entered the phone booth. A faint smell of urine caused his nose to twitch but he quickly found what he was looking for. A phone book of addresses, including residents and organisations, filed away in a side pocket. He laid it on the worktop. It was a long shot, he realised, but he flicked through the Ms, until a government department stood out in bold letters. Ministry of Public Enlightenment and Propaganda.

He knew the building. A palatial affair by the Brandenburg Gate. Propaganda in wartime Germany, he had gleaned from his training, was an essential art form. A way of controlling the people, especially when they were weary of a war many believed they could no longer win.

He dialled the number and inserted his coins.

"Minister's office." A young woman's voice.

"Good morning, Fraulein. Could you transfer me to the secretary of Herr Goebbels? I have some vital information of a sensitive nature involving the State Police. I think he would be interested.

"Hold the line."

A few seconds later, another woman with an assured manner answered.

"Fraulein Pomsel speaking. Herr Goebbels' office. How can I help?"

34

THE hours slipped by, again in pitch darkness, apart from brief intervals when dazzling light burned. She used those to sip water from an extra bottle Neumann's aide had provided. She also ate the bread roll, stale and crumbly, trying not to dwell on what might lie ahead. It proved impossible, especially when the shouts and screams returned, louder and more desperate even than before.

She slid in and out of consciousness, pressing her face into the mattress, forcing herself to remember the days when singing and bringing joy to an audience seemed the most important aspect of her existence. She still believed the beauty of a haunting melody or a passionate lyric could transport people to a special place where art and culture was valued beyond money and self-interest. But for culture to be relevant, for it to earn its place at the heart of society, there had to be freedom. The last few years, with food rationed and death all around, had taught her that music and performance was the privilege of those unaffected by bombs and tyranny.

Yet still it could bring comfort. Underneath her blanket she sang to herself to block out the sounds of torture, to calm her nerves. Not Wagner or Mozart. None of the classical composers, but songs from the musical theatre of the 1920s, imported from America. *Baby Face, California Here I Come, If You Knew Susie*. Songs of her childhood, full of optimism and humour that once she had listened to with her father via a crackly wireless.

When, finally, the cell door swung open once more, the two aides entered.

"Come with us." The command, clinical and stern, came from the man who had brought the only source of compassion the day before, along with water and bread.

"Where to?"

"No questions."

When Helena failed to move, the aides each grabbed an arm, yanking her off the bed. With forearms under her armpits they acted as crutches, half-carrying, half-dragging her out of the room, down a long corridor, feet barely touching the floor despite her protests that she could walk. They passed many solid doors along the way, all shut tight, although Helena could hear wails, the whine of machinery and the occasional heavy thud. There was a sharp, unpleasant, odour, not unlike stale urine. A man emerged from one of the rooms and stumbled towards them, his arms manacled, blood dripping from his toothless mouth. His eyes stared straight through Helena as they crossed, glazed and unseeing, two guards jabbing him on his way.

A shaft of light signified the last door on the right was open. The aides frogmarched Helena straight in and sat her on a hard, metal chair. No explanation, ignoring her appeals for information. One of the aides grabbed her arms, tying her wrists around her back with electrical wire that bit deep into her skin. The other aide wrapped a heavy chain around her waist and secured it to the back of the chair with a bolt. Helena's heart pounded. This was her worst fear. Tied, unable to move, at the mercy of men she believed possessed no mercy or compassion. She bit her lip to try to retain control, at the same time observing the room's contents.

A worktop ran down one side. Above it, steel implements dangled from hooks, the sort Helena associated with a butcher's shop. On another wall an extra row of hooks housed smaller, more delicate, tools, akin to the instruments in a dentist's surgery. A large white porcelain sink was set into the worktop, a crimson hue around the plughole. The smell of powerful cleaning fluid was pungent to the point of overpowering.

Helena did not require imagination to deduce the purpose of this room. She was unsure whether she could withstand torture. Jack had described operatives who stubbed cigarettes or sharp pins into their own arms to prepare themselves for the pain control that may be required. The very thought made her shiver.

"Please, I beg you, tell me what's happening."

The aides ignored her. Instead, one of them rummaged inside a cupboard, pulling out a piece of black material. He disappeared behind Helena and she was immediately plunged into darkness. The feeling of dread as the hood slid over her head and the drawstring pulled was overwhelming.

She sat there for probably 10 minutes, although it seemed longer, continuing to ask questions, yet receiving no replies. A faint chesty rattle as one of them breathed supplied the only clue the aides were still present. Heavy boots approached.

"You give us no choice, Frau Schulz." The cold delivery was unmistakable. Neumann. "I will ask you once again whether you know or have met Jack Martin, and whether you have indulged in activities of espionage in Berlin or elsewhere that would compromise the aims of the Fatherland. Activities, I remind you, that have led to the deaths of many German soldiers and citizens."

Deny. Deny. Deny.

Once again, Jack's mantra was Helena's safe place. "How many times do I have to tell you? I don't know this man called Jack. I would never do anything to kill anybody. I'm a singer." She battled to remain calm, but two days and nights of little sleep, sensory disorientation and horrific sounds, had manufactured a fearful tremor.

"I respect that. You're almost convincing, Frau Schulz. I wish it were true, I really do. You sound so believable and I have such admiration for your talents. But then we know you are trained in the art of acting."

She sensed him walking around her, three or four orbits, his voice rising and falling. Then he paused directly in front of her, his smoky aroma penetrating the tightly-drawn hood. "Of course, the art of acting, in reality, is not to act. Rather, it is to absorb the character one is playing so completely that, whatever the circumstance, one would always respond in the appropriate fashion. A good actor, such as yourself, playing an innocent victim, would always sound perfectly believable. Am I right?"

Helena was hot and breathing heavy, her oxygen levels compromised. She was tiring of Neumann's games. Exasperated by his droning voice. But she summoned one more appeal to reason. "I wouldn't be here if I was a good actor. I would have made up some lie by now that would have convinced you I'm innocent. I'm only here because I'm honest and truthful, and because I accepted an invitation from one of your German officers to do a good turn and sing at …"

The sonorous swish of metal on metal interrupted her thought. It took several moments to identify the sound of knives sharpening. The hairs on her arms and neck rose and she braced herself against the hard back of the chair for whatever was coming.

"Last chance, Frau Schulz." She sensed movement, detecting the stale sweat of a man standing over her. She wriggled and squirmed. She couldn't help it, a natural response to the thrust or swipe she anticipated.

Instead, she felt a rush of air against her legs as the door opened.

"Excuse me, Herr Neumann." A man's voice.

"What?"

"The telephone."

"Not now."

"It's Herr Goebbels."

***

It took Neumann around a minute to reach the office telephone. His irritation at being interrupted was tempered by a sense of apprehension. He was not accustomed to taking telephone calls from high-ranking German ministers, and everyone in Berlin was wary of Goebbels. He had recently been appointed Stradtprasident of Berlin. As well as this district city role, he remained in charge of Nazi propaganda, and was also Reich Plenipotentiary for Total War, challenged with finding an extra half million fighting men for the battlefield.

A hard core Nazi, known for virulent views on the Jews, his powers did not officially extend to military planning, but he had the ear of the Führer.

Neumann had run into Goebbels a year ago at a rally at the Berlin Sports Palace. He had been surprised at his short stature and his elegant appearance, yet stirred by his passion and ability to rouse his audience.

"Neumann here." His voice contained a lilt of curiosity.

"This is the Minister. My sources tell me you have Frau Schulz at police headquarters."

"That's correct. How did you know?"

"My job is to know everything, Neumann. Why is Frau Schulz being held?" Straight to the point.

"We have reason to believe she is involved in espionage against the Fatherland."

"Nonsense." A sharp edge to Goebbels' response alerted Neumann to be wary, but he was sure of his facts.

"We have evidence. Frau Schulz has been singing at a prison camp which has been supplying information, in the form of target coordinates, to the enemy. The dates and timings are conclusive. We believe she has been helping."

"Do you have physical evidence, for instance, codes or notes?"

"No, Herr Goebbels."

"Do you have witnesses? Anyone who will testify against her? Senior officers? The commandant?"

"No, but ..."

"Do you know who Frau Schulz is, Neumann?"

"Of course, but as well as performing at the State Opera, she is English by birth. She has every incentive to ..."

"She is part of our propaganda programme."

"Oh."

"Why the hell do you think she was allowed to sing at the prison camps? Not only does it show how well we treat prisoners, providing them with good food and entertainment, it puts the inmates in the mood to see the Nazi way is the right way, the only way. In a short time, we want these prisoners to profess that to the world, as well as fight alongside us. On the Eastern Front. Against the Bolsheviks."

"I really think ..."

Goebbels snapped, his reasoned tone turning decidedly ugly. "That's the point, Neumann. You don't think. Leave the thinking to those who know what they're doing."

"Mein Herr."

Neumann's mind was whirling. He was close to breaking Helena. He could sense it. His preparation these past 48 hours had been designed to infest her mind with doubts and fears. Few men or women, even those with professional training, were capable of withstanding the physical abuse that followed such psychological torture in the dungeons of Prinz-Albrecht. Within the day she would spill her secrets, he was certain.

But Goebbels was a formidable foe, possessing a sinister combination of zeal and arrogance. His *Total War* philosophy had been adopted by the Führer. Hitler had been best man at his wedding to Magda Quandt and had a soft spot for his six children. They were brothers in terror.

As if to ram home his influence, Goebbels ranted down the telephone. "Frau Schulz is not an ordinary opera singer. She is the Führer's favourite singer. Ignore that at your peril, Neumann."

The line went dead. Neumann paused for many moments before replacing the receiver, weighing his unusual combined position as a functioning member of the SS and the Gestapo with the express wishes of a political minister. Eventually, he trudged back down the corridor, re-entering the room where Helena sat hooded and bound.

"Frau Schulz, this is your lucky day. You are free to go." He signalled for the aides to untie her hands and release the chain around her torso. One of them ripped off the hood. She sucked in oxygen, the chemical taste no longer offensive.

"Why? What now?"

"As I said, you are free. A car will return you to your hotel. But Frau Schulz …"

"Yes?"

Neumann's eyes narrowed to the tiniest of slits and his words slithered out in a venomous hiss. "Don't, for a moment, think this is the end of the matter. I know what you are. Your voice and reputation may have saved you this time. But I promise you, Frau Schulz, we will meet again."

One of the aides helped her off the chair, the shock of the last two days having rendered her legs unsteady. He supported her down the corridor and out to the waiting car.

Neumann turned to the other aide. "Put a watch on the bitch. A couple of our best officers. I want to know where she goes, who she meets, what she has for dinner. Everything."

35

CARTER sauntered along the boulevard on the opposite side of the road from Hotel Adlon. It was the fourth time he'd passed this way in a matter of hours and the same cars remained.

They'd been easy to spot, both parked with unrestricted views of the hotel's main entrance, albeit pointing in different directions. The driver of the first car had barely moved in more than an hour, one hand on the steering wheel, smoking the odd cigarette, his face hidden in the shadow of a wide-brimmed hat. The occupant of the second car had alighted several times, opened the boot, pretended to sort through bags, scanned the street, and then returned to the front seat as if waiting for a hotel guest to transport. Classic techniques of the surveillance agent, except Carter thought they were sloppy, concentrating on the target, missing the big picture. First rule he'd learned in tradecraft school. Cover all bases. Secure an all-round field of vision.

Sloppy or not, it meant it was too dangerous for him to simply stride in and ask to see Frau Schulz. The Gestapo's watchmen would have briefed the concierge and receptionists, ordering them to report any activity involving Helena. Similarly, Gestapo technicians would have taken control of the hotel switchboard to monitor telephone traffic.

None of which disturbed Carter. It was as expected. He was rather pleased, and mightily relieved, that his telephone ruse to involve Herr Goebbels' office seemed to have worked. One of Karl's contacts had reported Helena's return to the Adlon. But the Gestapo were nothing, if not relentless. Their investigators may not have the physical evidence to tie Helena to espionage, but he knew it was only a matter of time.

He had to get her out. Out of Hotel Adlon. Out of Berlin. Out of Germany. First, he had to get into Hotel Adlon. A simple solution dawned. Book a room. As a Swiss banker, he was a perfect fit for the hotel's clientele. Then he remembered.

The first time he had visited the Adlon, he had indulged the concierge in conversation and spent the best part of an afternoon drinking and chatting with Helena in the lobby bar, watched by Albert, the barman. The second time, he had asked for Helena's room while announcing himself to the elderly receptionist, using his Swiss alias. Hotel concierges and receptionists interact with thousands of people over the course of their careers, but the Adlon staff could have witnessed few more striking than Carter and Helena, a Swiss banker and a beautiful opera singer. Carter was certain he would be remembered, but he knew someone who wouldn't.

***

Elke looked the part. She didn't usually wear make-up, but a touch of finely applied eye-liner, mascara, and red lipstick, added a decade of sophistication to her tender years. A summery floral dress, high heels, a dainty bonnet and a stylish overnight bag swinging from her arm, accentuated her womanly figure. Carter had also implored her to wear a smile, rather than her wardrobe of sullen pouts.

She had telephoned earlier to book a room at the Adlon and Carter had supplied the Reichsmarks.

The watchmen outside studied her entrance, but even with Berlin devastated and SS officers occupying several floors, the Adlon's civilian clientele was full of rich socialites. She blended perfectly. The receptionist enquired how long she planned to stay.

"One night only. I'm travelling to Leipzig by train tomorrow to meet with family."

"In that case, let's hope the night is quiet, Fraulein, and the trains are still running. Your room is on the third floor."

The receptionist handed her a key and Elke returned a warm smile, the sort Carter had ordered. The next task was to find Helena. Carter had no clue to her room number and had warned Elke not to ask. Nothing to attract attention.

After dropping off her bag in her room and jettisoning her bonnet, Elke headed for the lobby bar. It was quiet, a few officers in armchairs, two couples sipping cocktails before dinner. She ordered a gin and tonic. Most girls of her age would have felt intimidated by themselves in a plush bar with eyes drawn in their direction. Not Elke. She had grown up in bars, admittedly not as plush as this one. Yet the same principle applied. Hold your head high. Look comfortable and you'll feel comfortable. She had also picked up a newspaper from the lobby. A handy ploy for a woman on her own. It allowed her to peer over the pages to peruse the corridor to reception.

Half an hour and a steady flow of residents sauntered by. No sign of Helena. Elke contemplated entering the restaurant for dinner, but there were several dining rooms. It would be easy to choose the wrong one. She ordered another drink. The bar was filling up.

Her patience was rewarded a few minutes later when a waiter pushed his way into the lobby bar, silver tray in hand. He called to Albert. "Frau Schulz is taking room service this evening. Can you fix her usual?"

A sudden infusion of adrenalin caused Elke's cheeks to flush. This was a gift she was not expecting. Albert took his time serving other guests, to the waiter's annoyance, before finally attending to Helena's order. When her drink was ready, the waiter balanced the tray on the palm of one hand in customary fashion while heading to one of the elevators. Elke followed.

"Floor Seven." The waiter informed the lift attendant, who glanced at the cloudy cocktail.

"Frau Schulz?"

The waiter nodded.

"Fraulein?" The lift attendant enquired what floor Elke required.

"Seven."

"I'm sorry, Fraulein. That floor is reserved for long-term residents. A special pass is required."

"How silly, I meant six."

The attendant smiled benignly. "Of course."

When the lift reached the sixth floor, the doors opened and Elke strode out. She looked left and right, finally registering a sign denoting a flight of stairs. She sprinted down the corridor, climbed the stairs two at a time, emerging on the seventh floor where a flimsy cordon and sign warned guests it was restricted to VIP residents. The waiter was knocking on a door. Ducking behind a wall, she waited until he had gone, before edging down the carpeted corridor. She stopped at the same door, the number 725 in gold lettering emblazoned at eye level.

Left to her intuition, she would have knocked, entered, and blabbed the whole story to Helena. Carter had warned against that. He didn't want Helena to act on impulse and try to find him. That would lead the watchmen to his door, or Das Bar, either of which would compromise them both.

Instead, Elke slid a pre-written note Carter had given her under the door, and took the stairs down to the lobby bar where she ordered an expensive cocktail. Carter was paying. It would be rude not to enjoy such unexpected generosity.

***

The siren sounded around midnight. It was a little earlier than Carter anticipated, but it was a moonlit evening and the bombers were eager to unload their cargo.

Elke had retired to her room, but the alarm was her cue to action. She leapt up and ran down the stairs. Doors were opening everywhere as guests followed protocol and headed for the nearest concrete bunker. Staff steered them away from the lifts towards the stairs, ushering them out of the exits. Elke made for the rear door, normally locked and bolted, but opened in the event of an air raid for swift evacuation. Carter was there as planned. She grabbed his hand. "This way."

They made their way up the stairs, a few guests exchanging puzzled glances at two people running in the opposite direction to everyone else. By the time they reached the seventh floor the hotel was quiet, although a distant rumble suggested the action outside had begun.

The door to Room 725 was already ajar. Helena was standing in the middle of the room and when her eyes met Carter's she flew to him, throwing her arms around his neck, saying nothing, holding him tight for what seemed an eternity. Even when he tried to ease her away, she clung on, desperately exploiting the feeling of warmth and security to combat the sickening trauma of the last few days. Elke looked on, her embarrassed coughs eventually tearing them apart.

For an hour or more, they sat by the window, Helena relating her Gestapo ordeal at the hands of Neumann as distant explosions sent plumes of fire into the night sky. "It's like a torture chamber in that Gestapo headquarters. They're killing people for no reason. Neumann and his men enjoy it."

"I remember him that night at the bar. He's creepy and weird, the bastard of all bastards." Elke's contribution typically pithy.

Carter was sympathetic but measured, more interested in the way forward.

"We have to get you out, Helena. Once the Gestapo have suspicions, and now we know they do, they won't rest until they've got you in front of a firing squad, regardless of who you might know in high places. We should leave in the next few days. Felix is sorting fake papers. I've already put a plan in place."

"No." Helena's tone was strident.

"What do you mean, no?"

"I'm not leaving until I've got the second part of Sergeant Ripley's dossier."

"That was before the Gestapo picked you up. Now we know they're suspicious about the camp. They've matched dates and bombings and they suspect coordinates have been passed."

"I don't care. Ripley's risked everything. I'm not deserting him. I still have an invite to sing at the camp next week, and I'm going to be there."

"But they'll be watching you, searching you. Neumann will probably have the Gestapo following you. Have you got a death wish?"

"No, but I promised Ripley."

"Good for you, Helena." Elke piped up. "This country needs people to stand up and be counted.

"You can't stand up if you're dead." Carter threw Elke a furious look.

They sat in uncomfortable silence for several minutes, the rumbles outside growing less frequent, Carter weighing up whether Helena was the bravest, most-stubborn woman he knew, or the most foolish. Finally, he made a decision.

"Okay, one more performance, then you're out. Back to England. And, Helena …" He paused until she looked him in the eyes. "No ifs, no buts, you do everything I say."

36

IT was the same driver and guard as usual. The car pulled up in front of Hotel Adlon at three o'clock in the afternoon. Helena skipped out of the front door like a film star, floaty floral dress, hair cascading, dark sunshades lending an air of mystery. The glasses also allowed her an unobtrusive glance at the black vehicle down the street that had been parked for a week.

She had taken several short walks, noting the car always contained an occupant. This time there were two men in the front seat smoking cigarettes, the driver's window open halfway to allow the haze to escape.

Her driver pulled away and she sneaked a glance at the rearview mirror. As she anticipated, the black car slotted in behind them.

It took half an hour to reach the stalag, the driver dropping her outside the commandant's office. Reinhardt was waiting, along with an officer she had seen before and a woman she hadn't.

"It has been a long time, Frau Schulz. I'm sorry, I was away the last time you visited."

"I hope you'll come to the performance today, Commandant."

"Of course, but first there are some new regulations I must make you aware of. Please, in the office, if you don't mind." His manner was civil, almost apologetic, as he motioned for Helena to follow him into the office, although he signalled for the officers to stay outside.

As normal, they sat either side of his desk and Reinhardt indulged in a few minutes of meaningless small talk about music before fixing Helena with a serious frown. He seemed uncomfortable, reluctant to progress to the business end of the discussion.

Helena seized the initiative. "These new regulations, Commandant?"

"Yes, it's not my doing. I'm afraid the state police and their paranoia has decreed that, in line with other sub-camps in the area, all visitors must be searched on entering and leaving the camp. No exceptions. They're a bit jumpy about information being leaked. Would you mind if Frau Huber conducted a personal search? I'm afraid it will be comprehensive. Oh, and Officer Becker will need to search the contents of your bag."

Helena threw her head back and laughed. "Is that all, Commandant? I wondered why you were so serious. Of course, search me anywhere you like." Her demeanour was light and frivolous, but inside, her heart sank. The chances of smuggling out the rest of the dossier now seemed impossibly remote.

After the searches were complete, the Commandant accompanied her to the concert hall, where she checked the piano music with Michal as the men filed in. The hall filled quickly, all seats taken, prisoners standing alongside guards in the aisles.

"I'm Helena, from Lancashire." She launched into her first song from Strauss's Der Rosenkavalier, the first few bars prompting an appreciative ripple of applause from the audience. Scanning the hall, she searched for Sergeant Ripley's freckled face and ginger hair. Where is he? He's always in the front row. He loves his classical music. He's the one who campaigned for musical entertainment. Never misses a performance. Yet there was no sign of him. She found his absence disturbing, but her professional training allowed her to concentrate on the music.

The concert was around an hour long and though the men, caught up in the fervour of live music, predictably requested another rendition of *Land of Hope and Glory*, Helena was mindful to avoid anything controversial, especially with the commandant watching. She bowed her gratitude as applause rang out, announcing she'd see them again "God willing" in a fortnight.

As guards ushered prisoners out of the hall, Helena gathered her music sheets before approaching Reinhardt, her tone business-like. "Would it be possible to have a word with Sergeant Ripley about the next concert?"

"I'm afraid the sergeant is no longer with us. He was transferred a few days ago to a high-security stalag."

"Why?"

Reinhardt seemed reluctant to answer, his eyes sliding in an unusually shifty manner, while his voice lowered. There were guards and officers nearby. Was he warning her? That's how it seemed to Helena. Reinhardt cleared his throat.

"It sometimes happens. He had been with us a long time. The powers-that-be do not always decree that is healthy. Too much time and temptation to put escape plans, or worse, into operation. I'm sure you understand." Again, his eyes rolled.

"Of course, I understand." There was nothing Helena could do but forget the dossier and concentrate on her escape.

Reinhardt accompanied her back to his office block. Frau Huber subjected her to another search, this time insisting she strip naked, sifting through her clothing. When the officer was satisfied, Helena walked to the car, the armed guard holding the rear door open.

As she was about to climb in, she heard footsteps scurrying behind her. Michal, the piano player, with a book in hand. "Your music, Frau Schulz. Don't forget your music."

He handed her the book and she slid onto the back bench seat.

"Stop!" Frau Huber's long face stern, her bustling stride full of intent. "What is that?" She thrust her arm into the car. "The book, Frau Schulz, let me see."

"My sheet music, that's all. It's how I learn the songs."

With Reinhardt watching from the office veranda, Frau Huber flicked through the pages of notes and compositions, then, holding the book's spine, shook it vigorously. Finally, somewhat reluctantly, she handed it back.

The driver accelerated and the car slowly passed through the camp gates. A hundred yards down the road, Helena again glanced in the rear-view mirror. The black car was following.

37

THE camp was no more than 15 miles from the centre of Berlin, the first five made up of twisty roads through rural terrain, high hedgerows, crop fields of wheat and corn dominating.

Helena flicked through the music book, wrestling with a mesh of thoughts. The Gestapo must have rumbled Sergeant Ripley. That was the only explanation for his sudden departure so soon after her own stint in custody. Probably Neumann's doing. If he couldn't nail her, then he'd lash out at the camp commander.

Helena had never experienced true hate. By nature, she was an optimist. She liked to think the best of people, but the more she learned of Neumann, the happier she was to make an exception. He occupied the darkest crevices of her mind.

She made a conscious effort to banish him from her thoughts, flicking through the book she had handled on many occasions. Towards the back, her fingers detected something odd, a subtle difference. Several pages felt thicker than the rest. It could suggest damp or water damage, but the book was a prized possession, treated with reverence and care, although she had left it with Michal on her last visit to allow him to practise.

She studied one of the thicker pages in more detail and her heart began to race. There were several pencil marks on the score. At first she was irritated, wondering if Michal had ignored strict instructions not to write in the book. Writing never defaced her music scores, either pen or pencil. It was a lifetime rule, instituted by her music teacher as a child. She stroked the bottom edge of the page with her thumb. It separated marginally. Slowly, it dawned. A page containing the same score, probably from an identical copy of the book, had been stuck over the original sheet. She prised it free, just enough to reveal the page had a backing, on which were scrawled handwritten notes.

Now she understood. Sergeant Ripley, knowing he wouldn't be there to smuggle the second half of the dossier, had formed an ingenious plan to fox the increased security. She wouldn't know for certain until she arrived back at the hotel, but she was pretty sure she was in possession of the full dossier. A dossier that could send British traitors to the gallows. That's what Ripley had said. She closed the book, a smile playing on her lips, the thought of releasing the tension of the last few months and completing her mission raising her spirits. Summer days in an English rose garden came to mind, warm and heady with the fresh scent of blossom, the tang of chilled lemonade and the prospect of freedom. She closed her eyes, indulging the daydream.

A few miles further on, the driver swung the car around one of the tight bends, only to find an agricultural threshing machine blocking the road, its delivery arm extending over one of the high hedgerows. One of its wheels appeared to have stuck in a ditch, two men and a young woman in farming gear seemingly trying to set it free.

Helena's driver braked hard, jerking her back to reality. In the mirror, she noticed the black car behind also come to a halt, followed by a truck. The farm workers wielded spades, the swish of metal in earth promising progress, at least that's what Helena hoped, although she could detect little coordination in their efforts. After half a minute, the two men stopped digging. One sucked on a cigarette, the other stood hands on hips, a pronounced shake of his head suggesting the problem was not readily solvable. Finally, they broke from their huddle over the ditch. One of the farmers and the woman, both wearing bandanas, trudged towards the car, apparently to offer apologies.

"This doesn't look good." The driver voiced his frustration, revving the accelerator and swapping uneasy glances with the guard, who made to exit the car.

As he did so, the farmer casually pulled a pistol from the back of his trousers and shot the guard in the head from no more than six feet. The driver instinctively reached across the seat for the guard's rifle, but grappling for a long-barrelled gun in the confines of the car was cumbersome, and in the back Helena saw the woman quicken her stride. The bandana flattened her hair, acting as a rough disguise, but her features were unmistakable. Elke. She calmly made for the driver's side window, outstretched her right arm and shot the driver with a pistol as he squirmed. The first bullet struck him a glancing blow in the neck, the second hit him in the chest. To be sure, Elke fired a third into the body, now slumped across the front seat.

Two more shots sounded from behind. In the mirror, Helena, her body shivering in shock, brain numbed by the casual and callous nature of the executions, witnessed another gruesome episode play out, seemingly in slow motion, although later she realised that must have been a curious trick of her overloaded mind. The driver of the black car fell back in his seat and the passenger slumped forward, both with bullet wounds to the head. Walking back to the truck was a grey-haired man, wearing a beret, a pronounced limp on his right side. When he turned, she saw he was sporting a wide grin, gold tooth glistening in the late afternoon sunlight. Karl.

The next person Helena saw was Carter, strolling towards the scene from the direction of the threshing machine. He opened the rear car door and offered a hand to help her clamber out.

"What just happened? Tell me, the driver, the guard. What the hell just happened?"

"There was no other way, Helena. It had to be now or never."

"What do you mean?"

Carter put his arm around her shoulders, squeezing gently to quell her uncontrollable shakes, and led her to Karl's truck. They clambered in the back, while Karl, Elke and Felix, the *farmer* who had accounted for the camp driver, cleaned up. That involved driving the two cars with their stricken passengers through a farm gate, hiding them from the main road behind a mound of hay bales. Next, Karl jumped into the cab of the harvester, pumped the accelerator, rocking it out of the depression, before depositing it through the same farm gate. The entire incident had taken no more than a few minutes.

Karl proceeded to drive the truck with Carter and Helena in the back while Felix and Elke rode in the cab.

It took Carter some time to calm Helena enough to concentrate on the details of what had occurred. He explained that Karl had planned the ambush. He'd left a diversion sign at a crossroads behind them and Elke had placed another at a T-junction in front to guarantee they would not be disturbed. They had earlier tracked the cars to the stalag, knowing the Gestapo officers would follow. There was no other option but to take them out together.

"Did you need to kill my driver and the guard?"

"I'm sorry Helena, there really was no other option.

"What happens now?"

"First, tell me what happened at the stalag. Did you get the rest of the dossier from Sergeant Ripley?"

She told him about the increased security, the strip search, the fact that Ripley had been transferred within the last few days, and her inkling that somehow Commandant Reinhardt would not be entirely displeased to learn the Gestapo had been outfoxed.

"But if Ripley wasn't there, what about the dossier?"

She held up her music book. "Hidden in here, I'm sure." She told him about Michal, the handover, and the extra pages she'd found with hand-written notes. "It's written in code like the other half and stuck to the existing pages. If I didn't know the manuscripts so well, I would never have guessed."

"Who'd have thought? Mozart and Wagner helping the British cause."

Carter also asked about Jack Martin, but Helena had not seen any sign of activity at the solitary block.

As they debriefed, the truck pitched and swayed along country lanes for around an hour before swinging into an isolated lay-by protected by a line of tall poplar trees, south of Potsdam, on the road to Magdeburg.

Karl unclipped the tailgate, whistling gently through his teeth. He was enjoying this trip. "Okay, this is the meeting place. We're a little early. Time for a cigarette." He offered his packet around, Elke and Felix taking one, Carter and Helena refusing.

Karl and Felix smoked their cigarettes, assuming guard duty at either end of the lay-by. The night was black, low cloud scudding in from the west on a gathering depression. The prospect of air raids was minimal, but SS patrols would be out, even this far from Berlin. It would be foolhardy not to stay alert. The Gestapo pair and the stalag guards would also have been missed. Karl reckoned it would take until morning to find them, even if the search party plotted their route. The cars and thresher were well hidden, but there was always the chance the searchers could get lucky.

In the truck, the thought struck Helena that she had left Hotel Adlon for the last time. She had accepted long ago that her clandestine existence could not go on forever. But the reality of leaving Berlin, the city that had given her so much, a husband, a career, a wonderful enriching life she could never have imagined as a teenager back in Lancashire, suddenly filled her with sadness.

Carter pointed out a small leather case he'd asked Elke to pack for her. His rucksack sat beside it. He dug in his jacket pocket and handed over a lady's wallet. Inside were ID papers in the name of Frau Mary Schmid, containing Helena's photograph.

"You've thought of everything," she said.

"We're now officially man and wife. May I kiss the bride."

"I think that ship's sailed already." Helena laughed and immediately was serious again. "Where are we going? What happens next?"

Carter informed her they were waiting for a lift.

"Where to?"

"First, by road to Hanover, then train to Düsseldorf, and on to Belgium."

"But that's practically the breadth of Germany, must be four hundred miles, maybe more."

"True, but the route to Poland and Sweden is out, too much fighting. Travelling by train carries its dangers, but it's not as if we're downed airmen with American accents to give us away. We both speak fluent German and the Swiss banks have funded the Nazis in so many ways that we should be looked upon favourably. It's a good each-way bet."

Helena did not look convinced. "Why Belgium?"

"Why not? The Allies are pushing through France. They'll be into Belgium before we know it. I have contacts near Aachen, not far from the Belgium border. I used to handle a team of agents there. And who knows? We might even run into a British or American column."

"What if someone recognises me before we get there?"

"Ah." Carter had thought of that. He rustled in his rucksack, producing a silk scarf in pastel colours, functional rather than striking, the sort women wear as a hood, tied under their chin. "I wondered if you could wear this over your head. Actually, it was Elke's idea. Not exactly the height of fashion, but with your dark glasses, it could work." Helena's nose wrinkled, but she took the scarf."

"I was thinking more about the photo on the ID papers. It's the one from the Opera programme."

"We'll take that chance. Should be okay outside Berlin and the opera classes."

The sound of a diesel engine pulling into the lay-by and voices interrupted their conversation. Karl was shouting instructions.

"Looks like our lift has arrived," said Carter.

He jogged over to join Karl and Elke, who held a low intensity lamp, casting a gloomy light. The driver of the diesel truck killed his engine and eased his bulky frame out of the cab. A wide grin lit up his ruddy face as he extended a meaty forearm. Carter grabbed his hand and shook.

"Herr Schmid," said the truck driver.

"Great to see you again, Gunther."

It was the good Samaritan who had picked up Carter months ago on the road to Berlin. Carter had kept his business card, and remembered his parting shot, *"If you ever need stuff to shift, I'm your man. Just give me a call."* That's exactly what Carter had done.

They had settled on a price and Gunther had arranged his next provisions drop in Berlin to coincide with Helena's singing engagement at the stalag. Gunther asked no questions. Carter kept the reason for his transport deliberately vague. It suited both that way.

The farewells were brief. Staying in one spot for too long was not advisable. Carter shook hands with Karl and Felix, and went to hug Elke, who approached that natural personal connection with wide arms and stiff caution, rather like a stick insect selects its prey.

"Look after them, Elke."

She nodded and retracted in the same articulated manner she had engaged.

Gunther opened the back of his truck.

"Pleased to meet you, Frau Schmid," said Gunther, as he fiddled with the tailgate.

Carter chuckled. Helena shook her head, wondering how a Lancashire lass had accepted an acting role pretending to be the wife of a man who was pretending to be a Swiss banker. In the heart of Nazi Germany.

It was 200 miles to Hanover. She was tired to the point of exhaustion, nerves frayed, mind bewildered, far from convinced this exfiltration plan would work. But there was no alternative. No going back. She climbed awkwardly, reluctantly, into the truck, with the optimism of someone on the way to a firing squad.

38

THE pleasing aroma of fresh hay was in stark contrast to the toxic thoughts percolating through Neumann's mind.

He should have tortured the truth out of Helena when he had the chance. He shouldn't have allowed himself to be intimidated by Goebbels. He should have backed his own intuition. He was a bloodhound where traitors were concerned. Everyone knew that. He could smell them. Why the hell had he let her walk out of Gestapo HQ?

The veins in his neck bulged with anger as he stood in the centre of a field in the middle of nowhere, confronting the consequence of his decision.

Two Gestapo corpses lay crumpled in one car, two more dead uniformed guards in another. Around 30 soldiers peered and prodded into hedgerows, searching for culprits, looking for clues. Neumann knew the killers were long gone. The physical clues told him as much, the rigor in a couple of the corpses advanced to the stage where their arms could not easily be reclined, two of them pointing to the sky in the shape of building cranes.

The killings needed little piecing together. To Neumann's logical brain, the scenario was obvious. The convoy of stalag guards and Gestapo officers had been ambushed before it reached the urban outskirts of Berlin. The hit men were professionals. None of the deceased had managed to deploy their weapons. Their vehicles had been expertly concealed, meaning they were not discovered until the middle of the next morning, even though the non-arrival of the guards back at base had raised the alarm within an hour of the convoy leaving the stalag. Then there was the motive. Frau Schulz was gone. Proof she had been rescued from the Gestapo's round-the-clock surveillance. Proof for Neumann, as if he needed any, that she was guilty of treachery.

Neumann stared at the scene, the sheer impudence of Frau Schulz having set a challenge he could not ignore. He lit a cigarette, inhaling numerous deep drags, the infusion of nicotine aiding his focus. As he watched his men retrieve the bodies, he sifted possibilities.

Frau Schulz was responsible for smuggling coordinates out of the stalag, pinpointing targets for enemy bombers, probably over many months. Of that he was certain. Like any undercover agent, she would have gleaned much information that her handlers and their masters would deem valuable. It was inconceivable she had achieved all that by herself. There must be accomplices. A handler. A back-up team. An interruption from his deputy broke his concentration.

"Excuse me, Herr Neumann."

"Yes, Meyer." Neumann discarded his cigarette stub, grinding it into the grass.

"I've arranged for the bodies to be transferred to the mortuary. I'll ask the relevant departments to inform the families and ..."

Neumann nodded absent-mindedly, his eyebrows knitting as if in deep thought, before posing a question. "What would you do now, Meyer, if you were Frau Schulz's handler?"

"Get as far away from Berlin as possible. They know the game's up here. Time to get home for a debrief."

"Exactly what I was thinking. Tell me, Meyer, did anyone visit Frau Schulz at Hotel Adlon in the past week while our officers were watching?"

"No. The men were sure she had no visitors."

"Did she leave the hotel?"

"Only during air raids, to one of the bunkers, as well as a few short walks. One of the men would have followed her, I'm sure."

Neumann looked sceptical. "Meyer, can you speak to the manager at the Adlon. Ask if she had visitors. Not just this week, but over the last few months?"

"Of course."

Meyer turned to leave.

"And, Meyer."

"Yes."

"Not a word to anyone else."

***

The Adlon reception was teeming with SS officers. Meyer was not a fan. He considered most of them arrogant and aloof, accustomed to giving orders but shying away from heavy lifting. It seemed there was a conference scheduled in one of the banqueting halls, the clatter of boots and murmur of conversation resounding.

He pushed his way through the hubbub to the concierge's desk and showed his credentials.

"I'm enquiring about Frau Schulz."

The concierge looked quizzical. "What about her? I can ring her room, if you like."

"I think you'll find she's no longer here. We're investigating her present whereabouts, but I need to know if she had any visitors recently."

"Frau Schulz is a well-known performer, a busy one at that. I'm sure she'll have had several visitors."

"I'd like a list, please."

"As you can see, we're busy at the moment." He motioned to the chaotic din around him.

"I wasn't asking."

The concierge breathed deep and his shoulders stiffened, but, like most hotel concierges, he was shrewd and sharp-witted. He realised there was no future in crossing the Gestapo.

"Very well." He squatted behind the counter for several seconds, before emerging with a heavy, hard-backed, diary. Flicking through the pages, he arrived at entries from a month ago. Carefully, he scrolled down the hand-written items, each recording visitor activity among the civilian guests, a normal precaution in wartime Berlin. Military personnel were not included.

He wrote on a separate piece of paper, poring over the days, eventually reaching the current date. He handed the paper to Meyer. Six names. Four of them were women. One of the men was a fellow opera performer known to the hotel. The other was Herr David Schmid, the visit recorded at 7.45am, along with the fact that Frau Schulz was not in her room.

"Who wrote this?"

The concierge glanced at the initials. GW. "That would be old Gerhard."

"Get him. Now!" The order brooked no reply.

The concierge disappeared for around a minute, returning with the elderly receptionist.

Meyer launched straight in, a bony forefinger thrust at the diary entry. The receptionist slid his spectacles down his nose, bent his head and peered for a few seconds. "Looks like my writing."

"This David Schmid, what do you remember?"

"Not much. He wasn't here long. Frau Schulz had gone out early. I told him he'd missed her."

"Did you not ask what he wanted?"

"He said he was an opera lover, but he didn't look much like an opera type to me."

"What did he look like?"

"Ordinary sort of fellow. Average height. Dark hair. Wearing a hat and spectacles with black frames, I think. Or was that someone else?" The receptionist stroked his chin in contemplation before continuing. "No I'm sure it was him. I asked to see his papers. He was a banker, a Swiss banker with the Union Bank of Switzerland. I definitely remember that. Don't come across many of them these days. Spoke perfect German, bit of a harsh accent, quite distinctive."

"Thanks, Gerhard. You've been most helpful."

39

AN hour went by, then one more, and another, the truck's rattling engine slowly devouring the miles.

Carter had flattened several of the empty cardboard boxes used to carry Gunther's provisions, creating a makeshift bed for Helena. She used his rucksack as a pillow, exhaustion quickly rendering her oblivious to the pitch and sway of the ride. Carter also used the time to rest, although sleep refused to come, his mind insisting on checking and rechecking his plan, assessing and reassessing their chances of reaching the Belgium border.

He had managed to transmit a message before leaving Dolziger Strasse. He hadn't taken geographic precautions, trusting his ability to keep the message short and speedy, in the knowledge he would not be returning anytime soon, hopefully never. It simply read: *Running with The Wolf*. He replaced the transmitter under the floorboards, pulling the cupboard across. The possibility of Lieutenant Harris and his team using the information in any meaningful way was remote, but the message gave Carter a kind of closure. He'd signed off. Mission mostly successful. Almost complete. On my way home. If it were the last message he ever sent, then at least those who knew and cared for him would have some context to his final days.

After three hours, they arrived at a checkpoint, a squeal of brakes as the truck came to a halt.

Carter sensed Helena jerk awake and he leaned over, gently covering her mouth with his hand, a sliver of light from headlamps arrowing through a gap in the truck's tarpaulin cover. "Quiet." He whispered in her ear.

They could hear Gunther chattering with one of the guards, the conversation apparently affable, although details were unclear. Gunther was a frequent traveller down this route. His company was renowned for aiding the civilian war effort and the chances were he had come across the guard before. It sounded that way as the soldier waved the truck through without even a cursory check of the vehicle's contents.

"Where are we?" Helena's voice was croaky.

"Don't know, but it's pitch black again, so probably in the countryside. I guess we're about half-way. Good sleep?"

"What do you think?"

"It's not the London Ritz, I'll grant you. Not that I've ever stayed at the Ritz."

Helena wriggled into a sitting position, her back braced against the wall of the truck. They said nothing for many minutes and Carter thought she must have dozed off again.

"What happened to Bo?" The question sliced through the darkness, its plaintive nature stinging Carter.

At first, he didn't answer, hoping she may believe he had dropped off. In his mind, the jolting vision returned of Bo's splintered brain splattering against the wall in the back room at Das Bar. He could hear again the crushing sound of the gun firing. In his heart, he felt for the young children left without a father. He knew Helena loved Bo as though a favourite uncle. He had looked out for her and she for him. Their warm relationship was obvious from the first time he had seen them together, when she had tended Bo's shattered nose after the visit from the Gestapo.

She asked again. "I know you're awake. I'm not stupid."

"I know you're not."

"I've not seen or heard from him. He wasn't with the rest of the Das Bar team. You never mention him."

Carter searched for a story. He contemplated lying, pretending Bo was on a secret mission, accompanying downed airmen on a long journey to freedom. Or, fed up of dodging bombs, dealing with the Gestapo and surviving the fraught existence of the resistance, he had decided to leave Das Bar, flee Berlin, and join his family in hiding. Anything would be preferable to reality. But when he eventually spoke, the truth stumbled awkwardly from his lips as if wearing jackboots two sizes too big.

"He ... was ... a traitor, Helena."

"No. Bo? Never." She screamed in Bo's defence, blindly rejecting such outrageous calumny, before resorting to reason. "Half his family were French. He hated the Germans for starting this war. There was no way he would help the Gestapo, or the SS. No way."

"He gave them Jack. He gave them the airmen shot on the Polish border. In time, Helena, he would have given them you."

"Why? How do you know?"

"Because the Gestapo threatened his family, his wife and two small girls. They would have tortured them and then they would have killed them. You know that's what they do. Bo would have done anything to keep them safe."

"So, you killed him." There was disdain in her tone. He couldn't see her. He was glad for that, but he could imagine the scornful sneer on her face. He wanted to yell, *No, it wasn't me. I was a coward. I couldn't do it.*

Instead, he stayed silent. He had witnessed Helena hug Elke at the lay-by. Their relationship at times had been tetchy, but Helena had seen the good in the damaged young woman, and acted upon it. She had encouraged her, mentored her, remarked on her progress during her time at Das Bar, and been increasingly hopeful for her future. Carter didn't want to dash those hopes. Not now. Precious little good had come into Helena's life since he had met her, other than stress and tension, culminating in recent days in the psychological horrors at Gestapo headquarters. There was nothing to gain by leaving her with the lasting thought of Elke, her one hopeful woman-child, blasting out the brains of her *favourite uncle*.

Helena took his silence as confirmation, but, thankfully for Carter, pursued no more details. It meant the rest of the journey was strained, Carter eventually closing his eyes and succumbing to troubled sleep. There were two more checkpoints to negotiate. The first passed much like the earlier one, disinterested guards waving Gunther through, the truck barely breaking its rolling gait. The second was a close call.

Carter had insisted he and Helena stay in the back, rather than ride up front in the cab, mainly because he didn't want subjecting to unnecessary scrutiny at checkpoints. A Swiss banker and his wife travelling in a truck's cab, was unusual. They might arouse suspicion. He had to counterbalance that with a Swiss banker and his wife being found in the back of a truck, cowering behind a tower of cardboard boxes.

The final checkpoint was near the centre of Hanover, in the urban residential sprawl that had suffered terribly last October. More than 1,200 civilians had been killed in a single night of carpet bombing of the city, largely due to its strategic industrial importance. Tyres for military vehicles and aircraft were produced in three large Continental factories, other sites manufactured guns and tracked vehicles, while two large refineries produced aviation fuel and motor oils. Carter had chosen the city for none of those reasons. His interest was the sophisticated railway junction at the intersection of north-south and east-west routes. Miraculously, he had learned the hub was almost intact, apart from daily running repairs to the bombed track.

They were almost in sight of the railway station when half a dozen soldiers pulled over the truck as the first light of dawn cast a pale hue. Bombers had visited the city the previous night. Carter and Helena had detected as much from the tell-tale aroma of gas, dust and smoke.

"Pull over and open her up." The lead soldier shouted orders to Gunther.

"I'm empty. Just back from Berlin to pick up more provisions for the flak towers and bunkers. They're taking quite a pasting."

"So are we. Pull over."

Gunther manoeuvred the truck into a lay-by, its perimeter formed by rubble at the side of the road. Three soldiers stood guard, while two were detailed to search. The ranking officer checked Gunther's papers.

Carter heard heavy boots at the rear of the lorry, the searchers grappling with the securing ropes, cursing whoever had tied the knots. Both he and Helena laid flat on the truck's deck, behind boxes. It was a flimsy lair as the boxes were bound to be tossed aside during any significant search. The soldiers eventually managed to loosen the ropes enough to drag back the tarpaulin. They peered over the short tailgate, shining a torch over the truck's contents.

"Looks like empty boxes." One of the searchers shouted. "Do we need hands on?"

The officer rapped back. "Have you got something better to do? Check every box, you lazy bastards."

Carter's heart sank. He reached out, squeezing Helena's hand. She squeezed back, collective peril and impending capture eclipsing the previous awkwardness.

The tailgate swung open with a heavy clank. Boots resounded on the truck's metal floor, a torch beam zig-zagging, searching for anything of interest. Carter fingered his revolver, but he knew there was no point fighting. The odds were hopeless. He resigned himself to the predictable fate in store for a secret operative caught in enemy territory, hoping he could convince them Helena had been coerced at gunpoint. He was about to surrender when a radio crackled at the front of the truck. The officer immediately shouted orders.

"Leave that. Gas blast a couple of streets away."

The soldiers' boots thudded as they jumped down from the truck.

40

THERE was a rasp of irritation in the man's voice. "I don't need to check, Herr Meyer, we don't have anyone visiting Berlin named David Schmid."

"You're sure?"

"I've worked for the Union Bank of Switzerland for almost thirty years, most of those as head of the foreign department. I know all our travelling executives personally. There's no one called Schmid and no one fitting your description. Good day, Herr Meyer."

The phone line went dead.

Meyer marched out of the office, down the corridor, and knocked on Neumann's door.

"Yes."

Meyer entered to find Neumann standing, scrutinising the large scale map of Germany dominating his office wall, a lit cigarette dangling from his lips. Meyer related the phone conversation.

"Good work, Meyer. I knew it. This Schmid character is the handler. All we need to know now is where they've gone."

"Fastest route out of the country, I'd have thought. They know they've been rumbled. They're probably on their way to Sweden as we speak. Should I alert the checkpoints and ferry hubs? Frau Schulz is familiar to many. If they're travelling as a couple, they'll be even more recognisable."

Neumann went to flick ash into a glass ash tray on his desk, but it detached from the tip of his cigarette prematurely, landing in a little grey dust cloud on the carpet. He ground in the powder under the sole of his jackboot until it disappeared, immediately returning to the map.

With his pointing stick, he traced the route from Berlin to Sweden, via the Polish border, considering the options.

"No, Meyer, I don't think Sweden is their escape route."

"Why not?"

"Too many checkpoints around this area." He pointed again at the map. "Too much fighting. Too many imponderables with ferries, too dangerous to cross in small boats, and if they reached Sweden, how would they get back to England? No, it makes more sense to head west."

"But that would mean travelling hundreds of miles through Germany, then hundreds more through the occupied territories."

Neumann lit another cigarette. Nicotine was his crutch when he was anxious and his inspiration when he was thinking. He sucked smoke eagerly into his lungs and savoured the kick as the adrenal glands responded, raising his heart rate, sharpening his thought process.

"Frau Schulz speaks German like a native. It seems this Schmid character does too. Tell me Meyer, what's the best way to travel in Germany? Despite the war and all the bombing, what remains one of the jewels in the Fatherland?"

Meyer considered for a moment, searching for the answer that would please his master most, recalling a conversation from months before when Neumann had proudly divulged his engineer father had been a driving force in helping amalgamate the regional railways of the individual states of Germany into a powerful national enterprise following the First World War.

"The Deutsche Reichsbahn?"

Neumann smiled approvingly. "Yes, Meyer. The pride of Germany. The national railway is the country's lungs, supplying life and energy, directly responsible for so many of our triumphs. The annexing of Austria, the invasions of Poland, Denmark and Norway, the battle of France and the Balkan campaign, none of these would have been possible without the railway supplying the means of deploying huge volumes of troops rapidly."

"You think they're on a train heading west?"

"I do. West towards France or Belgium. That's where the Allies are making their push. But not a train from Berlin. Too risky. If we'd found the men they killed sooner, we could have hunted them down within hours. Driving to a station far from here makes more sense."

He pointed his stick again, slowly ticking west and south-west in the regular but staccato motion of a clock's second hand. There were so many possibilities. He alighted on towns and cities, small and big, almost all with stations and rail lines still intact, albeit with delays where bombs had damaged the track.

"Alert our regional headquarters in the west. Circulate their descriptions to all the major rail hubs. Tell the station managers to search out pictures of Frau Schulz and post them everywhere. Someone must have seen them. Someone must know where they are. We have twenty-four hours to catch them, or they'll be out of the country, gone forever."

Meyer scurried along the corridor to his own office. Neumann pinched the burning tip of his cigarette between his fingers, snuffing it out, surging adrenalin ensuring he was oblivious to pain.

***

Gunther Hagen searched out the policeman on the desk.

"I want to report two suspicious persons."

It was not an unusual occurrence and the officer, a member of the uniformed police force of Nazi Germany, waved dismissively towards a seat and told him to wait.

"No, you don't understand. They're at Hanover Station, waiting for a train. If you don't act now, they'll be gone."

Face lined and weary after a night dealing with the fall-out from yet another bombing raid, the officer again directed him to a chair.

"I want to speak to the Gestapo. This is a most-urgent matter of national security."

At last, Gunther caught the policeman's undivided attention. The Gestapo relied on a nationwide web of informers, encouraged to betray their neighbours, friends, even family members, if they suspected them of spying, harbouring Jews or enemy airmen, or acting against Nazi ideology. In some cases, the State Police paid for valuable information. Gunther had done his homework.

It was 30 minutes since he had dropped Carter and Helena at Hanover's rail hub.

He'd not asked where they were going, nor was he interested. They would have concocted some fake story, as Carter had done when they first met.

Herr Schmid? Carter was no more Swiss than he was an Olympic sprinter. Nor was Carter a banker. Gunther prided himself on his ability to read people and while Carter was convincing, there was something about their first meeting that did not gel. He couldn't put his finger on it from their conversations, although the more Gunther heard Carter speak, the more phrases reminded him of his English pen friend as a child. While they had slept in the truck's cab waiting to enter Berlin, Gunther had also felt the suspicious bulge under Carter's jacket and detected the contours of a revolver. No matter. These were dangerous times. Guns were easy to come by. As they parted, he had tested Carter on the geography of Deutsche Bank in Berlin and his answer was almost convincing, except that Gunther knew the bank had been closed temporarily that month for renovations to bomb damage. That clinched it. Schmid wasn't all he seemed.

When he received Carter's call, the money was too good to refuse. Gunther was travelling to Berlin anyway. Giving a lift to a couple was no hardship, especially as soldiers at checkpoints rarely searched his truck these days. The second part of Gunther's plan only struck him on the journey from

Berlin. The pick-up in the isolated lay-by and the heavy weaponry carried by Felix and Karl had convinced him he was carrying two spies, or at least members of the resistance, in all likelihood running for their lives. Gunther was no Nazi supporter, but the Gestapo would pay handsomely for such information. Business was business.

The policeman started to ask questions and scribble notes. He wanted descriptions of Carter and Helena, the exact location where they had been dropped. What they were wearing and carrying.

He picked up the telephone. "Gestapo headquarters, please."

***

Helena found the smell of steam engines warm and comforting. She didn't know why, but thought it might have something to do with the forge she visited with her father as a child. She remembered watching with wonder as the blacksmith hammered a horseshoe, metal glowing, the exciting scent of hot iron, fiery and peppery, on her nose.

The memory was rekindled as several engines blew off steam, white plumes rising, striking the ceiling where they hung, billowing, before dissipating like vapour from a boiling kettle, as if they had never existed.

She slipped her arm inside Carter's as they walked along Platform 5, taking their place in the queue. Their IDs stated they were a couple. It made sense to act like one.

Carter had purchased two tickets from the ticket office, where three harassed sellers struggled to keep pace with the snaking lines of disgruntled passengers. He'd been asked for ID papers, but scrutiny was sloppy. There were no problems. No questions.

After boarding, they elbowed their way along the train. Carter had supplied a travel warrant and paid extra to reserve seats in a compartment in the front carriage, as his tradecraft demanded. He swung Helena's small case into the overhead luggage rack, keeping his rucksack, containing both halves of Sergeant Ripley's dossier, by his feet, tucked under his seat.

"So far, so good." He whispered to Helena as they took their seats, across the way from an old woman travelling by herself and two middle-aged men whose dark pin-striped suits suggested they were business types.

"How many miles to Düsseldorf?"

"Quite a way. A bit shy of two hundred."

"I'll be happier when we get there." A sense of foreboding had crept up on Helena. Her shoulders shivered and she couldn't help looking around furtively, as if a Gestapo officer was hiding behind every seat.

"Act naturally." Carter whispered his advice, squeezing her hand, trying to infuse confidence.

"What's natural about any of this?"

The train jerked forward, searching for its familiar chugging rhythm. The front carriage had cleared the end of the platform when Carter glanced behind. A flurry of activity in the heart of the station concourse caught his attention. Men waving arms. He thought he heard shouts and definitely spotted the green uniforms of the ordinary police force. It was difficult to make out what was happening. The window was grimy, the action blurry, but Carter felt his stomach lurch.

"What is it?" Helena had glimpsed his worry lines.

"Nothing. The usual station chaos, that's all."

***

"A plane, Meyer. Get us on a flight in the next hour. I want to be there when we catch them." His face was hard as stone, fists clenched in the bellicose attitude of a man struggling to contain his anger. His eyes burned with menace, yet there was also a disconcerting calm about Neumann, his voice controlled, almost robotic, as if nothing could shift his focus from the job at hand.

The Hanover Gestapo had received Meyer's alert and descriptions of Carter and Helena. They had matched them with those Gunther had given to the police. A squad had raced to Hanover station along with regular officers, only to find the suspects had boarded the packed express train bound for Düsseldorf. It was then they had informed Meyer.

"Are you sure it's them?" That was Meyer's first question. The Hanover officer replied, "Almost certainly."

His second question was equally as obvious. "Does the train stop anywhere?"

"No, express all the way to Düsseldorf."

"Arrival time?"

"Impossible to say with any degree of accuracy. Scheduled arrival is eight o'clock this evening, but trains rarely run to time these days, especially over such a long journey. Depends on bomb damage on the line and whether the route is targeted."

It took Meyer almost an hour to organise a flight for himself and Neumann. The city of Düsseldorf and its airport had taken a hammering from the RAF in recent months. The runway there was severely damaged. But Meyer was creative and after a few calls he had formulated a plan. They would hitch a flight from Berlin on a FW 200 Condor, a handy passenger-cum-transport aircraft that was ferrying fighter plane spare parts to Essen airport. From Essen, they would drive to Düsseldorf, an hour's journey at most, arriving in good time to greet the train from Hanover.

"And then …," Neumann savoured the thought, "…we will see what Herr Goebbels has to say about Frau Schulz."

41

HELENA was asleep within minutes, the tension and trauma of the night combining with the soporific monotony of the train's rolling motion.

Her head lolled to one side, resting on Carter's shoulder. He allowed it to stay there, taking comfort from the peaceful rhythm of her breathing and the warmth of her presence. He shut his eyes, luxuriating for a few minutes, thinking about nothing, free of nervous trauma, bathing in the moment, pretending life was straightforward and soon he might be home.

Before long, he was back on the beach. In 1940. At the head of his column. Again.

"Okay lads, line up straight and orderly. Show everyone what we're made of. No reason to drop our standards just because we're on our way home. The next fishing boat's got our name on it."

I don't know whether I believed it. For days my men had been blowing up bridges behind them as the Germans pushed the Allies towards the sea and the chaotic retreat to the beaches ensued.

Glancing behind, all I could see were men from many nations, leaderless and defeated. Thousands of them. The mutilated. Men in shock, eyes glazed, tattered uniforms soaked in blood. In front, long lines out to sea, waiting patiently for rescue boats, chest deep in oily water from the shipwrecks offshore. All around, the stench of death.

Then the Stukas came from nowhere. Screaming, feet above our heads, spraying bullets. I hit the sand and yelled. "Down, men, down, get down." And when I rose, disbelief, terror, and an anger of which I thought I was incapable, raged within me, followed by despair. I was alone.

"Get down, get down ..." Carter repeated the phrase, panic in his tone, over and over, in English, his body writhing as if trying to exorcise the demons that had infiltrated his sleep these past few years.

Helena, awakened by his stirrings, held his head still and squeezed his face in her hands. "Look at me, Sam. It's all right, it's a dream, a bad dream." Her words, triggered by Carter's exhortation, also spilled out in English. Heads turned. Much murmuring. The two businessmen opposite glanced at each other.

Carter awoke, discarding grogginess and disorientation with remarkable speed.

"Sorry, hope I didn't disturb anyone. Happens sometimes." His voice calm, having returned to perfect German.

One of the businessmen fixed him with a doubtful expression. "You're English?"

"No, Swiss. We speak many languages. German. French. Italian. English."

"You dream in English? That's unusual."

"Not really." Helena waded in. "He's had some terrible experiences in recent years, like so many of us. Plays tricks on your unconscious mind."

The man nodded in a manner conveying sympathy and disbelief.

For the next hour, the train trundled through the German countryside, forests and fields sliding by, Helena musing on nature's inherent beauty and man's innate inhumanity. How could such a beautiful country be scarred with so much hate and division? How could mankind believe dropping high explosives on each other was an acceptable way to settle any disagreement? Why did the human race never appear to learn anything from its own history?

She pointed out a white windmill, its arms circling like an aircraft's propeller, ducks swimming on a pond in front of it. Then real aircraft, dozens of them, filled the window frame, silhouetted against a blue sky. Allied bombers, Carter observed, with protective fighters on the edges of the formation. For a few moments, anxiety rippled through the carriage. Used extensively in Germany, Belgium and France to move troops to the Fronts, trains were a legitimate military target. Yet the bombing of moving trains was inefficient. They were difficult to strike, and, in any case, German engineers were adept at removing shattered carriages from the lines and repairing track. These bombers were too high. They posed no threat. Concern eased.

The compartment was roomy and relatively comfortable, but too intimate for Carter and Helena to indulge in any serious conversation. The old woman spent her time knitting an oddly-shaped garment. It could have been a cardigan, but when Helena asked, the hissed reply was almost incoherent. The woman had no teeth.

After a while, one of the businessmen rose, stretching his arms. He slid back the compartment door and disappeared down the corridor, probably to purchase a drink from the on-board café, or use the toilet. When he hadn't returned after half an hour, Carter became suspicious.

"Back in a moment." He threw Helena a comforting glance, and swayed down the train in the same direction as the man, negotiating the overspill luggage littering the aisle of most carriages. Several children were playing a card game with their backs to the side of the train, blocking the corridor. He muttered a few encouraging words, careful to step over bare legs and knees. He bought a coffee at the café. No sign of the man. About to wander back, he caught sight of the train guard at the end of the corridor He was a big fellow with a belly that seemed to exit one of the compartments before he did. The guard was in deep conversation with a passenger. As the guard turned, Carter spotted the pin-striped suit alongside him. His heart sank. Damn! His unguarded, unconscious moment, had betrayed them. That was his conclusion and rarely did his instinct let him down. He trudged back to his own compartment, contemplating what to do next. If the man had convinced the guard of his suspicions, then Carter was certain a welcome party would await them at Düsseldorf.

The man returned to his seat a few minutes later, his studied gaze and smug expression convincing Carter he was right.

He said nothing to Helena. They were still many miles from Düsseldorf. No point saddling her with the angst his news would undoubtedly bring.

The next few hours passed without concern. The guard poked his head around the compartment a couple of times on his routine sweeps, Carter detecting an interest in himself and Helena that was not afforded the businessmen and the old woman.

***

Neumann watched the engine puff smoke rings into the night sky as it chugged towards the platform. The train was almost an hour later than expected, but that had given Neumann time to assemble his welcome party.

Meyer stood beside him, along with two other Gestapo officers he had borrowed from the Düsseldorf headquarters. A squad of six SS soldiers, four with rifles, two bearing machine guns, formed a guard along the platform. Neumann had requested the soldiers' presence for two reasons. One was to block any potential escape attempt. Carter and Helena would know capture as spies meant certain death. They had nothing to lose by running. The other reason was political. By involving the SS, Goebbels' propaganda department would be unable to cover up the decision to set Helena free from Gestapo custody. Neumann had kept a meticulous paper trail of Helena's time in custody, the details of their conversations, his suspicions, and the intervention of the propaganda minister. Not that the leading SS officer cared for any of that.

"Six soldiers and four Gestapo men to escort one woman into custody." The SS officer's sneer raised Neumann's hackles, but he took a deep breath. All that mattered was Frau Schulz's imminent capture. He didn't need to explain himself, but he did anyway.

"This is a woman who has eluded capture for many years, tricking and deceiving at every turn. A woman who has fed information to the Allies that has resulted in the deaths of many of our compatriots. This is not a woman to be taken lightly."

"A singer?" The tone of the SS man's response was no less disparaging.

"One, my friend, who would happily sing at your funeral."

They turned away from each other, shuffling frostily, neither disguising their obvious antipathy.

The train clanked and clattered into the station, shrill whistle and a hiss of steam signalling its arrival. When it stopped, the soldiers stepped forward to secure the doors, the guard emerging from the last carriage, waddling as hastily as he could muster up the platform towards the SS officer, attracted by the distinctive uniform.

"Thank goodness you're here. We have two spies on board. I think they may be English …"

Neumann interrupted. "Where are they? Which carriage? Show us."

"This way." Sweat ran down the guard's ruddy face as he trudged towards the front carriage, Neumann and the SS man in his wake. Passengers, bags and cases tugging at their arms, were trying to alight, remonstrating with the soldiers who yelled at them to stay on board. Neumann and the SS officer clambered into the first carriage following the guard, pushing their way through the throng. A few moments later the guard slid back the door to compartment six, pointing to where Helena and Carter were sitting. Except they were no longer sat there. Instead, an old woman packed away her knitting gear into a hessian bag, and two pin-striped suits stared back with startled expressions.

"Where are the man and the woman?" A frisson of alarm in the guard's tone. The businessman who had reported his suspicions spoke.

"Not seen them for twenty minutes. Maybe more. They both went to the toilet, but they can't be far, the woman's suitcase is still here." He pointed to the overhead luggage rack, Helena's leather case lay where Carter had stored it."

Neumann swung the guard around by his shoulders, the man's eyes wide with fear. "Has the train stopped anywhere since leaving Berlin?"

"No, it was slow going, but there were no scheduled drop-offs. It's an express service."

"That's not what I asked. Has it stopped anywhere, station, or otherwise?"

"Only for a few minutes."

"Where?"

The guard fumbled a handkerchief from his pocket and dabbed sweat from his brow. His cap was skewed at an odd angle and his flushed face had turned a deep shade of purple. "Not far back, in the countryside, a crane gang were moving debris from the track. They'd almost finished. The train was held for no more than two or three minutes."

"Damn you, exactly where was this?"

"I'm not sure. It was getting dark."

"Think, man."

The guard's hands were shaking. He'd expected gratitude, perhaps a reward, when he reported his suspicious passengers, not interrogation. His confused brain fought to remember the train's impromptu stop. "Around six or seven miles away. There's a line of beech trees at the start of the Aaper Forest. Quite distinctive. I remember seeing the outline as the light faded."

"For your sake, you'd better be right."

Neumann brushed roughly past the guard, motioning Meyer to follow.

42

HER shoes were flat and sturdy, quite the opposite of what she was used to wearing. For once, she was glad she had favoured pragmatism over fashion.

The drop from the carriage was around four feet, enough to break or twist an ankle if she landed awkwardly. The light had faded and the track below was uneven, packed with shale and concrete to steady the wooden sleepers. Carter had already jumped after locating the carriage's outside handle through the window to swing the door open. He had reasoned passengers would not notice, absorbed as they were by the sight of several items of heavy machinery, ducking and weaving like mechanical prehistoric creatures, as they cleared debris from the rails.

He urged Helena to sit on the floor and dangle her legs over the side of the train, before exhorting her to jump.

"Now!"

Carter's hands caught her around the waist, breaking her fall, but as she hit the ground her left leg buckled and her knee hit the sharp gravel, slicing into the skin. She stifled a yelp, fighting back nausea, at the same time motioning to Carter that she was unhurt. He then surprised her with his litheness, balancing on a metal lug protruding from the body of the train, enabling him to swing the carriage door shut. The guard would not be alerted to their impromptu departure.

He grabbed his rucksack and they headed for the beech trees, standing tall like sentries at the entrance to the forest. They hid behind a wide trunk and waited until the train chugged into life and trundled along its way, a worsening squall snagging at the steam.

"What now?" A hint of panic accompanied Helena's question. She was a city girl, accustomed these past years to luxury hotels and the traffic and bustle of London and Berlin. Survival in the countryside was an alien concept.

"First. Let's have a look at that knee."

Carter dug in his trouser pocket for a handkerchief and bent down to wipe blood from her wound. "You're lucky, it's deep, but clean. Sliced through a few layers of skin, that's all. How does it feel?"

"Don't fuss, it's fine. I've had worse shaving."

They exchanged knowing glances. "Okay, I'll wrap this around it for now. It'll help stop the bleeding." Carter double folded the handkerchief, tore strips down either side, then tied the fabric around her knee as a makeshift bandage.

Next, he dug inside his rucksack, producing a small torch and a pen. He unscrewed the top portion of the pen to reveal a miniature compass embedded in the stem, one of the inventions George Bacon had devised in his Beaconsfield office.

Carter calculated they were around 55 miles from their intended destination on the Belgium border, west of Aachen, where he was hopeful of linking up with resistance contacts capable of facilitating their onward passage. They needed to head south-west. Trains were now off limits. He considered walking but that would take many hours, require sound paths and good fortune, especially now patrols were certain to be searching for a couple of English spies answering their description.

They needed transport. A farm truck. A stolen car. Even a pair of bicycles. He wasn't fussy.

First, they needed to put miles between themselves and the train line before finding a safe place to spend the night, although it was immediately obvious there was no fast way to cover the ground. The squall had developed, the sound of lashing rain striking leaves reminding Helena of bacon and eggs sizzling in a frying pan. Not only was there no moonlight to steer their path, the terrain was heavy, unsteady under foot, festooned with thorny bushes and brambles. On top of that, they were soaked before they had travelled much more than a mile and a half.

They alighted on the cabin quite by chance. Carter had allowed a brief halt for a breather. As they sucked in oxygen, sheltering under the canopy of a maple tree, they heard the sound of rushing water close by. Carter went to investigate, discovering a swollen stream, perhaps a small river, snaking its way through the forest. He chanced switching on his torch for a few moments, the beam capturing white ripples of foamy water dodging between rocks and fallen branches. He flicked the torch to the left and it latched onto the window of a wooden dwelling, perched on the riverbank, raised on decking to allow for the occasional flood. A fisherman's cabin was his first thought, although it was a substantial building, suggesting it probably provided accommodation for several anglers at a time. He returned to the maple tree to fetch Helena, but when they tried the cabin door it was locked. Carter contemplated shooting off the lock with his revolver, but that was too risky. The sound could carry for miles, alerting anyone interested enough to investigate. Instead, he spied a pile of logs in a log store to the right of the cabin. One of the logs, around four feet long and four inches in diameter had not been chopped. It would provide a perfect battering ram.

With Helena holding the torch, Carter charged at the door lock with the log outstretched under his arm, his weight perfectly directed to provide a concerted force. The lock shattered, metal shearing, part of the door frame splintering.

"Open sesame." Carter dropped the log, a mischievous twinkle in his eyes.

Helena shook her head and entered, eager to escape the downpour. A sweep of the torch revealed a room more comfortable than anticipated. No chairs, but a wooden table occupied one corner. A fireplace dominated another wall, the surround blackened with soot. Cupboards and shelves stacked with fishing paraphernalia proved the cabin was in regular use, while pictures on the walls of several men, sporting smug smiles, posing with various types of fish, were a clue to the owners.

Carter immediately noticed a back door, bolted, and a candle lantern on a shelf, complete with a box of matches. Soft candlelight soon lent a warm and inviting hue, in contrast to the weather outside.

"Better dry off before we get the shivers." Carter ripped off his jacket and shirt, revealing a white vest underneath. He kicked off his boots and, without a thought for modesty, stepped out of his trousers, before hanging the clothing from hooks that lined one wall, probably inserted to dangle numerous forms of fishing bait.

Helena looked bemused. "You don't expect me to do that, do you?"

"Stay wet if you want to, but I'll be dry in half an hour. I know which I'd prefer. Don't worry, I won't look."

Carter was about to turn his back, but noticed a trickle of blood on Helena's leg.

He knelt down to inspect her knee. "What happened to the bandage?"

"No idea. Must have slipped off. I didn't feel anything."

He wiped the wound clean once more, this time with the bottom of his vest, applying pressure. Helena yelped, but insisted she was fine.

When he was satisfied the bleeding had stopped, Helena stripped to her underwear, following Carter's lead in hanging the clothing. As she did so, Carter searched the cupboards, alighting on a couple of rough woollen blankets, the coarse feel softened by the instant infusion of warmth.

For the next hour they sat on the floor, backs against one of the walls, blankets pulled around them like ponchos. They shared a bar of chocolate, delighting in the sweet, creamy texture, a luxury Helena had purloined from the Hotel Adlon.

Carter doused the lantern, concerned even the soft light might draw attention. The blackness was total.

"You never talk about family or friends. Why is that?" Helena's question ripped through the dark like a tracer bullet, almost physically jolting Carter. He pondered his response, before dipping into the training textbook.

"The first thing you learn about espionage is to divorce your secret life from that of family. It's the only way to keep them safe."

There was a lengthy pause, as if Helena was weighing the conviction of his answer. When she replied, her voice was measured, but tinged with sadness.

"No, it's not that. You say all the right things, as you just did. You joke and make light of everything, but your eyes betray you. Only someone who has been through unimaginable loss can recognise the same in someone else. There are signs."

Carter cleared his throat. "Such as."

"You can't sleep. You avoid getting close to people or starting new relationships. You start to isolate and detach yourself from anyone close to you. You work obsessively. Any of that sound familiar?"

Again, the pause was long, Carter's eventual reply containing a rasp of indignation. "There's a war going on if you hadn't noticed. We're all working obsessively. We've all been detached in some way from our loved ones. That's what happens in war. It's unpleasant, it's terrible, bloody awful, but it's normal."

"I know that. When I lost Siegfried, I didn't think I could go on. It was so unfair. He was a good man. For months, I cried every night. I was in despair, but I never hid my loss. I acknowledged it. I never tried to avoid it. Not like you."

For many seconds there was silence. Helena bit her lip. She doubted herself. Thought she'd gone too far. Maybe she was wrong about Carter.

Eventually, the silence was broken. Not by a grate of disagreement or a sneering cough, but by a sob. Just one, followed by a deep intake of breath and a heavy sigh.

"You're right."

"What do you mean?"

"We all handle grief differently. You had your friends and your fans. You faced your grief head on, in public, singing every night. I'm not like that. I didn't want to admit I'd lost Mary and Patricia. I wanted to keep them alive, in my thoughts, in my dreams, so I could pretend one day I could go home to them and everything would be like it was."

"What happened?" This time the pause was short, as if a dam had breached, everything Carter kept bottled up these past years spilling out in random directions like a hosepipe dancing on a lawn with the chaotic force of water passing through it.

He told her how he had arrived back from Dunkirk racked with guilt and shame, having lost so many men under his command. He had caught a train to the family dwelling in the Home Counties, yearning for the comfort of domesticity, only to walk down his street to witness three adjoining houses still smouldering from the night before, a lone fire engine standing guard beside the charred ruins, a testimony to the ferocity of the inferno that engulfed them.

"At first, I couldn't take it in. I thought maybe I'd made a mistake. Maybe it wasn't my house. I hadn't been home for such a long time, perhaps my memory was playing tricks. I'd read about that happening to survivors of the Somme in the Great War. Shell shock. Hard men who could hardly put a sentence together, who no longer recognised their wives and children, minds reduced to mush by the battering they'd endured.

"I dropped my bags and ran to the garden gate where two firemen were packing up some of their equipment. I've never felt such panic. I kept asking them, *'Where's Mary? Where's Patricia? Tell me they're alive.'* They shrugged, but I saw sadness and shiftiness in their eyes. As if they couldn't bring themselves to recount the horrors they'd witnessed. I knew then, but still I wouldn't let myself believe it. How could I be alive after all the men I'd seen die around me, and how could they be gone when they'd never hurt anyone? It wasn't fair, it wasn't bloody fair."

It was the first time Helena had heard Carter swear. She felt a tear roll down her cheek, sparked by the full extent of the emotional complexities Carter had kept hidden.

"Go on." Helena encouraged him to continue.

He described meeting the local vicar, although with no recollection of how, or when, or where. All he remembered was a vague feeling of kindness that the vicar had not wrapped proceedings in religion or sanctimony.

Instead, he had explained how Mary, soulmate, lover, confidante, best friend, and mother of his only child, was dead, killed by a stray bomb loosed by the Luftwaffe, probably with no more regard than to lighten the plane's load on its journey back to base. The family home was not on a strategic bombing route, nor close to any rail lines, airports, or munitions factories. Patricia was found lifeless in Mary's arms, as if she were trying to shield their daughter from the flames.

"A random incident, the vicar said. The sort no one can explain or justify, the only mercy that they would not have suffered as apparently it was a direct hit."

Yes, Carter hid his loss. Buried it deep a few days later, alongside his wife and child. He recognised that now. Not to deny his love, nor their existence, but to protect their memory in the darkest recess of his mind where his most precious thoughts were treasured.

"It was my way of coping." Another sob from Carter, this time brief, more controlled.

"I'm sorry, Sam. I didn't mean to pry. I didn't want to upset you, especially now. I just detected something inside eating away at you."

"Don't be sorry, Helena. I should be thanking you."

Carter felt movement under his blanket and slim fingers entwined his own, and squeezed.

The only sound as they sat in the darkness, holding hands, extracting psychological warmth and comfort from their closeness, was the rain pattering on the windows.

A sweet, soft voice, almost a whisper, broke the silence. And the melancholy strains of Lili Marlene, familiar and reassuring, filled the cabin.

43

NEUMANN hunched his shoulders against the slicing rain and readjusted his wide-brimmed hat.

"Look, Meyer. This is the spot. Matches the guard's description." He pointed to the mound of debris at the side of the rail track and the gouges in the earth caused by mechanical diggers. The machinery had gone but the diggers' calling cards were fresh.

"But where is Frau Schulz now? She could be anywhere. They may have followed the rail line and left at a convenient roadway. They may have set off across fields. Hitched a ride. Any number of things might have happened." Meyer's tone was designed to convey the hopelessness of searching a huge area of forest and countryside after dark in the middle of a storm.

Neumann was not to be deflected. He was close, maybe little more than an hour behind his prey. He could smell spies. He was sure of it. "They are here, Meyer." His hand swept in an arc, taking in the perimeter line of the Aaper Forest. "If I was running for my life on a night such as this, that is where I would head. A natural hiding place. A modicum of shelter."

"But it's a huge area and we have no dogs, no searchlights, only a tiny search party."

"Enough. You sound like that SS fool." Neumann clapped his hands to draw a line under the discussion. He was still smarting from an altercation with the SS officer at the station. Neumann had demanded the officer supply armed men and transport to launch an immediate search for two British spies.

The officer had taken exception to Neumann's zealous tone, the conversation descending into a political arm-wrestle. The officer reminded Neumann that the SS were formed to lead the New Order after the Nazis had won the war. They were members of a special club, chosen for their superiority. While he and Neumann might answer to the same boss in Heinrich Himmler, he was not about to take blind orders from a man who merely had a job, rather than a birth-right, and who made decisions on careless whims, such as chasing a female singer of no strategic significance around the country.

Neumann protested to no avail, the SS officer stomping away with a signal to his men to follow. At that point, the wise move would have been to muster reinforcements from Gestapo headquarters, but that would have taken time and with every passing minute Neumann could sense the trail growing colder.

Instead, he ordered his men to pile into their car and head back up the road adjacent to the track. They found the spot where the train stopped with ease. A simple matter of spotting signs of recent activity. No way was he giving up now.

"Let's move." Neumann ordered Meyer to take the wheel, while he sat in the passenger seat, the other two Gestapo operatives hunched in the back. A dirt track, probably used by walkers or tourists in more peaceful times, led towards the Aaper Forest, the car's headlights struggling against the lashing rain to illuminate the contours of the hill leading to the trees.

Fifty yards before they reached the forest perimeter, the incline and the waterlogged conditions forced the car to slew to one side. The engine complained. Meyer revved the accelerator, the car slid even further, slithering to a stop accompanied by a metallic wrenching sound. Neumann clambered out to find the nearside front wheel buckled against a rock. The car was going nowhere fast.

"Scheisse!" Neumann spat out his frustration.

"What now?" Meyer said.

"Chase them down on foot. This track probably goes no further than the trees anyway."

Meyer popped open the boot, handing two rifles and ammunition to the local officers, while he and Neumann grabbed a pistol each. Four powerful torches followed.

They tramped into the forest, Neumann ordering the locals to sweep to the left, while he and Meyer panned right. By keeping 50 yards apart, Neumann reckoned they could search a significant swathe of the forest while staying in contact. If his hunch about the forest was correct, he also had the element of surprise. His quarry had no idea he was on their tail.

Taking meticulous care, it took an hour to travel the first mile. A swampy smell of decay hung heavy, exacerbated by the sodden conditions. There was a false alarm when one of the Gestapo men came across the remnants of an old camp site. The sides of a small tent billowed in the squall and tin cans blew around the area, rattling against the rocks. Neumann signalled the others to surround the site and one of the rifle bearers inched forward to investigate. Eventually, he poked his rifle, followed by his torch, into the gap in the tent's front flap. A sleeping bag gave the impression of a body and there were remnants of food packaging, but it was soon obvious this was not a recent site. Probably an old resistance refuge for stranded airmen.

They assumed their positions once more, trudging through the undergrowth, torch beams sweeping back and forth, illuminating all manner of trees, branches pitching ghost-like in the wind.

If anything, the rain fell even heavier, tree canopies collecting pools of water before cascading in sudden deluges on anything or anyone below. An hour went by, then another, the mood increasingly less confident as dampness seeped through their clothing and drained into their psyches. Meyer was deliberating how to raise his doubts when an object caught his eye. His voice echoed through the darkness. "Here, I've found something."

Neumann and the others tracked sideways, honing in on his position. Meyer pointed his torch. Stuck to a bramble, thorns forming tiny tent pegs, a white piece of fabric, stained in places, flapped in the breeze. Neumann ripped the torn handkerchief from its anchor. He nodded three or four times, as if ticking boxes in his head

"Blood, Meyer, wouldn't you say? Fresh blood at that." The question did not require a response. Neumann's jutting jaw and smug expression said it all. His instinct had been correct.

Not only was he on the right trail, he was almost in touching distance.

44

A BEAM of light streamed across the ceiling. To Carter's sleep-fogged brain, it appeared far away, like the twinkle of a distant ship at sea.

A few seconds later another beam danced across the far wall of the cabin, this time jolting Carter awake, a nervous lurch of tension in his stomach. He nudged Helena in the ribs, at the same time clasping a hand over her mouth. Her eyes flicked wide, radiating fear.

Carter signalled for silence and eased into a standing position, away from the windows, at an angle that afforded a clear view in front of the cabin, but would not betray his own position. His heart sank.

Four torch beams travelling in measured fashion towards them, in the thick of the forest, but no more than 100 yards from the cabin. Having led numerous search parties, he recognised the protocol. The pedantic tread, spread of personnel, sweeping motion of the light source. These were not resistance fighters, nor anglers returning from a day's fishing.

"Quick, we need to get out." His whisper urgent as he grabbed his clothes off the hooks and pulled them on.

Helena hitched herself against one of the timber walls. She stepped towards her own garments, immediately crumpling with a thud and a curse that Carter hoped the lashing rain would camouflage.

"What is it?" Carter dropped to his haunches.

"My damned knee. It's stiffened up. Must be worse than I thought."

"Let me help." He swung a forearm under one of her armpits and heaved her to her feet. "Try again."

Once more Helena attempted to put weight on her damaged leg and again she let out a painful squeal as it buckled. The light beams grew brighter.

"I'll carry you." Carter's tone increasingly desperate.

"Don't be an idiot. We'd never make it. You go. Go!"

"I'm not leaving you."

"Yes, you bloody are." Fiery determination and cold reason in Helena's voice. "You've got the dossier. That's why we're doing this. The reason we're here, in the middle of a godforsaken forest, in a country that's gone to hell in a hand cart. If you don't get the dossier out, this has all been for nothing. I'm not having that."

He hated himself for agreeing, but he knew she was right. The lights were almost upon them, the beams converging as the hunters targeted the same spot. If Carter and Helena surrendered, as sure as night follows day they would be interrogated, tortured and shot. The dossier would be lost forever.

Carter's training emphasised the pragmatic. The big picture. War was squalid. At times it involved the deaths of thousands on the battlefield, soldiers soaked in honour and blood, fighting for a just cause. At others, it was fought on a pitifully small scale, like now, an officer with a grudge, a woman with a sense of right and wrong. Big or small scale, however, almost always there was a waste of innocent lives.

The depressing thought danced in Carter's mind as he swung the rucksack containing the documents over his shoulder, bent down on one knee, and thrust his revolver into Helena's hand. He tilted her neck and kissed her full on the lips, before pulling away. "I've met a lot of agents, many of them fools, liars, traitors or drunks, if I'm honest. But never one as brave as you, Helena. If only we'd met in another life."

"If only ... now go!" She pushed him away.

Carter unbolted the cabin's back door and slipped out into the wild night, head spinning, a terrible ache in his heart.

***

The waiting was worst. Not knowing who or what was outside. The torch men were in no hurry. Their beams continued to straddle the cabin, searching out every nook and cranny.

Helena sat on the bare boards, out of sight, cursing her knee, watching the surreal light show on the cabin's walls. The dancing beams reminded her of opening night at the Berlin State Opera, peering into powerful stage bulbs at an audience cloaked in blackness.

She had managed to wriggle into her skirt and blouse, and pull on her damp overcoat. Her ears strained to listen to whispered voices, the language undoubtedly German, but the words clipped and indistinct.

She tried to stay positive. Perhaps the men were from the local police. Maybe searching for downed airmen. The ruined region of Düsseldorf had suffered as much as any German city at the hands of Allied bombers. Barely a night had passed in recent months without air raid sirens sounding. Maybe, just maybe, the search party had nothing to do with her.

Yet reality kept crushing hope. In response to the ambush following her final performance at the stalag, she knew her description would have been circulated to every station, airport and police force in the land. The train guard would have reported the *Swiss couple* missing. It was hardly surprising the authorities were on her tail.

Her fevered musing was interrupted when the light show ceased. Everything went dark, blacker than ever. Her night vision struggled to respond. The thud of a footstep vibrated on the decking outside, so close and determined that a shiver of fear ran up her spine. Instinctively, she curled up with hands protecting her head. More heavy scuffling, then the crack of wood splintering and the zing of bullets ricocheting around the cabin. For what seemed like more than a minute, but in fact was a few seconds, Helena's senses were overwhelmed. Paralysed. She didn't think it was the end, but only because she couldn't think. A rush of wet air stung her face as the door swung open and a man's voice bellowed.

"Don't move."

She had no intention of moving as torchlight flooded the cabin. Propped on one elbow, she raised a hand to shield her eyes. Her nostrils detected the smell of men's sour sweat and sodden clothing. Then he spoke, and all lingering hope evaporated.

"Frau Schulz. I'm so pleased to keep my promise." Neumann, silhouetted in the shattered doorway, a triumphant grin in place. He tipped his head and a trickle of rainwater dripped from his hat, pattering on the wooden floor. "I said we would meet again and here we are for another friendly chat. I don't think Herr Goebbels will be advocating on your behalf this time."

Helena remained silent, but squirmed into a sitting position, her back against a wall.

Neumann noticed blood seeping from the wound on her knee. "Nasty gash. Is that why your so-called Swiss friend, Herr Schmid, left you behind? Not very gallant of him."

"He's more of a gentleman than you'll ever be." Helena's reply dripped venom. She saw no point in denying Carter's existence. It was obvious Neumann must have tracked them from Hanover, while countless witnesses on the train would testify that they were travelling together.

Neumann motioned to Meyer to fire up the lantern, flooding the cabin in soft light, in contrast to the harshness of the torches. He also ordered the rifle-carrying officers to stand guard outside, a command they reluctantly obeyed considering the rain persisted, albeit lighter than before. Leaning against the table top, Neumann made himself comfortable, jettisoning his hat on one of the angling hooks and wrenching off his sodden overcoat. He lit a cigarette, snuffing the match flame between thumb and forefinger, taking two deep drags, before fixing Helena with a sinister stare.

"Who does your banker friend really work for?"

Helena's lips tightened.

"Did he kill two of our men and two prison guards in Berlin?"

Again, Helena refused to acknowledge the question.

"Where is he now?"

No answer.

Neumann showed no frustration. He was accustomed to dealing with captives who did not comply with his initial interrogation. He sucked on his cigarette, blowing smoke in concentric circles.

"There are two ways of dealing with this. You can answer my questions. I'm sure you understand that would save a lot of discomfort. Or you can stay silent and force us to improvise with our usual interrogation techniques. That would involve much more discomfort."

Helena fashioned a look of contempt. "What does it matter? You're going to kill me anyway."

Meyer was standing by the window, shuffling his feet. He was uncomfortable. He had been for some time. He viewed Neumann's relationship with Helena as an obsession unbecoming of a senior member of the Gestapo. Neumann had rank and file members to do his dirty work. Lots of them. Instead, he chose to fly across the country on a whim, chasing two suspects through the countryside in the dead of night in filthy weather. It made no sense, except that Neumann was playing a dangerous game. That was becoming increasingly apparent. He wasn't out here in the Aaper Forest to catch enemies of the Fatherland. He was here to make a point, to prove Goebbels wrong. To take on one of the Führer's trusted aides. In Meyer's estimation, that was way past dangerous. It bordered on suicidal. Yet Neumann was a difficult man to control, one who neither sought, nor took, advice.

Meyer tried anyway. "Perhaps we should return to Düsseldorf and continue the interrogation there? I'm sure Frau Schulz would remember more with dry clothes and time to think"

"When I need your counsel, Meyer, I will ask for it." Neumann's accompanying glare told his deputy to back off. "Frau Schulz is not in need of dry clothes or thinking time. I would like to know what made her become a spy and act against the country that gave her everything. A career, fame, money, the adulation of so many, including those in the highest echelons."

Helena despised him for pointing that out. Hated him because she recognised the truth in his words. Germany had given her everything she ever desired as a young girl growing up in a cotton-mill town in Lancashire. She would never have risen to national prominence as a singer in England. She knew that. Her soprano range was ideally suited to the epic productions of the Berlin State Opera and the music that the Führer and his acolytes promoted. She was in the right place at the right time, or at least that's what she thought when her husband, Siegfried, had lured her to Berlin as a young woman with the promise of stardom.

"I love my life in Germany, but I hate what the Nazis have done to this beautiful country. To the Jews, to culture and music. The Führer and his administration will go down in history as the most wicked rulers the world has ever seen. You, and people like you, are part of that. Without the Gestapo generating fear in homes across the land this dictatorship would have fallen years ago. The trouble with people like you is you can't think for yourself. You believe what you're told to believe and if that involves genocide then so be it."

For a moment, Neumann looked impressed. He was not used to being harangued, especially by a woman whose eloquence matched her beauty. His admiration did not last long. Flicking his cigarette to the floor, he stubbed out the end under his boot. A metaphor, perhaps, for what he had in mind.

Suddenly, he was tense, leaning forward, towering over Helena, who sat with her legs underneath her, jaw jutting in defiance, desperate to show no fear although her terror already had surfaced unseen in a warm trickle between her thighs.

"I've heard enough of this drivel. I'll not be lectured by someone who betrays whichever side is convenient." Neumann rose from the table and drew the pistol from his belt. He towered over Helena, who had concealed Carter's revolver behind her back, yet realised she could never grab and fire it undetected, or in time.

"One last chance." Neumann outstretched his right arm and pointed the gun at Helena's head. "Who are you working for, and where is the *Swiss man*? Three seconds. Speak now, or you'll never sing again."

Helena's eyes were transfixed on Neumann's index finger, gently rocking back and forth on the trigger. He started to count in his clipped, soulless manner. "One ...two ...". She heard him, but her mind was numb. She was used to singing in tune, controlling her breath, hitting the high notes. She had never undergone survival training, apart from a few generic tips from Jack Martin. She had not been taught coping mechanisms as a captured spy in enemy territory, or delaying tactics when faced with life or death situations. Hell, she had never even fired a gun.

"Three!"

45

THE shot sent Carter into panic. His body shook, his mind struggled to reason. *Why shoot Helena now? It was too soon. The Gestapo interrogated and tortured. Took delight in prising secrets. Then they killed. Shooting Helena before they had extracted information about her contacts at the stalag made no sense.*

Yet all Carter could think of was her crumpled body, cold and lifeless, on the cabin floor.

From his vantage point amid a rhododendron bush around 50 yards away, he could see Neumann playing with his black pistol, blowing smoke from the barrel. He could see Meyer, too, but only from the back, tall and statue-still.

With the aid of his compass, Carter had tracked north, south-west and due east, meticulously counting his paces to arrive at his present position, facing the front of the cabin.

Discovering two guards bearing rifles either side of the building, occupying wide stations to allow a clear field of vision, he had settled down to plan his attack.

There was one major problem. On his departure, he had thrust his revolver upon Helena. It had been an instinctive decision to give her the opportunity to end any interrogation on her terms. On reflection, it had not been the wisest move. The chances of her taking out even one of the Gestapo team were not favourable, given that she had no combat training. It also meant he no longer had a gun, while the Gestapo team had four.

Think, Sam. Think. All that training as a special forces' operative. Learning how to act and react under pressure when time was short and stakes high. Something Carter had excelled at on punishing training days in the private hamlet of Achnacarry in the Lochaber region of the Scottish Highlands before being accepted as an MI9 agent.

Yet that shot changed everything.

He no longer thought or cared about himself. Nor was his mission to deliver the dossier of paramount importance. All he wanted was revenge. For Helena. Minutes ago he was planning a rescue. Now his soul burned with murderous intent.

Training kicked in. First, he had to neutralise the guards. Their positions told him they were well versed in strategy, yet there was a disgruntlement about their demeanours which gave him encouragement. Hunched against the miserable weather, one of them sat on a large boulder by the stream, puffing on a cigarette, the other stood stamping his feet to generate circulation under the canopy of a beech tree. Neither of them had shown much interest when the shot was fired, as if inured to the workings of Gestapo bosses. Crucially, neither could see the other, their line of sight obscured by the angle of the cabin.

Carter made his decision, peeling off to his left where the guard was smoking. He moved swiftly, soft footsteps taking him back through the trees so he could approach the guard from behind. He contemplated searching for a heavy branch to act as a club, but the chances of taking out the guard with one blow were slim and any commotion would seal his fate.

He crept forward to within five yards. The guard sucked hard on his cigarette, savouring one last drag before flicking it into the stream. That was another reason for taking this man first. The rushing water would smother any sound.

Falling to one knee, Carter removed a lace from his boots, one Felix had supplied back at Das Bar when kitting out the downed airmen.

He knotted the lace at either end and pulled it tight with his fists, testing the tension of the steel-reinforced garrotte. It felt good. The guard cursed as he rose tentatively from the rock, as if the damp had penetrated arthritic bones, using his rifle as a crutch to help him stand.

Carter was on him before he became fully upright, flinging the garrotte around his neck and pulling as tight as his strength would allow. He felt the ligature bite immediately, blood oozing from the man's neck, the guard gurgling in tune with the babbling stream. It was all over in seconds, the man's writhing ceasing as the ligature scythed through muscle and bone, crushing his windpipe. His body went limp and Carter lowered it to the ground, all the while his ears straining for any sign that his actions had been detected. There was none.

The cabin acted as a shield as he proceeded to snake around the back towards the other rifle carrier, his plan hinging on both guards being neutralised before Neumann and Meyer exited the cabin. Thick-set and taller than the other, this man was a tougher opponent, but fortune, the inclement weather, and the element of surprise, favoured Carter. As he sneaked into position, the guard laid down his rifle, stooping to squeeze his waterlogged trousers. Carter seized his chance, springing forward, locking the garrotte in place, attempting to deactivate the second guard in similar fashion to the first.

This time the man took longer to succumb, his bulk cumbersome, awkward to overwhelm. The guard reached behind him, clawing at Carter's clothing, kicking backwards, snatching at his face, his lunges wild and desperate as life ebbed. One grab secured a tight hold on Carter's hair and for a few brief moments it seemed he might yield as the guard wrenched follicles from his scalp. Yet, somehow, Carter clung on, his grip on the garrotte tightening, his fingers bleeding with the effort, until eventually the pain in his scalp subsided as the guard ceased to struggle. It was only then, when once more he could hear the babble of the stream and feel the sting of the rain on his cheeks, that the enormity of Carter's savagery eclipsed the endorphins released by the thrill of the hunt. Feeling a man's pulse stop beating, his muscles and tendons twitching, jerked him back to reality. He felt sick, almost vomited. Exhausted by the effort, he collapsed on his back, lying in the mud by the guard's body, sucking in oxygen.

For a few fleeting moments, as always in times of stress, he revisited his recurring nightmare. Back on that Dunkirk beach with the rest of his men on the day the Stukas came. A sense of futility almost overcame him, probably would have done if the thought of Helena, dispatched so ruthlessly, hadn't steadied his resolve.

He staggered to his feet, grabbed the guard's rifle and made for the cabin's rear entrance, the one he'd exited an hour before after pulling the door shut, wedging it in place with a rock so it appeared bolted to any casual observer. He listened at the door, the rushing stream muffling the sound of German voices. But he distinctly heard laughter. It was the thought of merriment that lit his fuse.

Military strategy, allied to basic common-sense, told him to track back to the front of the cabin, stay in the open, and wait for the two officers to emerge from light into the dark of the night where he could pick them off with ease. But he didn't. Instead, he took the direct, some might say foolhardy option, displacing the rock and charging into the cabin with rifle raised ready to fire. No thought of taking prisoners. Kill or be killed.

Meyer was his first target, standing by the far wall, holding a pen and notebook, an expression of shock and bemusement on his face. Carter fired two bullets and saw them strike, one in the chest, the other in the neck. Meyer toppled slowly, seeming to implode within his own footprint, like a tall chimney in a controlled demolition. Carter swung towards Neumann and immediately wished he had followed the military textbook. The rifle was unwieldy in the confined surroundings and the Gestapo officer was ahead of him, reacting a split-second quicker to the first shots.

Carter saw Neumann raise his black pistol and dived for the floor, anticipating the thud of bullet into meaty flesh. The crack of the shot bruised his ears, but he felt nothing. He rolled sideways, readjusted his rifle, searching for his target, wondering how Neumann had missed at such close range. Then he saw him, the Gestapo man's body straddling the table top, arms swinging, mouth and eyes open forming a mask of disbelief, a single bullet hole in his forehead.

Sat hunched on the floor in the corner of the cabin, Helena was shaking, Carter's revolver in both hands. Their eyes met, and Carter experienced an emotion that transcended relief. A visceral outpouring of such intense yearning that his lower lip trembled and a single tear ran down his cheek.

"Helena, you're alive. I thought ... I thought ..."

Helena tried to mouth something, but the words wouldn't come. Instead she sobbed, her shoulders heaved. Carter, not trusting his shaking legs, crawled on his knees to her, enveloping her in a comforting embrace. Still she couldn't speak. They sat like that, his nose buried in her hair, her head resting on his chest oblivious to the slime and mud on his sodden clothing, for several minutes, rocking gently back and forth, the tightness of their embrace inducing calm. Eventually, she spoke.

"What kept you?"

They both laughed, the normalcy of the glib phrase penetrating the wickedness of a wild and dramatic night.

"But I heard the shot, what happened?" Carter was eager to learn the details.

"I thought Neumann was going to kill me. He was on edge, impatient. He pointed his gun at my head, giving me three seconds to tell him about you. He counted down, too quick for me to even think. At three, he shot a bullet so close to my head I thought I'd been hit. My brain was pounding. I couldn't hear properly for minutes. Still can't. He was playing with me, enjoying my fear."

"The bastard."

"He'd have killed me with the next bullet, for sure. But I didn't tell him anything, honest." Helena's tone was earnest.

"I know, I know. I knew you wouldn't."

"How did you get past the guards?"
"Put it down to good luck, and clever friends."
"Who?"
"Never mind, just colleagues good with gadgets. Come on, we'd better get moving."

***

They retraced their steps in the forest, Helena limping, Carter half-carrying her over the roughest terrain. They reached the spot where Neumann had abandoned the Gestapo car and Carter attempted to restart it. Stuck solid.

As there was no chance of escaping without transport, Carter left Helena in the shelter of the car and set off down the road adjacent to the track, jogging 200 yards, walking 100 yards, eating up the ground, using his torch sparingly, always on the look-out for a vehicle.

A few miles outside Düsseldorf, he came upon a small hamlet, no more than 10 houses. Trucks filled the driveway of some. Outside another, a black car was parked. It caught Carter's eye, mainly because it was a Mercedes 770, one of the most popular cars in Germany in the past decade, the Führer had been known to drive one himself with customised bulletproof windscreen.

It was the sort a Swiss banker might drive, thought Carter.

Not for the first time that night Carter got lucky. He tried the driver's door and it opened. Now came his special training. He fiddled in his jacket pocket for Bacon's compass pen. By turning the top anti-clockwise it revealed a screwdriver head with which he could remove the steering column panel, revealing a bundle of wires. With his torch between his teeth, and one eye on the front door of the house the car belonged to, he isolated the yellow, black and red wires, using the sharp screw head to cut them. It was fiddly, but with patience and feel he intertwined the wires, forming a connection to bypass the job of the key, completing the circuit between the battery, ignition and starter motor. The engine purred into life. There followed an anxious moment as he sought the fuel gauge. Almost full.

Perfect. Ten minutes later he picked up Helena and headed for Belgium.

"I could get used to this." Helena was impressed with Carter's choice of motor.

"I thought you were used to the good life."

"Not nearly as much as you might imagine. Just because I have a room in the Adlon. Or should I say, had?"

The play on tense somehow brought home the enormity of the last few hours. Helena went quiet. She was heading out of Germany, her country of choice, her nation of opportunity, probably for the last time. As much as she couldn't wait to see the back of the last few wretched years, it was a sobering thought.

They made good time. The roads were in surprisingly good condition and they drove for an hour before meeting the first road block. Carter handed over their papers.

"Herr Schmid." The soldier read his name out loud.

"And Frau Schmid." Carter offered their relationship before the soldier had seen Helena's papers.

"Very well. All seems fine. Better stay on the road south, well away from Aachen. There's a monumental fire-fight kicking off there right now." The soldier handed back the papers, but while doing so shone his torch inside the car. The beam alighted on Carter's trousers, caked in mud, although most of it had dried.

The soldier's tone was stern. "What happened here?"

"Had to change a wheel a few miles back. Filthy night, but it had to be done." Carter's explanation was swift, textbook succinct.

The soldier nodded, waving them through.

They did as the soldier suggested, bypassing all roads to Aachen, driving another hour or more before reaching the Belgium border. It was still German-held territory, but Carter felt somehow safer when they sailed through another checkpoint, the border guards uninterested in their papers, into an Allied country.

Driving off the road, they stopped in a clearing, a line of trees masking the car from view.

"Let's try to get a couple of hours sleep." With adrenalin dissipated, the night's exertions had wearied Carter to the point of exhaustion. He lay back in his seat, head resting on the leather upholstery. The night dark as pitch.

After a minute or so, Helena ordered her thoughts. "Thank you, Sam, for everything tonight. I'll never forget what you did. Without you, I daren't think what might have happened. You saved my life."

She waited, listening in the blackness for his reply. It came in the form of a gentle snore.

***

Carter awoke with a start, a metallic knock on the car window. A rap of authority.

Dawn was breaking, the air damp and the light watery, as so often after a big storm. He could sense activity all around. Heavy boots stomping, doors clanking. He reached for his revolver, blinking bleariness from his eyes. Soldiers with rifles, armoured vehicles. His heart sank. The Mercedes was surrounded.

He heard a shouted order. "Out of the car. Now!"

Helena woke beside him. "What's going on?"

"Out of the car. Hands above your head." The order sterner this time, the soldier's face pressed against the windscreen, young, fresh and determined. For several moments neither Carter, nor Helena, could determine why the order was strange.

Then it dawned. It was barked out in English, laden with a lazy drawl, like characters in films from across the Atlantic.

Carter dropped his gun in the foot-well, slowly opened the door, and clambered out. Helena exited her side too. Around 20 soldiers, in drab olive uniforms, many dragging on cigarettes, looked on.

"Well, what do we have here?" The lead soldier's demeanour changed from concern to curiosity.

"We're English," said Carter.

The soldier gestured towards his colleagues. "Say howdy to the Ninth Infantry Division of the American First Army."

Helena's shoulders relaxed. "Thank God."

46

September 1944. London.

SHE fidgeted with the crucifix on a gold chain around her neck. She always did that when she was nervous.

It was a long time since Helena had been in England and she had never visited the War Office. A secretary from Brigadier Pritchard's department had booked her into the Ritz on Piccadilly the night before and she had spent the morning familiarising herself with the topography of wartime London. She sauntered past the Houses of Parliament, continued down the Embankment, stopping to marvel at Tower Bridge and the bomb-damaged St Paul's Cathedral. In many ways, it was not dissimilar from Berlin. A meandering river, ruined buildings, shattered glass, debris, the taste of dust, a wasteland of destruction with the odd vision of architectural beauty standing proud and undefiled. Survivors amid the carnage. Of course, London also had the English accents Helena had missed so much this past decade.

Her walk took her full circle, arriving at the junction of Horse Guards Avenue and Whitehall on time at 1pm, only to find the Brigadier running late. Shown to his office, she sipped tea for 20 minutes from a China cup. A shortbread biscuit lay untouched on the accompanying saucer.

The Brigadier arrived babbling apologies.

"Frau Schulz. So sorry to keep you waiting. I hope my secretary has taken good care of you."

"Yes, of course. Please call me Helena."

The Brigadier motioned for Helena to sit with him at the head of the conference table and a couple of minutes later three others entered the room and took seats. The first was Lieutenant Harris, followed by the Brigadier's secretary carrying a notepad and pen. Carter was the last to enter, throwing Helena an encouraging smile.

The Brigadier kicked off proceedings. "Good news this morning. I hear the American First Army has finally taken Aachen, the first German city to fall to the Allies. A bloody battle by all accounts, best part of six weeks of fighting with the loss of many brave men, but there's no stopping us now. The Nazis' days are numbered."

"Amen to that." Lieutenant Harris rarely missed an opportunity to agree with the Brigadier.

"Let's get down to business." As the Brigadier spoke, he patted a brown folder in front of him, the letters 'TS' emblazoned in red ink in the top left-hand corner. Even Helena, a novice in the complexities of military jargon, could work that one out. *Top Secret.*

"The cryptanalysts have deciphered the coded dossier you delivered and I have read it. I have to say it's a damning catalogue of British treachery. If the named traitors come before a court of law, and I'm sure one day soon they surely must, this dossier will see men hanged. It confirms our suspicions that the Germans were trying to form a unit comprised of disaffected British soldiers and airmen in prisoner of war camps, many of whom have connections with the British Union of Fascists. They would be known as the British Free Corps, the intention being to train them to fight the Russians on the Eastern Front. Thankfully, we believe only a handful have turned traitor, but it's important to honour the thousands of soldiers who fought and died so bravely in the cause of freedom by ensuring all traitors face justice."

Helena held up a finger and the Brigadier signalled permission to speak.

"What about Sergeant Ripley? Do we know what's happened to him? He's the bravest of all."

"Currently, we don't know the whereabouts of Ripley, a courageous and resourceful man, as you say. We believe the Germans have moved him out of Berlin, probably to a high-security prison somewhere in Upper Silesia. It's likely he has faced interrogation, but his dossier confirms names and supplies the vital evidence to convict, even in his absence. There is one more thing, Helena."

"Yes."

"Would you be prepared sometime in the future to testify in court about what you saw and who you saw in the stalag?"

"Of course."

The Brigadier's tone became more grave. "None of this can be mentioned to anyone at any stage, not friends, confidantes, lovers, or family. Everything is covered by the Official Secrets Act, not to be taken outside these four walls. I expect the statute of limitations to last for many decades. Do you understand?"

Helena's nod was almost imperceptible, her lips tight, eyes sad. She knew secrecy and silence meant she could never explain her actions to her family, silence that would be taken as certain proof that she harboured Nazi sympathies. She faced life as a pariah in the country she loved. She could never go home to her beloved Lancashire. The realisation brought mist to her eyes.

"I'm sorry, I need to hear you, Helena."

"Yes. Yes. I understand."

The Brigadier turned to Carter. "When you were last in this office, you promised you would deliver the truth. You have been as good as your word. Tell us how you came across Helena and how you managed to escape Berlin with such vital information."

Carter proceeded to recount the story of the past nine months. Das Bar. Meeting Bo Schneider. Liaising with the resistance. Learning that Helena was The Wolf. The sighting of Jack

Martin in the stalag. The smuggling of Sergeant Ripley's dossier. And the final escape from the clutches of the Gestapo.

He spoke for almost half an hour, the Brigadier's secretary scribbling a verbatim note of proceedings.

When Carter had finished, Brigadier Pritchard signalled to Lieutenant Harris. "I think it's time."

Harris rose from his seat and left the room. A minute or so later he returned, followed by a man in a suit that hung loosely from his shoulders as if several sizes too big. He wore a stubbly beard flecked with grey and while his demeanour bore the gaunt hallmarks of a man who had experienced harsh times, his eyes twinkled with promise of fun and mischief. Helena glanced up as the men entered. Her gasp was audible.

"Jack. Oh, Jack … I thought you were …" She jumped out of her seat and skipped around the table, flinging her arms around his neck, hugging him tight as tears flowed down her cheeks.

After many moments, Jack Martin gently prised her from his grasp and took a seat, stretching to shake Carter's hand across the table.

"Long time no see." Jack spoke first.

"Shame about your crummy flat."

"Wasn't that bad. Did you find the Johnnie Walker?"

Carter chuckled. "Didn't last long."

Lieutenant Harris interrupted to explain that Jack Martin had been held in solitary confinement in the Berlin stalag as a suspected spy after being captured in Grunewald Forest. He had been saved by the Czech airman he had been carrying. When the airman had been shot, Jack had stumbled, struck his head on a rock rendering him unconscious underneath the body of his dead comrade. The SS had dragged him away, soon to discover that he was the secret agent given up by Bo Schneider.

Such characters were routinely executed by the Nazis. But, in a fortuitous collision of opportunity and timing, the Germans were eager to trade him for a captured agent of their own. Following a few nervy attempts at a handover, Jack had eventually returned to England, via Poland, a few days after Helena had spotted him in the stalag.

As the lieutenant spoke, Carter watched Jack, noticing his eyes never left Helena. A couple of times they shared meaningful glances across the table, their faces breaking into spontaneous smiles as bright as the autumn sun. Carter was surprised at his own reaction. He should have felt joyful. He knew that. But his head was filled with dark thoughts. Somehow, he felt vulnerable, as if his relationship with Helena, whatever that might be, was under threat.

A few minutes later, Brigadier Pritchard brought the meeting to a close, informing Carter and Jack Martin that a formal departmental de-briefing would take place in the coming weeks.

"I hope to see you again soon, Helena. In the meantime, thank you once again for your courage and for your service. Enjoy our hospitality and hopefully you can catch up with family."

Helena felt a shudder run up her spine.

***

There was a blustery breeze blowing when they emerged from the large neo-Baroque building that housed the War Office on Whitehall.

They stood on the corner under one of the distinctive domes, Carter and Jack with hands thrust deep in overcoat pockets against the chill, Helena, shivering slightly in her cotton dress, positioned between them.

The conversation was a shade awkward. What do you talk about when everything you've done and said of any note for years is governed by the Official Secrets Act? They swapped details on where they were staying and Jack enquired about Max, his blind neighbour from Dolziger Strasse.

He also asked if Helena was still singing. She didn't reply, the thought hijacked by the diesel rumble as a convoy of big Army trucks trundled by, although Helena had already come to terms with the fact she would probably never sing professionally in public again. Too many memories of nasty men and Nazi coercion.

After five minutes containing polite mundanities and awkward shuffling of feet, Carter announced he'd better be going. He wasn't good at small talk.

"I'm off, this way." He jerked a thumb, pointing towards the Thames.

"Okay." Jack motioned in the opposite direction. "This way for me."

They both looked at Helena, who offered Jack her sweetest smile. "It's really great to see you again, Jack." She reached up on tiptoes, leaned into him, kissing him tenderly on the cheek, at the same time hugging him tight around the waist for many seconds.

Then she pulled away, slipping her hand into Carter's. They walked down Whitehall towards Westminster Bridge, neither saying anything, nor knowing what the next day would bring. All they knew was that they would face it together.

Acknowledgements

Trawling through social media some years ago, I spotted a post by a women's group commemorating the birthday, on January 25th, 1906, of their *Woman of the Day*. Her name was Margery Booth. She came from Wigan.

The location tweaked my interest as Wigan, located between the industrial cities of Manchester and Liverpool in the north-west of England, is my home town and I had never heard of Margery Booth. It transpired that I had walked past the house where she was born, in Hodges Street, on many occasions in my youth, unaware that it was the birthplace of one of Britain's most courageous and selfless wartime spies, albeit one unknown to many.

Margery's extraordinary true story became the inspiration for the fictional tale of Helena Schulz, the main character in *The Singing Spy*.

Margery trained as a singer in Bolton before taking private tuition from Eileen D'Orme in Knightsbridge. She later attended the prestigious Guildhall School of Music, prior to emigrating to Germany. She passed an audition at the Berlin State Opera in 1928 and five years later was the only English prima donna in Berlin, singing in German, French, Italian and Spanish, quite a journey for a working class girl from a Lancashire coal and cotton town.

In 1935 she sang in London at the Proms and by 1936, her contract required her to spend seven months of the year in Berlin, singing on 60 nights at the State Opera. Touring was allowed outside this time and in April she fulfilled one of her greatest ambitions, singing at the Royal Opera House in Covent Garden when she played Magdalene in Wagner's opera *Die Meistersinger*.

Later the same year she married Dr. Egon Strohm, a journalist, radio reporter and academic from a brewing family in the Black Forest, whom she had first met years before as a student in London. To avoid a media circus, the ceremony was held in secret by special licence at All Saints CE Church in Rawlinson Road, Southport, on August 26th, 1936. Margery and her family had moved to Clifton Road, Southport, when she was eight.

At the outbreak of the Second World War, Margaret was trusted by the Nazis. She had sung for Adolf Hitler, attended dinners with prominent Nazis and even received gifts of flowers from the Führer. She was invited to sing at a prisoner of war camp in Genshagen, in the south of Berlin, where she met and later agreed to work with John Brown, a British officer, MI9 agent and prisoner, smuggling out coded information at great risk to herself. At one point as suspicions grew, she was arrested and interrogated by the Gestapo, but released, never revealing any secrets, eventually escaping Germany in March 1945.

After the war, information she supplied was instrumental in helping to convict William Joyce, aka Lord Haw Haw, whose radio broadcasts were one of the Nazis' most famous propaganda tools, and John Amery, son of a British MP. Amery made many propaganda broadcasts for Germany and supported Italian dictator Benito Mussolini. He was also the originator of the British Free Corps, a volunteer Waffen-SS unit composed of former British prisoners of war. Amery was captured by Italian partisans in Milan in April, 1945, and handed over to the British authorities. He was hanged for high treason in Wandsworth Prison on December 19th, 1945. Joyce, born in the U.S. and of Irish descent, but who had falsely claimed British nationality to obtain a British passport, became the last man to be executed for treason in the UK when he was also hanged in Wandsworth on January 3rd, 1946.

Sadly, Margery was rejected in many quarters when she returned to Britain, where she stayed for a while in a safe house in Bayswater. An only child, her mother, Florence, and her father, Levi, had divorced and both died in 1933. Because Margery had assumed German citizenship and had connections with influential political figures, she was wrongly thought to be a Nazi sympathiser. She never sang professionally again and emigrated to the United States, where she died of throat cancer in the Montefiore Hospital in the Bronx, New York, on April 11th, 1952, at the age of 46. In 1947, Margery had managed to regain her British citizenship, but attempts to nominate her for a posthumous award have fallen on deaf ears. The lone public recognition of her courageous exploits is a blue plaque on the foyer wall of the Queen's Hall, Wigan.

It states: *Margery Booth 1906-1952. Opera singer and British spy during the Second World War. Born in Wigan and performed at Queen's Hall in 1935. 'The once forgotten is now remembered'.*

Thanks to Wigan historian Graham Taylor for his chronicling of Margery's story and the Notre Society for their work in securing the blue plaque recognition.

My heartfelt gratitude and admiration, however, go to Margery herself for making the fictional tale of Helena Schulz possible. Aspects of their stories run parallel but timelines, relationships, and other details, have been changed to aid the dramatic flow.

Another courageous woman deserving of mention is Russian emigree Marie 'Missie' Vassiltchikov, whose book about life in Berlin, *The Berlin Diaries 1940-1945,* is a remarkable historical document. It provided a sharp and personal insight into life under the Nazis in the German capital.

Many thanks to Michael for his expertise and creativity, and the team at FCM Books.

Most of all, a big thankyou as always to my wife, Carole, for her editing skills, meticulous proofreading and all-round support.

About the author

A journalist by profession, Frank Malley began his career as a news reporter on the Post & Chronicle evening newspaper in Wigan in the late 1970s. He went on to work as a columnist and deputy sports editor with the Daily Express in London and as chief writer with Press Association Sport, covering World Cups in football and rugby, five Olympics, and sporting events across the globe. He began writing books after turning freelance and to date has published seven novels, as well as three non-fiction titles. He lives in the Bedfordshire countryside with his wife, Carole.

***

If you enjoyed The Singing Spy, the author would appreciate a quick review on Amazon, Goodreads, or your favourite book website. Reviews are vital. A few words matter.

Also by Frank Malley

The 13th Assassin

The Hit List

The Killing Circle

Codebreaker

(An omnibus e-book edition of the Emily Stearn thriller series)

When the Mist Clears

If It Looks Like a Duck

Simply the Best

Living on the Deadline

Champions

Available in paperback and on Kindle from Amazon

Printed in Dunstable, United Kingdom